WILDE AT HEART

TONYA BURROWS

Entangled Publishing, LLC
2614 South Timberline Road
Suite 109
Fort Collins, CO 80525
Visit our website at www.entangledpublishing.com.

Ignite is an imprint of Entangled Publishing, LLC.

Edited by Heather Howland
Cover design by Heather Howland
Cover art from Shutterstock

Manufactured in the United States of America

First Edition September 2015

ign♦te

Chapter One

He shouldn't be here.

Scratch that. He abso-fucking-lutely should not be here.

Even as the thought tracked through Reece Wilde's head, he pushed open The Bean Gallery's front door. 9:00 p.m. on New Year's Eve, and the coffeehouse was dead silent. Its tables, each depicting a different famous painting, sat empty of the usual eclectic crowd of patrons. No college students cramming for exams. No hipsters philosophizing over lattes. And certainly no businessmen stopping for a convenient caffeine fix before their next meeting.

That was how he'd discovered this place. Just a quick stop between back-to-back morning meetings to re-caffeinate before back-to-back afternoon meetings.

And this was where he first saw Shelby Bremer, the woman who held a starring role in his every sexual fantasy for the past several months. The woman who was so fucking far off-limits, she might as well have the words "access de-nied" tattooed on her forehead.

When they first met, she'd been a patron here, eating breakfast over in the corner at the table painted like Van Gogh's *Starry Night*. Reece glanced over at that table now. Someone had stacked the chairs on top of it in preparation for closing time, but he could still see her sitting there so clearly, the image of her short skirt and combat boots seared into his mind like a brand. Normally, he wouldn't have given a woman with pink-streaked blond hair, tattoo sleeves, and an eyebrow ring a second glance, but there was something about her that fascinated him. As he'd waited in line for his coffee, he hadn't been able to take his eyes off her. When she noticed him staring and blew him a kiss with her mid-dle finger, a switch had flipped inside his head, and his vi-ciously repressed sex drive roared to life. Everything in him demanded he take her, dominate her, bend her over that badly painted table and leave his handprint on her ass for that saucy gesture of defiance. The need had been so instant, so intense, it scared the ever-loving hell out of him, and he'd scrammed as soon as he had his coffee in hand.

But he'd come back. Day after day. She was always at the same table, and she'd started watching for him, a spark of interest and heat in her blue eyes. Although they had never said a word to each other, he'd all but given in to the inevitability of the two of them fucking sooner or later. And for the first time in a very long time, that idea didn't make him want to run in the opposite direction.

Then he'd found out she was his brother's fiancée's sister.

Which was exactly why he shouldn't be here.

Shelby worked at The Bean Gallery now, and she had

the closing shift tonight.

Not that he was stalking her or anything like that. Just keeping tabs at the request of his brother. Eva—his soon-to-be sister-in-law—constantly worried her half sister's impulsive nature would lead to Shelby hurting herself or burning down the house, and whatever Eva worried about worried Cam. So Cam had recruited his brothers to covertly keep an eye on Shelby.

And this visit was just Reece's brotherly duty. Just like all the others.

Right.

His fantasies hadn't ended just because Cam had asked him to keep tabs on Eva's little sister. Hell, if anything, the request had only revved him up because now, not only was Shelby something exciting and exotic, but she was *forbidden*. The hacker in him loved the forbidden. He couldn't look at the woman without wanting to strip her naked and taste every tattoo on her body, and Cam sure as hell wouldn't consider *that* a brotherly duty.

Voices floated out of the back room, and Reece stopped short, caught by his own indecision halfway between the door and counter.

He should leave.

Yeah. Leaving would be a good plan, because he had no logical reason to be standing here other than the fact he couldn't stay away. And if he didn't leave now, he wasn't going to until he got a taste of Shelby and put this goddamn uncharacteristic infatuation with her to rest.

He didn't move.

One of the other baristas appeared first, a middle-aged woman with gray-streaked brown hair and brown skin baked to cracking. Reece vaguely recalled her name was something like Jane or Jenna, but he'd never exchanged more than a few pleasantries with her. The second to emerge was Stephanie, a sweet, bubbly college student who worked at the coffeehouse part time. She was ready for a New Year's party in a glittery dress that covered about as much skin as a Band-Aid. Sky-high shoes dangled from her fingers. She was young, but she had class in spades. Give her five years and she'd grow into the kind of woman Reece should be interested in, the kind of woman his ultra-conservative business associates would approve of. Instead, all of his focus zeroed in on the woman trailing Stephanie through the door.

Shelby.

His pulse kicked up despite reminding himself she was related to Eva. For fuck's sake, she was practically family. In a few short days, when Cam and Eva tied the knot, she *would* be.

And just like all the other times, the reminder did nothing to douse the firestorm of lust burning through him.

Her outfit tonight was relatively tame for her—black cropped jacket over a black tank top and a ruffled purple plaid skirt—and still, he wanted to see what was underneath. Hell, she could be dressed in a burlap bag and he'd want to see underneath. Her hair spilled over her shoulders in a shock of turquoise and purple, and he noticed a new piercing, a small turquoise gem glinting from her nose.

That shouldn't be sexy.

Goddamn, but it was.

"Are you sure you don't want to join us, Shel?" Stephanie was saying. "It's going to be the party of the year!"

"No, my sister would kill me." Shelby's voice carried a

permanent sensual rasp, the kind of voice that brought to mind twisted sheets and writhing bodies, and it worked on him like a drug, making him jones to hear her speak again.

Jane-slash-Jenna finally noticed him standing there and skidded to a halt. "Sorry, we're closed. You'll have to come back after the holiday."

Shelby glanced over at him, at first uninterested, but then she did a double take and grinned. "It's okay, Jana. Hey, Suit and Tie."

Jana. Right. That was her name.

The older woman scowled. "You know him?"

"Yeah, and if I had to guess, he's my babysitter for the night." Shelby sighed and met his gaze. "Did Eva send you?"

Fuck, no. Eva would castrate him—slowly—if she knew he was here, but he wasn't about to lay it all out on the line in front of an audience. "She thought someone should give you a ride."

Shelby lifted a brow and he realized a half second too late how sexual that had sounded. He added, "Home. A ride home."

"Of course she did."

Stephanie made a face. "I don't know why you let your sister boss you around like this. You're a grown-ass woman."

"I owe it to her," was all Shelby said in reply, then shooed the two women toward the door. "Go on. I'll see you girls in a few days. Happy New Year."

"Same to you," Jana said and left, still scowling at Reece as she passed.

"Happy New Year," Stephanie chirped, but then paused halfway out the door. "Don't forget I start student teaching on the fourth, so my availability's going to change."

"I've already left a note about it in the office so I'll remember when I start the next schedule."

"Thanks. You're the best." With a flirty wave at Reece, she followed Jana out. Shelby crossed to the door and waved as she clicked the lock into place then flipped the sign from OPEN to CLOSED.

"So," Reece said, searching for a way to break the awkward silence. "They made you a supervisor?"

"Don't sound so surprised." She moved from window to window, drawing down blinds over the glass. As soon as the last window was covered, she whirled to face him, hands on her hips. "Are you stalking me, Rolo?"

He made a concerted effort to relax his jaw before he broke his teeth. "My name is Reece."

"It's all candy to me." She lifted a shoulder and breezed past him. "Do you honestly think I haven't noticed all the drive-bys? And, c'mon, you used to be a one-coffee-a-day guy. Now you're here at least three times a day."

"Maybe I need the extra caffeine."

Her nose crinkled. "You do look exhausted all the time, but I doubt caffeine will help with that. You should go on a vacation."

"I don't take vacations."

"*Humph.* You really should. You need to pull that stick out of your ass before it does permanent internal damage."

He closed the distance between them. "You have no fucking clue what I need."

She paused on her way back to the register and glanced over one shoulder, eyebrow raised. Her piercing glinted in the overhead light with the movement. "Wow. That sounded like a threat. Or…was it a promise?"

Dial it back, he told himself. He stopped, still a good five feet away from her, and released a pent-up breath. "I'm only here to give you a lift home."

"Uh-huh." She opened the register with a key and took out the cash-filled tray. "Well, I have some things to do first, so make yourself comfortable."

She took the tray and credit card receipts into the back room. He waited a handful of moments and debated his own intelligence before he finally followed. Of course he was going to follow. He couldn't seem to *not* follow this woman. As if he were a dog and she were his mistress in control of his leash.

And, okay, that thought should not have lit him up like a damn light bulb.

Jesus, he was a sick fuck.

He found her at a desk in the office behind the kitchen area, counting out the day's bank deposit. Her tongue poked out of the corner of her mouth in concentration, and the sight of the pink tip peeking from between her purple-painted lips was somehow both adorable and insanely erotic. For a second, he could only stand there and fantasize about all the things that tongue could do to him, and the room grew uncomfortably warm. He loosened his tie, tried to find a train of thought that was less…explosive.

"Uh, you seem to have settled into the life of a responsible adult."

She held up a finger in a classic *hang on* gesture and finished counting, then wrote down the amount and stuffed the bills into a plastic deposit bag. She dragged her tongue over the flap and sealed it closed, then smirked up at him. "Word of advice, Hershey. Insulting me is not the best way to get into my skirt."

"It's Reece. And what makes you think I want into *your* skirt?"

Her gaze dropped pointedly to the front of his trousers. "That boner you've been rocking since you walked in wasn't enough of a clue? Unless you're just *really* turned on by coffee. In that case, weird. But to each his own."

Reece shifted on his feet and, as unobtrusively as possible, folded his hands together in front of his body. At that moment, he kind of wished he'd melt into the floor, because the heat burning across the back of his neck almost surely meant he was blushing. And he *didn't* blush. Goddammit. "It's not...uh, I-I'm not..."

"Oh, you mostly certainly are, sweetie." Standing, she gathered the deposit bag and turned to the wall safe behind the desk. Once the money was closed inside, she propped herself on the edge of the desk and studied him, amusement dancing in her eyes. "You're cute when you're flustered. I like that about you."

"I don't get *flustered*."

She raised a sculpted brow and the hoop there glinted in the overhead lights. Her expression said it all—*the hell you don't*—and frustration roared through him, chasing away the embarrassment. Nothing ever went smoothly when Shelby was involved. Nothing was ever easy, and if he had any goddamn sense left in his head, he'd bail out now.

Instead, he dropped his hands to his sides and stalked forward, not entirely sure what he planned to do until he caged her against the desk with an arm on either side of her body and crushed his lips to hers. He just couldn't stand not knowing if her kiss was as spicy as her attitude. And, holy fuck, she *ignited* in his arms as if he'd set a match to her. Fingers raked through his hair, nails dug half-moons into his scalp. Even though he was the one who had her caged, he suddenly felt trapped, captured.

Never breaking contact with his mouth, she pulled herself up to sit on the desk and used his tie to drag him into the spread vee of her legs. His mind scrambled through all the reasons they shouldn't be doing this.

She was Eva's little sister.

Cam would kill him.

They were in her boss's office…

And his body was saying *who the fuck cared?* He needed her out of his system. He needed to be able to think straight again and not like a teenager with his first crush. Most of all, he needed her to scream his name. His *real* name, not the stupid candy-themed nicknames.

He broke away from her lips and went to his knees in front of her, trailing his hands from her hips to her knees and then back up her inner thighs.

She wasn't wearing panties. Why did that not surprise him? And she was all slick and soft and she moaned when he parted her, slipped a finger inside. Her inner muscles clenched, and he liked the tremble that shook through her body. He added a second finger, watched her head fall back and her nipples bead against the fabric of her tank top. He smiled before adding his mouth to the action, tasting her, circling her clit with his tongue until she finally cried out something that might have been his name. He couldn't tell with the roaring inside his head and his own body about to combust—

Shit. What was he doing?

He jerked away from her and, panting, stumbled several steps back.

"Reece?" His name came out on a surprised gasp. "What's wrong?"

Jesus. What wasn't? This was all wrong. His attraction to her and…everything. "I should…leave. Yeah. I'll go."

She was leaning back on the desk with her thighs parted, eyes heavy, cheeks flushed, but at his words, she bolted upright. "*What?*"

He still tasted her on his lips, and it took far more willpower than he imagined to walk the six feet to the office door. "Go home, Shelby. This never happened."

"What?" she said again.

"This. Never. Happened. And it won't happen again." He couldn't look at her as he stepped into the kitchen. Ran trembling hands through his hair. Took a moment to gather himself…

And only then did he notice the smoke, stinging his nose with a strange burned coffee scent. Thick and black, it billowed along the ceiling, poured in from the front dining area, where he saw the dance of fast-moving yellow flames.

Jesus, no wonder he was dripping sweat. He hadn't heated up. The room had.

"Fire!" He whirled to grab Shelby from the office, but she was already behind him. Fear chased away her indignant expression, and her complexion drained of color, leaving her so pale her faded purple lipstick stood out in stark contrast.

She raised a hand to her mouth. "Oh my God."

"Where's the nearest exit?"

She pointed across the kitchen to a spot on the far wall. Where the smoke was heaviest, naturally.

"Yeah, of course it'd be there." He stripped off his suit coat and wrapped it in a makeshift bandana around her face, tying the arms behind her head.

"Wha—what about you?" she sputtered.

He untucked his button-down shirt and lifted the front to cover his mouth and nose. "All right?"

She shot a glance at the thickening smoke and firmed up her shoulders. Nodded. Her show of bravado would have been convincing if he didn't feel her trembling when he closed his hand around hers.

"Stay low. We'll be out of here in no time."

Chapter Two

The walk to the fire exit seemed endless, each step taking them deeper into the blackness, until Reece shoved open the fire exit and pushed her out ahead of him. Shelby's eyes and lungs burned, scoured raw by the smoke that rolled from the door behind them, thick and black. It seemed to reach out and wrap itself around them as if it planned to drag them back inside to their deaths.

Her heart was trying its damnedest to swan-dive out of her chest. When she saw those first dark tendrils creeping across the ceiling, she had never been more frightened in her life. Which was saying something, since she'd landed herself in some pretty scary situations over the years.

But the whole time, Reece never let go of her hand, and she drew strength from the connection. It calmed her. Allowed her to function past the fear that threatened to paralyze her. If she had been alone, she honestly didn't know if she'd have made it out of the building.

Across the street from The Bean Gallery, the shock finally caught up to her, and she lost her footing on the ice-slickened sidewalk. Reece was right there, his arm a solid weight around her waist, keeping her upright. She tilted her head back, stared up at him through blurry eyes. His tidy white dress shirt was no longer tidy or white, and soot streaked his face, coated his hair.

"I have you," he said softly and tightened his grip.

Reece Wilde—genius, workaholic, millionaire muckety-muck—had *her*, the girl from the way wrong side of the tracks. And he wasn't just slumming it for a night like she first suspected. Oh, no. Because if that was the case, he wouldn't want to be publicly associated with her in any way other than through their siblings' upcoming marriage, and he'd be outta here before the fire department showed. Instead, he looked as if he had no intention of leaving. Which maybe was a good thing since he was all but holding her up at the moment.

No, tonight hadn't been about slumming. Had it been his clumsy attempt at…courting her? He was just that type of guy to court a woman, all hero with a core of pure goodness and solid honor. He was the type of man to stick around. His freak-out in the office when she would have let him do just about anything to her on that desk proved as much, made her realize how uncomfortable he was with the whole idea of a slam, bam, thank you, ma'am.

So, yeah, he'd stick around. Maybe for good, which kinda scared the hell out of her, because she didn't do permanent anything. Except for her tattoos, but that was different, because they were the storybook of her life, the forever-present reminders of her mistakes and her triumphs. But in every other aspect of her world, she was completely, 100 percent anti-permanent. Hell, even her hair color changed every other week.

Reece was the human equivalent of tattoo ink. She was henna.

But for a moment, with his arm around her and the heat of his body easing her shocked shivers, she did wonder…

Oh, no. What was she thinking? She so wasn't about to rehash *Pretty in Pink* with him. For one thing, he didn't need her kind of trouble in his life.

She shrugged out of his arms and turned to watch the fire eat away her one chance at a normal, straight-and-narrow life. Smoke and flames roiled from the broken front window and blackened the outside brick. She rubbed her hands over her eyes and only then did she realize his suit coat was still wrapped bandana-like around the lower half of her face. She yanked it off and scrubbed away the tears that made her vision go all wavy.

Dammit, she loved that place. Had put her heart and soul into it. And now it was gone.

A siren wailed somewhere close by. The firefighters were on their way, which meant her sister, detective extraordinaire, wouldn't be too far behind. And along with her sister would come Reece's brother.

"You should go," she told him, still staring at the flames. "We both know Eva didn't send you here tonight. You'll catch hell from Cam."

He made a noncommittal sound and didn't move. She faced him. "I'm serious. Go before they see you."

"You think I'm afraid of Cam?" A hint of a smile turned up the corner of his too-serious mouth. "I used to dig up worms in our backyard and chase him around with them until he cried. I'm not afraid of my little brother."

"Maybe not. But you should be very afraid of my big sister. If Eva finds out what we were doing in there before the fire broke out…"

If she wasn't mistaken, a flush filled his cheeks underneath the soot. "We're both consenting adults. And as I said, it's not happening again."

"Humph. Tell Eva that. See how well it goes over. I'll give you a hint: lead balloon."

"It'll be fine."

"Keep looking on the bright side, Starburst. One thing, though. You weren't planning on ever having children, were you? Because Eva will make sure you don't."

He winced.

She patted his shoulder, then on impulse stood on her toes to kiss his cheek. He was just too damn cute. "Do us both a favor and leave. Please. It will make this about a billion times easier for me, okay?"

He stared down into her eyes for a long moment, and she hoped to all things holy he couldn't read any of her secrets. Because she got the feeling he could, and it chilled her to the bone.

"Please," she said again on barely a breath of sound and held out his jacket. As grateful as she had been for it during their dash through the smoke, she didn't want Cam or Eva to see her with it now.

The fire engine's lights flashed red and yellow against the snow clouds hovering over the city. They were less than a block away at this point, and she feared he was going to be stubborn, but he finally gave a short nod and took the jacket.

"We're going to talk later."

He left her standing on the sidewalk and climbed into an SUV that was worth way more than she'd ever made in her lifetime. She wished she could hate him for it, but when she tried, the worry she'd seen in his eyes edged out all the negative emotions and filled her with the warm fuzzies.

Ugh. That man was dangerous.

The fire truck screamed to a stop in front of the building, and they wasted no time hooking up their hoses. Streams of water filled the air and within minutes, they had the fire under control.

One of the firefighters came over to her with a blanket. It was just cold enough that the mist from the hoses was already freezing into ice on his helmet and, for the first time, she realized how cold she truly was. And here she thought it was only shock.

He draped the blanket over her shoulders. "Are you okay? Do you need medical attention?"

She shook her head. "I'm fine."

"What happened here?"

She opened her mouth to tell him how she was preparing the bank deposits before leaving for the night—true—when she noticed smoke and escaped out the side exit—also true—but a car pulled up behind the fire truck, lights flashing in its grill. The fireman glanced over, and then did a double take when Eva and Cam slid out of the vehicle.

"Hey, Detective Cardoso. Someone call homicide?"

"No," Eva said, and her tone was all *omg-I'm-going-to-lock-Shelby-in-a-plastic-bubble-and-never-let-her-leave.* "Deluca, this is my sister."

Shelby managed to keep her wince internal. Someday

she wanted Eva to say that without looking like she just bit into a lemon.

"Oh." Deluca's eyes narrowed as he looked from Eva—tall, thin, dark hair, and olive skin—to Shelby—petite, curvy, turquoise-and-purple-for-now hair and fair complexion—and then back again.

"Half sisters," Shelby explained helpfully, then regretted drawing attention to herself, because Eva whirled on her.

"What the hell happened?"

Shelby sucked in a breath and gave her sister the story she'd been about to tell Deluca. When she finished, Cam frowned and scrubbed a hand through his dark hair. It was a thoughtful expression, which was so Cam-like she kind of wanted to hug him. Always steady and solid, he was the rock of Gibraltar in his family. She couldn't wait until he became her brother-in-law.

"Anybody here with you?" he asked.

Oh, shit. Steady, solid, and way too frigging perceptive. "No, not now."

"On the way in, I thought we passed…" He trailed off, shook his head. "Nah, forget it. Was it arson or an accident?" he asked Deluca.

Deluca shrugged. "Won't know until the fire's out and one of our investigators can get inside. But, I gotta tell ya, just between you and me, that broken front window is looking suspicious."

"How so?"

"Well. If something had exploded inside the building and broke the window, there would be shards of glass on the sidewalk, but there aren't."

"Meaning something from outside the building broke

the glass," Cam said. "Something like a Molotov cocktail thrown through the window."

"You got it."

Arson? Shelby's stomach flipped over, and she hugged the blanket tighter around herself. Oh God. If Reece hadn't been here with her…

Someone wanted her pushing up daisies.

Maybe it shouldn't surprise her, given the life she'd lived up until a few months ago, but it did. It really did.

Holy batshit, Robin.

"Shit," Cam muttered, succinctly echoing her own thoughts. "Mind if I take a look?"

"Once the flames are out, sure." As the two men started toward the fire truck, she heard Deluca add, "We'll need to contact the owners—"

"I'll do it!"

They stopped, turned, and Shelby realized she'd sounded far too eager. "I mean, the blow might be softer coming from someone they know. I'll contact them."

After a beat, Deluca nodded. "You do that."

Stupid, she scolded herself as she watched them walk away. Stupid, stupid. Should've told the truth. Which, yeah, meant she'd have a lot of 'splaining to do. The kind of explanations she really wasn't ready to give and some she couldn't.

Behind her, Eva cleared her throat. "Shelby."

She glanced over, saw her sister's arms crossed, boot tapping out an impatient rhythm in the slush on the sidewalk.

"I can tell something's going on," Eva said.

"Besides my place of employment burning to the ground as we speak?"

"Besides that. Did you start the fire? It's okay if it was

an accident. You just have to come clean."

Shelby blew out a breath. Of course Eva thought that. In her sister's mind, she was a walking jinx. "No, I didn't start it. You heard the hottie fireman. He thinks it was arson, and Cam seems to agree."

Eva ran her hands through her loose, bed-tangled hair. Didn't take a genius to figure out what she and Cam had been up to before they heard about the fire.

Which, of course, made her think of Reece. And the bone-quaking orgasm he'd been on the verge of giving her.

Despite everything, a blossom of lust unfurled low in her belly. The way he'd touched her had been…unrestrained. Sweet, a little clumsy, and uncharacteristically enthusiastic. So not what she'd expected from Reece stick-up-the-ass Wilde.

And, dammit, she wanted more.

Was there a female equivalent of blue balls? Because she had a mean case of it, which the adrenaline rush had only exacerbated.

Eva waved a hand in front of her face. "Planet Earth to Shel, come in."

Shelby shook her head, dislodging all thoughts of Reece. "Sorry. What?"

Eva frowned, concern etching lines around her eyes. "Are you okay? Maybe we should take you to the hospital."

"No, you don't need to do that. I'm exhausted and zoned out for a sec. No biggie. What were you saying?"

"Oh God. Shelby, you scared me, you know?" Eva stepped forward and wrapped her up in a hard hug. "You were here closing by yourself, and when I heard the call come across the scanner…"

Shelby held her just as tightly and breathed in the leathery scent of her sister's jacket mixed with the clean scent of soap from a recent shower. It did wonders to calm her still-racing heart. "I'm so sorry, Evie. But I'm okay. Honest."

"Whatever's going on with you, you know you can tell me, right? I can't promise I won't get mad at first, but I'm always here for you, no matter what."

"I've never doubted that."

"So then what aren't you telling me?"

Oh, so much. So very much that she didn't even know where or how to begin.

She clung to her sister and watched the firemen douse the last of the flames. The front end of The Bean Gallery was nothing but a blackened shell now, and tears pricked her eyes. And for a heartbeat, warm and comfortable in her sister's embrace, she considered spilling everything. All she had to do was open her mouth and start talking.

But then she caught sight of a familiar face in the crowd of bystanders that had begun to gather on the sidewalk, and her heart dropped to her toes.

Shitballs. And here she'd thought this night couldn't possibly get any worse.

Chapter Three

"What are you doing here?"

Reece glanced up from the spreadsheets on his laptop to see his brother Vaughn lounging in the doorway of his office. It was a tiny room in the back of the Wilde Security building and Vaughn filled the doorframe with his body.

"I could ask the same of you," Reece said, avoiding the question. "As best man, shouldn't you be with the groom, making sure he gets to the plane on time tomorrow?"

"Cam's so goofy in love with Eva, he's not going to miss that plane for anything." Vaughn lifted a shoulder. "And I wanted to check some things before we leave."

"Lark." Reece didn't bother making it a question. He knew damn well Vaughn was like a starving pit bull with a bone when he latched on to something. And he'd latched on to Lark Warren's disappearance with all his teeth, though nobody could figure out why. As far as Reece knew, Vaughn had only met Lark once at their youngest brother Jude's wedding last fall, but he was bound and determined to find the woman now. Which was proving more difficult than any of them could have guessed since the real Lark Warren was a sixty-eight-year-old who had died of a heart attack three years ago, shortly before Vaughn's "Lark" appeared in D.C.

Reece returned his attention to his computer, but the numbers on the screen were starting to blur together. Time to lose the contacts and break out the glasses, he decided, and opened the top drawer of his desk, found his contacts case, solution, and glasses. He stood. "You have to let her go, Vaughn. This obsession isn't good for your health."

"Jesus. I'm not a fucking fragile china doll."

"Never said that." He stopped in front of Vaughn and waited for his brother to step back, out of the doorway, to let him pass.

Vaughn didn't move. "You didn't have to say it."

At six feet tall, Reece wasn't a small man by any stretch of the imagination, but he was the shortest in the Wilde family and had to look up to meet his younger brother's gaze. "You *were* seriously injured less than two months ago. You shouldn't even be thinking about coming back to work yet, not to mention chasing this woman's trail across the country."

"I'm fine." But even as he said the words, he pushed away from the doorjamb, and his jaw tightened with a suppressed wince.

"Yeah, you look it." Reece strode past him to the bathroom and started the preparations to remove his contacts at the vanity. Vaughn's walking cast clomped across the floor, then a chair scraped back and a computer booted up.

"Did you hear about the shit Shelby got into the other

night?" Vaughn asked.

He fumbled his contact and it landed somewhere on the floor. "Fuck!"

"What?"

"Nothing. Dropped my contact." He groped around for his glasses and slid them on, but didn't bother searching for the lost contact. He returned to the main room where Vaughn was sitting at his desk, typing.

"Should get corrective surgery like Cam did," Vaughn said without looking up.

He'd considered it several times over the years, but what did it say about him that he hated the idea of losing even a day of work to get his vision fixed? Probably nothing good, so he shoved the idea aside.

"What did you say about Shelby?" Jesus, he hoped he'd managed to keep his voice casual, because his heart was pounding a hole in his ribcage.

Vaughn still didn't look away from his screen. "Yeah, that girl is a walking disaster. The Bean Gallery burned to the ground during her shift on New Year's Eve."

In the faint blue light of the computer screen, he watched Vaughn's expression closely, trying to decide if he were being baited. But he saw no hint of it. Besides, there was no way Vaughn could know. No. Way. He had to relax before he gave himself away. "Is she all right?"

"Yeah, she's good. Shaken up, Cam says, but uninjured. They're calling it arson."

Arson.

For a second, everything stopped. The sound of Vaughn's fingers on the keyboard, the hum of the fluorescent overhead lights, Reece's heart. Everything.

It was arson.

Jesus, he never should have left the scene.

Then something in Vaughn's tone snapped him back to the here and now and had alarm bells clanging inside his head. "Don't tell me they think Shelby did it."

If the authorities believed Shelby started the fire, he'd have to come clean, admit he'd been there with her, and the only fire she'd started was the one in his blood. Which would be uncomfortable for them both, but better than having her accused of a crime.

"No," Vaughn said. "The evidence is pretty clear that someone threw a Molotov cocktail through the front window. The investigator assigned to the case is a good one, but Cam still wants us to look into it ourselves when we get back from Vegas."

"All right."

Vaughn finally gazed up from his computer, his blue eyes narrowed. "That's it?"

"That's what?"

"Your only reaction is 'all right'? No bitching about the expense of taking on a case we won't get paid for?"

"Eva's going to be family in two days. By default, that makes Shelby family, too. If it involves her safety, it's something we need to investigate, expenses be damned."

Vaughn froze for an instant, then very slowly turned in his seat to stare. "You *look* like Reece, but you can't possibly be him. Real Reece has conniptions over money issues. So where's my real brother, and who do I have to kill to get him back?"

"You've been spending too much time with Jude. His smartass is rubbing off on you. It's not attractive."

"Good thing I'm not trying to attract your ugly ass then."

"Fucking younger brothers." Reece rolled his eyes to the ceiling in a silent plea for patience, then started back to his office. "Go home, Vaughn."

"I will. But first I need to contact Gabe and Quinn, give them Lark's description, since HORNET is all over the country. Figure if I cast a wide enough net, she's bound to get caught in it."

Reece paused in the doorway and glanced back. Vaughn was again working on his computer with laser-like focus. He was good with technology, but Reece was better. The least he could do was take some of the pressure off, and maybe Vaughn wouldn't run himself into the ground during his search.

"I'll look into her financials, see what I can dig up."

Vaughn met his gaze, eyes full of gratitude in the instant before he glanced away. When he spoke, his voice came out soft, a little rusty. "Thanks."

Jesus. Vaughn really was tied up in knots over this woman. Out of all the craziness in the past year—Jude reuniting with his lost love Libby, Cam and Eva taking their friendship to the next level, Vaughn nearly getting blown up, and whatever the hell was going on with Greer—this had to be the craziest. Vaughn just wasn't the kind of guy to commit to a woman, but he sure as hell was committing everything he had to the search for Lark.

Reece returned to his office, sat behind his desk, but ignored the expense reports on his screen. Instead, he clicked over to the internet and ran some searches on Lark. He got about what he expected: the engagement announcement for Lark and her ex-fiancé, an article about said fiancé's nasty past and her disappearance after he was caught for his crimes. For a while, speculation was he'd killed her before he was caught, but Vaughn didn't seem to think so. And now that they knew she had been living in D.C. under a stolen name, Reece had to agree. She was in the wind, but was it because she was a frightened victim or a criminal?

He'd dig more later. Right now, he had to get those reports done for DMW Systems, the software company he'd built from the ground up after leaving the army. Currently, most of his contracts were government, but he hoped to take his company into the private sector and was in the process of securing a major investor who would help cement DMW's spot as a top competitor in the field. Everything had to be perfect or it wasn't going to happen. Irving James III was about as old school as old school money got and the fact he was even considering investing in a tech company was a miracle in and of itself. Reece's "good old fashioned family values" and "patriotism" had drawn the billionaire's attention. Now he had to find a way to keep it.

He worked until he realized the outer office had gone silent. Straightening in his seat, stretching his arms over his head to work out the kinks, he checked the clock on his screen. After two a.m. No wonder he didn't hear any noise out there. Vaughn probably called it quits hours ago since they were scheduled to be on a seven thirty flight to Vegas.

By his estimation, Reece had just enough time to get home, pack, shower, and maybe if he was lucky, even squeeze in an hour of sleep.

He reached to close the lid of his laptop, and his email dinged. Probably shouldn't look at it if he wanted that hour of sleep…

He opened the program.

The sender's name wasn't one he recognized, but the subject line hit him like a punch to the solar plexus.

SCANDAL! DMW SYSTEMS CEO HAS SEX WITH BARISTA AT COFFEEHOUSE.

What. The. Fuck?

He ran a virus scan, found none, and opened the attachment. Sure enough, there was a grainy video, like from a cheap security camera. It showed Shelby sitting on the desk with him between her legs and the screen went black right before he pulled away, leaving the viewer to interpret what happened next. Text appeared, followed by a string of numbers he could only assume was a bank account.

If you want this video to stay secret, pay up. $20,000.

Reece sat back in his chair, ran his hands through his hair, and just stared at the screen. This could not be happening. Not now.

Of course, logically speaking, this was the perfect time to hit him with blackmail. So it had to be someone he knew. Someone who had access to, or at least the ability to access the coffee shop's security footage. Someone who knew his government contracts were running out this year and he *needed* Irving James's investment if he wanted to keep both DMW and Wilde Security afloat. Someone who knew one moral misstep on his part would bring everything he'd built crashing down.

But who?

He stared at the bank account number. He could trace it but that would take time, a commodity he was preciously short on at the moment. And there was no guarantee it would lead him anywhere. If the blackmailer was smart, and Reece had to assume so, it would be an offshore account under an assumed identity.

He could try tracing the email, but it was from a free service provider anyone could sign up for. And again, he had to assume the blackmailer was smart enough to know how to cover his or her tracks in cyberspace. You don't blackmail a computer geek if you aren't confident in your own hacking skills.

Which left him with only one choice. Pay.

He rubbed his damp palms on his thighs and tried to think of another solution, *any* other solution, but he came up blank.

If he paid now, he'd have to keep paying. And paying. And paying. He knew how it worked. As long as the blackmailer had that video, he was vulnerable.

But what choice did he have?

"Goddammit." He signed on to his bank account and sent the wire transfer, then shut down his computer. At the very least, that money should buy him some time, but he couldn't worry any more about it right now. He had to go home, shower, and pack. He wasn't about to ruin Cam's wedding, refused to burden his brothers with the possibility of Wilde Security going bankrupt. After all the shit they'd had thrown at them recently, they deserved a worry-free celebration.

He'd handle this. Wilde Security was going to be okay. His brothers would be okay. Even if he had to pay every last penny he had, he'd make sure of it.

Chapter Four

Weddings didn't get much shorter or sweeter than Cam and Eva's. It was a no-frills affair in the smallest of the hotel's chapels. But despite that, and after much argument, Shelby had managed to talk her sister into wearing a gorgeously simple linen dress instead of a pair of jeans and her favorite leather jacket.

As Eva walked down the aisle, the cream color glowed against her caramel skin. And going by the look on her groom's face, the tastefully deep V neckline was well appreciated. Cam even gave Shelby a thumbs-up behind Eva's back because that man was no dummy. He knew who had the fashion sense in the family, and it wasn't his bride. Eva elbowed him in the ribs, and he grinned unapologetically as they turned to face the officiant.

Ugh. Those two were ridiculously adorable together.

Always had been, even back when they were struggling to keep their relationship in the "friend" category. It was about time they figured out how right they were for each other, and Shelby's heart melted when things got sappy at the exchange of vows. Even Cam's hard-ass identical twin, Vaughn, serving as best man, looked uncomfortably moved. He shifted on his feet and stared hard at a spot on the floor.

Shelby knuckled away her own tears and let her gaze wander over the scatter of wedding guests, mostly family and a herd of Cam and Eva's cop buddies. The remaining three Wilde brothers occupied the entire first row of seats on Cam's side of the aisle. Jude, the youngest, grinned and pulled his wife Libby into his side as she dabbed at her eyes. Greer, the oldest, always looked about three steps beyond exhausted and today was no different, but a small smile still tilted up the corners of his hard mouth.

And then there was Reece.

Pressed and polished as ever, he sat straight-backed in the pew and watched the proceedings with a calmness she couldn't understand. Color and noise and chaos followed her every move, so his intense stillness was intriguing. Was he really as calm as he appeared, or was there a typhoon swirling under that reserved exterior? Either way, she could so easily imagine him as a Victorian gentleman, born in the wrong era.

At least until he looked at her.

Oh, yes, there was the typhoon. All that energy, locked up inside, waiting to be tapped.

His hazel eyes all but singed as his gaze traced her body. A muscle ticked in his jaw. Without a doubt, he was thinking about stripping her out of her dress, and he wasn't happy about it. The scene from the other night played out in the air between them. If she closed her eyes, she would feel his hands holding her thighs apart again and his unadulterated enthusiasm as his tongue circled her clit. Heat flashed through her, settled low in her belly, and her inner muscles trembled. She'd gone uncomfortably damp between her legs, and the thong she was wearing wasn't doing anything to help the problem.

Reece finally broke eye contact, glancing away when Jude leaned over and said something to him.

Shelby released the air caught in her lungs and refocused on the wedding, her heart thundering. Given her current situation and all the shit it was bound to bring down on her, she shouldn't want the man. Oh, but she did. And had since the first time she laid eyes on him.

This was going to be a complication.

Then again, when did she ever do things the easy way?

The wedding wrapped up and Cam hooked an arm around Eva, dragging her in close for a kiss. Then, to a chorus of rowdy applause, they were introduced as the new Mr. and Mrs. Camden Wilde.

Cam and Eva lifted their joined hands in the air in triumph as if they'd just won a marathon together, and the cheers exploded. And, okay, maybe they had won something. Not many people found their soul mates.

Shelby had never seen Eva happier than in those moments after the wedding as the newlyweds fielded well-wishes from their friends, and a little seed of jealousy bloomed deep inside her heart. She wanted a piece of that happy for herself. Maybe not all of the marriage crap and certainly not the whole "golly gee" *Leave It to Beaver* family her sister had always dreamed of, but it would be nice to have the kind of connection Cam and Eva had found with each other.

She didn't need or deserve the entire happy pie. But was a sliver too much to ask for?

Probably.

She'd made more than her fair share of bad decisions, some of which she'd spend the rest of her life paying for.

Her gaze sought and met Reece's again. Only this time, she was the one to glance away after an instant. She was fooling herself. A respectable man like him would never forgive her sins. Especially since one of her sins was coming back in a big way.

And might just ruin him.

Every time he glanced up, there Shelby was, her electric blue dress drawing his gaze like a magnet. Someone should have told her that dress was far too sexy for a wedding, especially a wedding where two-thirds of the guests were single guys looking to have a good time in Vegas.

Okay, Reece admitted to himself as she turned away, the dress wasn't *that* revealing, considering Shelby's usual attire consisted mostly of corsets and miniskirts. Yes, the flared skirt was short and the black lace bodice left her shoulders bare, but all the essentials were covered. Still. It took every ounce of control he possessed to keep from taking off his suit jacket and wrapping her up in it, hiding her from the interested eyes of Cam and Eva's cop buddies.

He pinched the bridge of his nose. What was wrong with him? He had far more pressing concerns than Shelby

Bremer's choice of clothing. Like, for instance, finding his blackmailer. Or keeping both of his businesses afloat so his brothers didn't end up jobless. Really, sex should be the absolute last thing on his mind.

But it wasn't. Not when he was in the same room as Shelby. And that was a first for him. She was chaos on two gorgeous legs, and he hated chaos. Preferred neat, tidy, precise. So why did he find *Shelby*, of all women, so enthralling?

The room went pin-drop silent, pulling him from his thoughts, and he searched for the source of the sudden tension. At the back of the chapel stood a tiny blonde woman clutching the hand of a distinguished silver-haired man. Take away Shelby's tattoos and wild hair color, and this woman could be her twin. But she wasn't one of Shelby and Eva's long lost siblings, of which they had a ton. No, this was Katrina Bremer, the woman who had birthed an army of children and had abandoned most of them—all except for her two youngest girls. Instead, she'd given them a hellish childhood filled with drugs and a revolving door of questionable boyfriends. Abandonment would have been kinder.

"Mom?" Eva said, and Cam's arm slid around her waist in a fortifying hug. "What are you doing here?"

Katrina released her grip on her newest man and walked forward. She had gained weight since the first time Reece had seen her three months ago. At the time, she'd been strapped into the back of an ambulance—skinny, dirty, and high as a kite—on her way to the hospital for a psych evaluation after attacking Shelby and Eva. Now her blond hair was clean and braided, her dress unwrinkled and modest.

She stopped a short distance from Eva and clasped her hands nervously in front of her. "I wanted to see my daughter's wedding."

"You weren't invited," Eva snapped.

Shelby stepped between them and held out a hand as if to hold her sister back. "Evie…"

Eva whirled on her. "Did you tell her about this?"

"Of course I did. She's our mother."

"Yeah, and there's a reason I didn't invite her, Shelby. I didn't want her here." She shrugged out of Cam's grasp and stabbed a finger accusingly toward her mother. "How could you even want to see her after the way she attacked us?"

Shelby glanced back at Katrina, then rolled her lips together and straightened her shoulders, preparing to face off against her much taller sister. "She wasn't well back then, but she is now."

"Bullshit."

"At least she's trying now. She's been clean since that night, and she's engaged to a nice man, a former cop like you and Cam—"

"Engaged?" Eva spared her mother and the silver-haired man a disgusted glance. "Oh my God. Shel, we've been down this road before. Over and over and over. She's *never* going to change."

"I don't believe that. People can change."

"Not her!"

"Eva," Katrina said softly, tears streaming down her cheeks. "Honey, I know I've not been a good mother to you, but I am so, so sorry for what I put you girls through. I was selfish and…sick."

"See?" Shelby said and wrapped an arm around her mother. "Give her another chance."

"No." Radiating disbelief, Eva shook her head. "No! I've

given her more chances than she deserves." She turned that accusing finger on her sister, poking Shelby's chest. "I've given *you* more chances than you deserve, and all I ever get in return is disappointment. I can't—" Her voice caught and she shouldered between her sister and mother, leaving a heavy silence in her wake.

Katrina tried to hug Shelby, but she shrugged off the embrace and ran for the exit, too. Nobody moved for a solid three seconds after the chapel door banged shut behind her.

"Shit," Cam said under his breath and chased after his wife.

Reece hesitated for only a heartbeat before he followed. He found Cam pacing the floor in the hallway outside the women's restroom. "Are they in there?"

"Eva is." Cam dragged his hands over his head. "Goddamn Shelby."

"Hey, she was only trying to help."

"Yeah, well, Eva can do without her brand of help. You have no idea what a mindfuck it was for Eva growing up as the daughter of that woman."

"Shelby's her daughter, too," Reece pointed out.

"But that's the biggest difference between them. Shelby bounces back from everything. Eva doesn't. She carries the hurt forever." He stopped moving in front of the bathroom door and stared at the female stick figure like he wanted to set fire to it. Finally, he muttered, "Fuck this," and pushed inside.

Reece stood in the empty hallway and debated his next step. In a conference room several doors down, the reception revelry was already in full swing. A room full of cops with an open bar in Vegas? Yeah, he should probably go in there and keep things under control until the bride and groom returned.

He took a step in that direction, but a flash of blue at the other end of the hall caught his attention and he glanced toward it in time to see Shelby step into the elevator. He didn't think, just moved, striding down the hall and catching the door before it slid shut.

Shelby sighed and wiped at her eyes with both hands. "What are you doing here?"

"Making sure you don't do anything stupid."

She jabbed the button for the thirty-second floor. "Yeah, 'cause I'm full of stupid ideas."

"I didn't say that."

"You were thinking it. Reckless, wild, immature. Selfish." Her sigh was heavy with resignation. She tucked a strand of turquoise-and-purple-streaked hair behind her ear. "I know what you think I am."

"Shelby." She wouldn't meet his gaze, so he grabbed her by the shoulders and made her face him. The air sizzled when he touched her, the spark that had been between them since day one flaring red-hot. "You have no idea what I'm thinking."

Some of the shadows left her eyes. "Oh, I bet I can guess." She traced a fingernail down his chest, stopping when she reached his belt. "You're kinda transparent when you get like this, ya know?"

Reece tried to keep his face impassive even as his body internally combusted. "You're trying to distract me."

"Doesn't take much." Her hand dropped lower, cupping him through his pants. "And maybe I need a distraction right now."

"Cut it out, Shelby."

"You don't really want that, do you?" She squeezed him and his brain short-circuited, all of his good intentions evaporating in an explosion of heat and lust.

In a burst of movement, Reece grabbed her wrist and shoved her against the wall, trapping her there with his body. His gaze was fire as it dropped to her mouth and his body practically vibrated with all those dirty fantasies of his he tried so hard to keep a tight lid on. "Don't push me, little girl."

Little…?

Oh. Did he really just call her that?

Hell, no.

It was time to show him who was actually in control of this situation. She had him. Hook, line, and sinker. He just didn't know it yet.

Shelby shoved up on her toes, stopping only when her lips hovered inches below his. With her free hand, she reached down between their bodies again and found him hard, his erection straining the front of his perfectly pleated trousers. She wrapped her fingers around him and stroked him through his pants.

"I'm pushing," she whispered next to his mouth. "So what are you going to do about it?"

He closed the distance between their lips in a hard, take-no-prisoners kiss. He was demanding, unforgiving, as his tongue invaded and stroked and the rest of the world faded away. He released his grip on her hand to cup her breast, freeing her to plow her fingers through his soft dark hair.

Yes. He was the perfect distraction, exactly what she needed. To forget the rest of the world and just…feel.

He grabbed her ass and lifted her up until she had to wrap her legs around his hips or topple. She threw out an arm to keep upright, felt several of the floor buttons press under her palm, but who the hell cared? Reece was kissing her again, devouring her as his hand eased up her inner thigh under her skirt—

The elevator doors opened and a throat cleared. An older couple stood on the other side, dressed up for dinner. The man was trying to hide his smile, but his wife didn't bother.

"Excuse us," Reece said. He set Shelby down on her own two feet again and hauled her from the car by the hand. As soon as the doors shut, he pushed her against the wall and dropped his lips back to hers. "Where's your room?"

She laughed against his mouth. "This isn't my floor."

He swore and let go of her long enough to reach for the elevator's button, but she caught his hand and pulled. The alcove by the ice machine was dark, the bulb overhead burned out. She dragged him inside and tugged his shirt free, running her hands over all the delicious muscle of his back.

He growled in the back of his throat and banded his fingers around her wrists, stilling her hands. "Not here, Shelby."

"Why not?" She let her nails bite into his skin.

"We're going to get caught." Even as he protested, his erection jumped against her stomach, and his grip on her wrists loosened.

"But that turns you on, doesn't it?" Holding his gaze,

she guided his hand between her legs to the place already soaked with her desire. "It does for me."

"Jesus." He stroked her through her panties then shoved the strip of fabric aside and dropped to his knees in front of her. "This is crazy."

At the first swipe of his tongue, her legs threatened to give out, and she leaned into the wall for support. "Oh, but you're so hot when you get crazy."

His lips closed around her clitoris. The light suction sent shivers racing through her body, followed by wild flashes of heat. Her stomach muscles clenched, her hips bucked against his mouth. She'd never been with a guy who was so enthusiastic about going down on her. He was good at it, too. Knew how to use his lips and tongue and even the light scrape of his teeth to wring every ounce of pleasure out of their encounters. "Oh God. Reece—"

"Shh." He gazed up, his eyes dark, and slid a finger inside of her. "Don't make a sound." A second finger joined the first and stroked a spot inside that made her go lightheaded. "Make any noise at all and I stop, understand? Nod."

She wanted to smack him for that command, but when he stroked her again, her legs nearly gave out. She smothered a groan and nodded as another shiver of pleasure rippled down her spine.

He chuckled, and his breath fanned over her clit in a hot caress. Her thighs trembled. Hard. She locked her knees, bit down on her lower lip to keep from crying out. Then his tongue returned to tease her, his fingers found that spot again, and she melted. She lost herself in the orgasm, head spinning, body shaking uncontrollably. Heat swamped her, blasting away every worry, every thought, except one—she wanted him. All of him. Naked, pounding into her, sweat-slicked and out of control. God, did she want him.

When she finally floated back to herself, she opened her eyes to see Reece licking his fingers as if savoring the taste of her. And that was the biggest freaking turn-on ever. She reached for him. "Reece."

At the sound of her voice, his eyes snapped open. He scrambled to his feet, smoothed down his tie, and walked away without a word.

He. Walked. Away.

Shelby stood there, leaning against the wall, body still humming like a live wire. What the hell? She had been putty in his very talented hands. What kind of man walked away from that?

It was like that night at The Bean Gallery all over again.

Oh, no. He wasn't getting away with this oral-and-run routine a second time. It made her feel dirty—and not in a good way. He obviously enjoyed having his mouth on her, so why did he never want to go further than that? Why was she never allowed to reciprocate?

She walked out into the hall, glanced both ways. He was long gone, but that didn't matter. She knew where his suite was—right across the hall from Cam and Eva's. She jabbed the button to call the elevator.

Yeah, it was past time for Reece Wilde to get his.

Chapter Five

Jesus. Was he out of his goddamn mind?

Stupid question, Reece thought, and grabbed a bottle of bourbon from the complimentary bar in his suite. When it came to Shelby, he had no fucking sense in his head.

That girl was trouble with a capital T. In so many ways.

He yanked his tie loose and didn't bother with a glass, downing the bourbon straight from the bottle. He relished the burn as it slid down his throat, but it did fuck all to put out the fire raging in his blood. He pressed a palm to the ridge of his cock. Maybe if he drank enough, the damn thing would lose all interest in sassy tattooed women with impossible hair colors who tasted like spice and honey.

At the memory of Shelby on his tongue, he swore and took another long pull of the bourbon. He wasn't one to get sloshed to solve his problems, but tonight—yeah, tonight it seemed like the perfect plan.

He raised the bottle to his lips for a third hit, but a fist pounded against his door hard enough to rattle the chain. Oh, shit. Let it be Cam or Vaughn. Maybe Greer. Hell, he'd even take Jude. Anyone but—

He pulled open the door and was thrown back against the wall by a whirlwind of turquoise and purple and indignation.

"*You.*" Shelby took the bottle from his hand, knocked back a swallow, and pushed the door shut with one high heel. Then she pointed into the room. "Bed. Now."

He kept his face impassive. "I don't think so."

"Well, I do. That's the second time you've walked away. It's not happening again."

"I don't understand the problem. You had an orgasm. I gave you what you wanted."

"You have no clue what I want." She fused her mouth to his and her tongue invaded, seeking, claiming, branding.

Trouble, he tried to remind himself even as he clamped his hands around her hips. So much goddamn trouble.

And he didn't care.

Never had when it came to Shelby Bremer.

She broke away from the kiss and dragged him by the tie across the suite's seating area to the bedroom. The king-size bed sat kitty-corner between sweeping windows that offered a glittering panorama of the Vegas strip. Reece had a half second to consider hitting the remote to close the blinds, but forgot all about it when she shoved him down on the mattress and straddled his hips. She pulled on the knot of his tie until it fell loose, then whipped it off from around his neck.

"Wrists."

A thrill coursed through him. "No."

She wiggled out of her thong and swung it around her finger once before tossing it aside and grinding against his erection. Even through the layers of clothes still separating them, he felt her heat and the wetness from her earlier orgasm.

"Do you want this?" she demanded. "Don't lie."

He couldn't control the rumble growing in his chest. "Jesus, yes."

"Then you do what I say when I say it. Wrists."

Trembling, he held his arms out to her. Shelby looped the tie around his wrists, then secured the ends to the heavy wood bed frame. The room temperature shot up a good ten degrees as she slid down his body, popping open each button on his shirt. She trickled bourbon on every inch of skin she exposed and lapped it up. His muscles quivered under the long strokes of her tongue.

When she reached the edge of his pants, she sat up and undid his belt, unzipped his trousers, and freed him.

"Mmm." Her breath fanned over his cock. "You've been hiding a lot behind those suits huh, Hershey?"

"Reece," he gritted out between clenched teeth.

She laughed and drizzled bourbon on him, then circled his tip lightly with her tongue, sending electric shocks through his body. He strained against his bonds, wanting more than anything to dig his fingers into her hair and keep her hot little mouth on him. She continued with the light teasing until his entire body shook, and every breath he dragged in was a chore.

"Shelby…" Jesus, was that his voice? He sounded like he'd swallowed a handful of rocks.

"What?" she whispered against his hip and cupped his balls in one hand. "Tell me what you want."

"Your mouth."

"Where?"

He barely managed to strangle the words out. "On my cock."

"Now that's no way for a nice, straitlaced boy to talk." She bit his hip hard enough he was sure she left teeth marks, but the pain only intensified the pleasure, and his eyes all but rolled back in his head.

Jesus. Christ.

She was going to kill him. He'd die tied to this bed in a Vegas hotel room, and he'd be happy about it.

"Don't move." She traced her tongue down his length before sucking him in all the way, and he was lost. His world narrowed to Shelby, her mouth, her hands, and the throaty sounds she made as she tasted him. He didn't care about the family drama, the blackmail, propriety. All that mattered was the wild need she awoke inside him. He wanted to flip her over the bed and leave his handprint on her perfect little ass before plunging into her, and the frustration caused by his immobility only sharpened the edge of pleasure slicing through him. Heat pooled at the base of his spine, his muscles quaked, and his balls drew up tight. He wasn't going to last, and she wasn't showing him any mercy, assaulting him with her tongue and a light scrape of teeth that sent him into orbit.

Unable to hold still any longer, he curled his fingers around the tie holding his wrists, planted his feet on the mattress, and used the leverage to thrust against the soft, wet heat of her mouth. She moaned and the sound vibrated up his shaft, nailed him in the gut, and that was all it took. The orgasm ripped from him, left him breathless and boneless, all but a shuddering puddle there on the bed. Shelby relaxed on top of him, her head resting on his hip, her breath fanning over his still-hard cock. Her skin felt hot against his, and slight trembles vibrated through her into him. Damn, he needed her to release his hands so he could do for her what she had done for him.

"Shelby." His voice came out raw, and he had to clear his throat. "Let me taste you again."

For a moment, she didn't move. Then she pushed herself up and looked at him. Her cheeks were flushed, her turquoise and purple hair tousled, her lips plump and wet, and he was mesmerized by the sight of her.

At least until she said, "No," and got up off the bed.

Reece blinked. "What? Wait, where are you going?"

She pushed her hair back from her face, then draped a blanket over him. She found his cell phone in his pants pocket and pushed it into his hand. "Maybe the casino. Or a dance club. Haven't decided yet, but I plan to get shitfaced and forget this day ever happened."

"You can't just leave me like this."

"I don't understand the problem. You had an orgasm," she said from the doorway, throwing his own words back at him so sweetly his teeth ached. Then she was gone.

"Shelby!"

He heard the outer door click shut and groaned, dropping his head to the pillow. He gave his wrists a good tug, but that only tightened the tie. He tried again and the material constricted hard around his wrists.

Jesus. What kind of knot had she used?

He looked at the phone and groaned again, then hit the speed dial.

Fuck. He was going to regret this.

"**D**on't. Say. A. Word."

Greer just stared at him for an endless five seconds, then finally shook his head and walked into the bedroom, drawing a pocketknife from his jacket. "I'd guarantee something like this from Jude. Expect it from Vaughn. Hell, even Cam, I wouldn't be surprised. But you?" He cut the silk material in one clean slice. "I could live a million years and I'd've never expected to find you tied to a bed with your cock hanging out."

Reece sat up and rubbed his hands together, trying to work some feeling back into his fingers. "I told you, not a word."

Greer scooped up Shelby's thong with the tip of his knife and raised a brow. Leopard print. Because of course it was. "Not really a good look for you, bro."

"You know damn well it isn't mine."

"Yeah, and I'm intrigued." Greer flipped the thong toward him and it landed on his face, the lacy strap getting caught on his nose. He snatched it away, but not before he got a lung full of Shelby's scent. Lust shot through his blood and settled in his cock.

Jesus. Even with his brother in the room, her scent lit his fuse and set him off like he was a fucking firework. He needed to find her and when he did…

Oh, she was going to pay for this.

"I'd always kinda wondered if you were a tightly closeted gay," Greer said, and that snapped him out of his lusty thoughts as good as a punch in the balls. "Or…I don't know. Asexual?"

For a second, Reece's mouth didn't work. "Y-you *what*?"

"It's fine if you are," Greer added. "I don't care who you fuck. Or don't fuck. That's your business. You'll always be my brother, no matter what."

"I'm not gay. Or—asexual."

"Well, yeah, I know that *now*," Greer said with the faintest hint of a smirk.

"Why the hell would you think...no, hang on. I'm not having this conversation naked." He climbed out of bed and fastened his pants, then stripped off his unbuttoned shirt, which was damp from the bourbon, and folded it, set it on the end of the bed. He'd have to send it to the hotel's laundry or it would stain.

As he turned to face Greer again, he grabbed the bourbon from the nightstand where Shelby had left it and took a long pull. He had a feeling he'd need alcohol for the coming conversation.

Greer eyed him. "Take it easy. You already smell like a distillery."

"Body shots," he muttered. And because the memory heated him up more than the bourbon, he took another pull from the bottle.

Greer made a choking sound. "Body shots?"

He lifted a shoulder. "What happens in Vegas..."

Greer pinched the bridge of his nose. "Christ, I need a drink. No," he added when Reece offered him the bottle. "Not that one. I'll get my own."

It was for the better, Reece decided and followed his brother to the living area. He planned to drink until he could no longer feel Shelby's lips on him, until her scent left his nose and stopped fucking with his brain function. That would probably take every last ounce in the bottle. And then some.

He dropped to the couch and stared out the windows at the glittering neon of the strip. "What the hell made you think I'm gay?"

Greer grabbed a beer from the fridge and popped off the cap without a bottle opener. "Because you've never shown any interest in women."

"And I have in men?"

"No. I just thought you were confused or embarrassed or—I don't know. You haven't seemed interested in sex, period, which is what led me to the asexual conclusion."

"I've dated."

"Yeah? Who?"

Reece fished through his memory for a name, any name, and came up empty. There had been women, here and there, but…

Yeah, he had nothing.

Greer pointed the neck of his bottle like a finger. "Exactly."

"I've been busy."

"Yeah, you had an empire to build. Money to make."

If he wasn't mistaken, sorrow tinged Greer's tone, and that kind of pissed him off. "We both know Wilde Security wouldn't exist right now if I hadn't built that empire. It's the only thing keeping our heads above water."

Greer paced over to the floor-to-ceiling windows and drank his beer in silence for several minutes. The neon lights from the street below played over his hard-planed face, highlighting the dark shadows under his eyes. Jude had once said Greer looked like their dad. And until that moment, Reece hadn't really paid enough attention to see it. He did now, though. Those broad shoulders filling out a six foot, five inch frame, dark hair buzzed to the scalp and even darker eyes, a square-jawed face made of hard edges... Jesus, Greer was Dad's clone and the realization tightened like a vise around Reece's heart.

Twenty years later, and he still missed his parents every single hour of every single day.

"Would it be such a bad thing," Greer murmured, "if we went under?"

Alarm had Reece sitting up straighter. "Are you kidding me? Cam left a good job with the police to work for us. Vaughn gave up any number of promising careers in the private sector, and Jude? What else would he do? They're counting on us."

"Yeah," Greer said, and it seemed the weight of the entire world rested on that one word. He rubbed the back of his neck. "You're right. Forget I said that. I'm tired."

"I've noticed. Don't you sleep anymore?"

"We're not talking about me," Greer said abruptly and jerked his thumb toward the bedroom. "This...thing between you and Shelby needs to stop."

Reece tried to keep his features blank but had a feeling he'd already given himself away. Still, he tried to laugh it off. "Shelby? Are you kidding? No, it wasn't her."

Greer lifted a brow. "Word of advice, stay away from the poker tables. A blind man could read your tells."

"Fuck." Reece dropped his head into his hands. "Don't say anything to Cam. Or Eva."

"It's not my place to, but I'm telling you now, end it."

"There's nothing to end."

"Yeah, looks it." Greer walked to the door, but stopped before opening it and glanced back. "Just remember Shelby's...well, you're playing with fire. And not a nice, controlled one either. She's a wildfire and I'd hate to see you get burned, bro."

Wildfire. That was an apt description of Shelby Bremer. Hot, oddly seductive, and dangerous as hell.

Reece brooded by himself for several minutes after Greer left and swilled the bourbon, watching the light glint off the amber liquid as it sloshed around inside the bottle. He'd regret drinking more. His head was fuzzy, skin warmed by the alcohol. He set the bottle aside and levered himself up to pace over to the windows, but a rattle from the hallway caught his attention, like someone was trying to get into his room.

Had Greer come back?

Or...Shelby?

He walked over and waited a beat for the knock, but none came. He reached for the knob and a white envelope slid under the door, landing on his foot. His name was printed on the front in a handwriting font.

A hard lump of dread settled in his gut as he picked it up. From the weight and feel of it, he had a good idea what he'd find inside. He sucked in a fortifying breath and ripped open the envelope, dumping the contents out on the small foyer table. Photos. Of him and Shelby, his hand between her legs as he held her trapped against the wall. And then with his head between her legs.

Heart thundering, he yanked open the door even though he knew the person who had dropped this was long gone.

Yup. Hallway was empty.

He shut the door and grabbed a handful of tissues from the bathroom before returning to the table. He didn't dare handle the photos on the off chance his blackmailer had left fingerprints.

The quality of the photos wasn't good, printed by an inkjet printer on cheap glossy paper. But nor were they bad enough that he'd be able to legitimately deny the photos were of him. Anyone with eyes could see that he was the man kneeling between Shelby's legs.

So much for the whole what-happens-in-Vegas-stays-in-Vegas thing.

Jesus, could he make it any easier for his blackmailer?

Except he never expected his blackmailer to follow him all the way here. That was weird. He was no expert on the subject, but he knew that was not normal blackmail behavior.

Okay. So it's another piece of the puzzle.

One that actually told him quite a bit more about the person behind this. The blackmailer didn't just want money from him. If that was all, why the unnecessary expense of chasing him across the country? No, this person wanted something else. To ruin him? A distinct possibility.

He used a tissue to spread the photos out and studied each one closely. The person who took them had to have been in the hallway, too, but Reece had been too focused on Shelby to notice if anyone had followed them. He hadn't seen anyone when he walked away from her, either, but now that he thought about it, he did hear the elevator bell seconds before he pulled away from her—it was the sound that had brought him back to his senses. Had that innocuous ding been his blackmailer fleeing the scene?

On the back of the last photo, he found a message printed in the same cursive font as on the envelope.

What will your business associates think of you slumming it?

Fury lit him up. He wasn't slumming. Not with Shelby.

Okay, so his business associates might think that, but only because they were all stuck-up assholes. They considered sleeping with anyone who had less than a million in the bank "slumming." In some circles of older money, Reece himself was considered plebeian because he was self-made, from a family with a long history of career military and blue-collar workers.

Shit. He had to tell Shelby about this. He rubbed a hand over his face, stubble rasping against his palm, and stared at the photos. As much as he'd rather not, these pictures were of her, too, and she needed to know. What if it didn't just stop at pictures? Already the blackmailer had tiptoed over the line into stalking territory.

What if he was putting her in danger by not telling her?

Chapter Six

Shelby was in a dismal mood, and not even the chaos of vibrant lights and sounds on the casino floor cheered her.

This whole day had sucked.

Well, okay, not the entire day. She quite liked how it had ended and relished the thought of Reece tied to the bed, having to call one of his brothers for help.

Served him right.

But the rest of the day? Ugh. Was it possible to request a do-over from the big guy upstairs? She gazed toward the ceiling, but she'd never had much luck praying. Besides, she'd never set foot in a real church in her life—the chapel here in the hotel was the closest she'd come. If a big guy was up there granting prayers, he wasn't gonna listen to her.

The bartender arrived with her cocktail and she plucked the stick of cherries out of it, biting off the top one.

She really hadn't meant to ruin Eva's wedding day. She had only wanted…hell, she didn't know. She wanted a mother. Like, the real deal, not the spacey excuse for a mother she'd been born to, and part of her yearned to believe Katrina had changed. But Eva was probably right. Katrina would slip back into her old ways sooner rather than later, and did she really want to put any faith in that woman?

No.

The hurt and betrayal in the days after their mother attacked them last fall had been a bitter pill to swallow. Shelby absolutely didn't want that heartbreak ever again.

So cheers to fucked-up childhoods and crappy mothers. She lifted her glass and toasted her reflection in the mirror behind the bar. She'd drink tonight and wallow in her self-pity, then tomorrow she'd find Eva and apologize. She could admit now she'd only told their mother about the wedding out of some selfish need to be loved.

Stupid.

Who'd ever love her? Her own mother couldn't, and her sister barely tolerated her.

Shelby realized too late that tears had escaped her eyes and were rolling freely down her face. "Dammit." She whisked them away with the back of her hand and lifted her glass to take a healthy drink. Movement in the mirror drew her attention, and she gazed up into the eyes of the one man she absolutely did *not* want to see.

"Jason." She shook her head and downed half of her cocktail in one swallow. "You fucking followed me to Vegas?"

Jason Mallory stood behind her chair, blocking her in with his big, tattooed body. His hands landed on her shoulders. "I need an answer, Shelby."

"How about 'fuck you'. Is that answer enough for you?"

His fingers tightened. "Are you already forgetting our

arrangement? Prison wouldn't look good on you."

"I'm not forgetting." She spun and held out her wrists. "If you're going to arrest me, do it."

He stared at her for a long time, jaw clenched, then knocked her hands aside. "I'm doing you a favor here. The least you can do is honor our arrangement."

"The last time I *honored our arrangement*, someone died and my father ended up in prison."

"Because you put him there."

She let a shuddering breath go and turned back to her drink, downing a large gulp. "I'm not helping you hurt Reece."

"If he's done nothing wrong, you won't be hurting him."

"He's done nothing wrong."

"That's for you to find out." His gaze went over her head to the mirror and tracked someone near the elevators.

Oh God. It was Reece. And no doubt he was looking for her.

Reece stepped off the elevator and studied the casino floor, searching for Shelby's distinctive hair. He was holding out hope she hadn't bounced off to one of the other casinos on the strip. Or, Christ help him, a dance club.

He scanned the bar area and—

There. A flash of turquoise headed toward the front door in a hurry.

Reece ducked and maneuvered through the crowd and opened his mouth to call her name, but stopped. A man was following her—huge, bald, long dark beard, covered in tattoos.

Shit, that couldn't be good.

Outside the hotel, the guy grabbed her arm so hard he spun her around. She teetered on her ridiculously high heels and even from this distance Reece saw the flash of fear in her eyes. Anger sliced through him, startling in its intensity, and he picked up the pace, reaching her just as she twisted out of the man's grasp and lost her footing. She tumbled to the sidewalk and the man reached inside his lightweight coat.

Armed.

The guy had a gun. Was he planning to use the weapon on Shelby?

Reece didn't think, just let instinct take over, honed by his near religious devotion to the dojo. He braced himself and sent a kick flying toward the guy's side, felt a solid connecting blow rattle up his leg. The man howled, and the gun clattered to the sidewalk. Several stares turned in their direction as Baldy scrambled for the weapon.

Reece stepped in front of Shelby, but the guy had lost interest as more people stopped to gape. He must have decided there were too many witnesses, because he bolted across the street, headed in the opposite direction of their hotel. He'd be long gone before any of the bystanders finished calling 911, and Reece didn't particularly want to stick around for an encounter with Las Vegas's finest, either. He pulled Shelby to her feet and hustled her into the teeming crowd gathered to watch the Bellagio's fountains dance to Frank Sinatra's *Fly Me to the Moon* against the glittering palatial backdrop of the hotel.

As water soared into the air in synchronized bursts, he

caged her against the balustrade and used his bigger body to hide her distinctive appearance in the crowd, just in case the guy got any stupid ideas about circling back and trying again.

She was shaking, little trembles racing through her, and yet she smirked up at him. "Nice roundhouse, Hershey."

He backed away just enough to meet her gaze while still keeping her shielded. "What was that all about?"

"It was…nothing. No big." She lifted a shoulder and tried to shrug away from him, but he was not letting her get away so easily. He banded his arms around her and lowered his face to hover inches above hers. To anyone nearby, it'd look as if they were lovers stealing a romantic moment in front of the fountains.

Hah. Couldn't be any further from the truth.

"That was not nothing," he said. "He had a gun. What's going on, Shelby?"

She licked her lips. "I…" For a heartbeat, genuine fear showed in her eyes before she dropped her gaze. "I think he wanted something from me."

"Like?" When she didn't respond, he added, "You're not carrying a purse."

"I dunno then." Her tone was casual, as if a near mugging was something that happened to her every day. "But he's gone. You scared him off. My hero. So why did you come looking for me anyway?"

Okay, she wasn't ready to talk about it. Yet. But he'd get it out of her sooner or later, so for the moment, he let the subject drop. "Besides the fact you left me tied to my bed?"

Her smile was the picture of innocence. "Besides that."

Grumbling, he lifted his head to glance around. Didn't

see Baldy anywhere nearby. Good. He led her away from the crowd, his hand entwined with hers. Just another happy couple taking in the sights and sounds of the Vegas strip together.

Shelby swung their joined hands and oohed and aahed over all the lights like nothing had happened. Her ability to deflect was astounding. Even better than Cam's, and that was saying something since Cam was the master.

But Reece didn't have the luxury of ignoring his problems. He had to deal with them, and fast. He waited only until the crowd thinned out enough that he could talk without being overheard, then drew a fortifying breath. "I came to find you because I'm being blackmailed."

Her mouth actually dropped open, and she pulled him to a stop. "What?"

"Technically, we both are, because someone has video footage from the security cameras at The Bean Gallery."

She scoffed, shook her head. "No, that's not possible."

"Then it's a damn convincing fake, because it sure looked like us. I received the video with a demand for money unless I wanted the video leaked. And I don't."

She said nothing for several beats, then turned away. "Who can blame you?"

The note of dejection in her voice caught him completely off guard. "Shelby—" He had to run to catch up to her and grabbed her hand, pulling her to stop. "Hey, the reason I don't want it leaked has nothing to do with you."

She arched a brow. The ring there glinted in the neon of a sign promoting a burlesque show. "Oh no?"

"No!" When she remained unconvinced, he pushed out a breath. He had not expected this, hadn't expected the hurt she was trying so hard to shrug off. He closed his hands around her shoulders and waited until she met his gaze. "Look, I'm in the middle of a very delicate negotiation and any…indiscretion on my part will ruin it." And possibly ruin both DMW Systems and Wilde Security in the process. He needed this deal to keep both of his companies going, but telling her on this busy street felt too much like exposing his jugular and inviting everyone to come slice it open, so he kept his mouth shut.

"Indiscretion?" she echoed.

He winced. He was screwing this all up, wasn't he? "Uh, not that I think what we've done is, but—"

"Forget it." She shook her head. "I know you're way out of my league and tonight and the other night—they were lapses of judgment on your part. I get it, really. So what can I do to help?"

"Nothing. I only told you about it to warn you. If that video or the photos I received earlier tonight go public—it could tarnish your reputation as well."

She snorted. "Oh, Hershey. You can't tarnish something that was never polished to begin with."

"Stop." He caught her chin between his fingers before she turned away. "Someone massively fucked with your head, didn't they?"

Her lips tightened, and stubbornness shone in every line of her face. "I'm stating the obvious. Everyone might think I live out in la-la land, but I'm a realist. I know what I am. I know what you are. 'Oh, East is East, and West is West, and never the twain shall meet.'"

Surprise coursed through him, and he dropped his hand. "*The Ballad of East and West.* Kipling."

Color stained her cheeks. "I *can* read. In fact, I enjoy it."

He blinked. This woman had the ability to throw him off like nobody he'd ever met. "I-I didn't mean to insinuate — "

"Like I said, forget it." She waved a hand dismissively, turned away, and froze in her tracks. "Oh, shit."

Reece followed the direction of her frantic gaze to Baldy, a half a block away...

And headed right toward them.

Chapter Seven

"In here." Reece ducked into the first available building, dragging Shelby behind him with a hard tug on her hand, and they came face-to-face with Elvis in a black and pink fifties-themed diner. As if that wasn't surreal enough, a woman in a blue poodle-skirt sat at a table nearby, popping her gum as she tapped out a text on her phone.

Shelby giggled, and the sound was slightly hysterical even to her own ears. But this was all so ridiculous, and the shell-shocked look on Reece's face was the cherry on top.

"Hello," Elvis said. "Are you here to get married?"

Reece choked. "Uh, what? Married? No. We're just... passing through." He grabbed her hand again and tried to pull her across the tile floor, but Elvis gave her an idea. A crazy idea, sure, but what was life without a little bit of cray-cray?

"Wait." She dug in her heels. "This is it. This is the answer to both of our problems."

Reece glanced back at her like she'd lost her mind. And maybe she had, but since Jason, goddamn him, was determined to force her hand, she couldn't see another way out of this mess.

"Give us a minute?" she asked Elvis. He nodded and both he and his assistant slipped away.

Reece whirled on her. "We're not getting married."

"Just hear me out, okay? I know it's nuts. We're east and west. But you need the blackmail threat to go away and if we're married, those pictures and video become sleazy. No longer blackmail material. You can secure your business deal and then we can get it quietly annulled and go our separate ways."

He opened his mouth. Closed it again. Opened. Closed. Like a fish gasping for breath. Finally, he shook his head and muttered, "It would solve my problem, but what's in it for you?"

Oh, bugger. She hadn't thought this far ahead. She should have known he'd not go blithely along with such an insane plan without asking questions first, but how much to tell him?

What's in it for me, you ask? Well, if we do this, I can unobtrusively get all up in your business, give Jason the information he wants, and maybe, just maybe, he will finally let me go.

Yeah, no. The truth was 100 percent out of the question. She bit down on her lower lip, glanced toward the door, and settled on a version of the truth. "I, uh, kinda need money."

His eyes darkened and he shrugged off the hand she'd set on his arm. "I should have known."

"I'm sorry. I wouldn't ask but I…" *Okay, deep breath*

and spit it out. "I lied to everybody. I, um, kinda *own* The Bean Gallery."

"You *what*?"

"Yeah. Surprise." She tried for a smile, but it withered under his blistering stare. "I borrowed money from some bad people and bought it when the owners put it up for sale in November, then I told Eva I got a job there."

Reece pinched the bridge of his nose. "Let me get this straight. You *bought* a *business* when you have *zero* management experience?"

She shrugged. When he put it that way, it did sound ridiculous, but she was a fast learner and until the arson, The Bean Gallery had been doing just fine. "I thought it would be a good way for me to go straight and do something right for once, but now it's gone and I don't have a way to pay back the money I owe."

God, her stomach hurt. The lies came much too easily now.

"Shelby…" Clearly exasperated, he dragged a hand through his hair, tousling the neat strands. "What about insurance? Surely you had the store insured."

"Yes, but the people I borrowed from…" She motioned to the door behind them and let Reece draw his own conclusions about why Jason had been following her. "They're not content to wait for an insurance payout and as long as there's an arson investigation going on, I'm not going to see a dime."

Reece said nothing for a long time. "So the man chasing you…?"

"Yes. That's why." It was the truth. Mostly. Or at least a version of it. But, God, she needed Reece to believe because this half-truth was her only way out. "They sent him after me. I…think they want to make an example out of me."

"You *think*?" he demanded. Then after a beat of silence, asked, "How much?"

"One hundred thousand."

"Jesus Christ, Shelby."

"C'mon, your car's worth more than that. It's pocket change to you."

He rubbed the back of his neck, sighed. "How bad are these people?"

Oh, God. She didn't want to tell him.

His eyes narrowed. "Shelby?"

"They're…" She winced. "The Headhunters."

"The motorcycle gang? Are you fucking kidding me?"

"Mom used to date one of their guys." Another half-truth. She was digging herself into a deeper hole, but she couldn't tell him the full truth and wasn't that the story of her life? "I grew up around them, and they seemed like a safe bet."

"A *safe* bet? Jesus. You wouldn't know safe if it bit you on the ass."

"And you wouldn't know spontaneity if it smacked you upside the head," she shot back.

Reece made a low grumbling sound in his throat and paced away from her. A few seconds later, he whirled back. "The Headhunters are a criminal organization, no different than the mob. Would you have borrowed the money from the mob?"

"No! Of course not. I have a brain."

His expression clearly asked, *Then why the fuck don't you use it?* But to his credit, he didn't say it out loud. "They're absolutely going to make an example out of you if you don't pay up. That's their M.O."

"Yeah, not a newsflash. Why do you think I'm running from them? I like my legs unbroken, thank you very much. Even more than that, I'd really like to keep breathing for the next fifty or so years."

"All right," he said abruptly, startling her.

"Whoa, wait. Was that a let's-get-hitched all right or — "

"Yes. As much as it pains me to admit this, you have a point. Marriage will solve my problem until I can figure out who's behind the blackmail."

Shelby exhaled hard. Okay, Reece didn't sound thrilled about it, but he did agree it was their best option. The sense of relief that swamped her left her lightheaded, almost giddy. She might be able to pull this off after all. Solve both of their problems and keep herself alive and out of prison. Maybe after this was over, she'd even have a shot at a real life, away from people like Jason, away from the world she was born into, the world she wanted out of but kept getting dragged back to.

"But," Reece added and her heart dropped. "If we want to pull this off, you have to stop being..." He motioned to her with both hands.

"Stop...what? Being me?"

"Exactly. My wife can't have blue hair and tattoos and piercings and...all of this. It has to go."

Shelby somehow managed to keep her wince inward and gazed down at her inked arms. "I can't get rid of my tattoos."

"You can cover them up."

But...she liked her tattoos. She liked being her. Well,

for the most part. And the thought of changing herself for even a little while caused her stomach to twist. Changing to please a man was far too much like her mother for comfort. Maybe this wasn't such a great idea after all.

Except what other choice did she have? Reece was her golden ticket, her shot at getting out of all this crazy and making herself a better life. If she had to change to get his help, she'd do it. She'd just think of it like a temporary witness protection program.

"Okay." She worked up a bright smile that hurt her cheeks. "Let's do this."

S ometimes when life takes an unexpected turn, it leaves you awed and excited. Other times, it just leaves you feeling off-kilter and queasy, like you stepped off a carnival ride.

Reece felt as if he hadn't yet gotten off that ride. The world was whirling around him at nauseating speeds and he couldn't think, couldn't breathe—

What the hell was he doing?

He stood at the jukebox-slash-altar, next to the overly cheerful Elvis, with his stomach doing corkscrews. In the ninety minutes since Shelby had disappeared with Elvis's assistant, he'd woken up his shocked lawyer back in D.C. and had a prenup drawn up, which he then gave to the assistant to take to Shelby. He may have lost his mind, but he wasn't about to take any chances when it came to his companies. Not when his brothers and one hundred other people counted on him to keep their paychecks coming.

The prenup came back signed and was filed along with the marriage license and—holy fuck, was he really going to do this?

Yes.

He never pictured himself getting married but, yes, he was going to go through with it. He couldn't keep paying the blackmail. Without a doubt there was another email already sitting in his inbox, demanding more money. And he couldn't very well leave Shelby in danger when he was more than able to help. So she was right—this was a win-win short-term solution for the both of them. Shelby would get her money, and he'd have time to figure out the identity of his blackmailer.

A business arrangement. That was all this was. They'd do the ceremony thing and then outline some rules and—

The doors at the back of the room opened. Shelby stepped through and everything stopped. His racing thoughts. His flipping stomach. All the nerves eased away, and a strange sense of peace filled him.

She wore a classy 1950s-style dress in bridal white, but she had added a splash of color with a poufy underskirt that matched the purple in her hair. The ensemble screamed "Shelby" and a smile tugged at the corner of his mouth. How she managed to inject her own style into this was beyond him, but he admired her for it.

Too bad she'd have to tone it down once they returned home. His smile faded at the thought. It wasn't fair to ask her to change herself, but it was the only way this cockeyed scheme had any hope of working.

Next to him, Elvis broke out into song. It took him a second to place the lyrics: "Can't Help Falling in Love."

Jesus.

By the time Shelby reached them, she was laughing so hard tears streamed from her eyes. "Oh my God. You should see your face right now. Priceless."

Reece leaned toward her, lowered his voice. "Why is he singing?"

She dropped her voice to match his. "Because he's Elvis."

"He could have picked a different song."

"Like what? 'Jailhouse Rock'?"

Reece groaned. "Can we get this over with?" he asked, interrupting Elvis halfway through the second verse.

To his credit, Elvis didn't miss a beat as he switched into officiant mode. "Do you have the rings?"

Fuck. No. Rings hadn't even crossed his mind.

But there was the assistant carrying a box shaped like a pink Cadillac. Inside were two rings, both plain silver except for the colorful abalone shell inlay around each band.

"They had a selection of rings here," Shelby said, sounding uncharacteristically unsure of herself. "I picked these out while you were dealing with the paperwork. I mean, I know this is just for show...but are they okay?"

He accepted the thinner band—Shelby's ring—from the assistant and marveled at the glint of light off the shell inlay. All the tiny swirls of silver and green and purple and black. It managed to be both practical and fanciful, and didn't that describe the pair of them to a T?

He picked up her hand and slid the ring into place. "It's perfect."

Her smile lit the room and, yeah, in that second, it was perfect.

Chapter Eight

Shelby climbed into the back of the limo provided to take them to their hotel. It was just as chintzy as the rest of the wedding had been, with blue suede 50s decor, and a gaudy JUST MARRIED sign on the back window. She kind of loved it.

Reece, on the other hand…

She settled into the leather seat across from him. He was adorably rumpled, his hair tousled, his tie askew, his jacket wrinkled. If she was pressed to give a name to his appearance she'd call it "shell-shocked," or maybe "flabbergasted" was a better term. When he reached to open the mini fridge and spotted the ring on his finger, he froze, stared at the band for several heartbeats, then grabbed the complimentary bottle of champagne instead of the water he'd been reaching for. He popped the cork and downed half the contents in one breath, his throat working with each swallow.

Damn. That was sexy.

The temperature in the car inched into uncomfortable

territory, and Shelby shifted in her seat, crossed her legs under the skirt of her dress. Sure, all of the Wilde brothers were good looking, but Reece? With his long, lean muscles and cutting hazel eyes, he was sex walking around in a perfectly tailored suit. She'd always thought so, since she first saw him at The Bean Gallery, back before she knew he was Cam's brother.

And now they were married.

Weird.

She twisted her ring around on her finger and couldn't take his silence a second longer. "So. Interesting night."

He made a noncommittal sound and sat back, loosening his tie with a quick tug that did absolutely nada to douse the firestorm of lust building inside her.

What would he do if she crawled over there and straddled his lap? He was her husband now, after all. Wasn't that expected behavior on a honeymoon?

She entertained the fantasy of hot limo sex for a few minutes, but never made a move toward him. She knew better. They may be legally married, but it wasn't real. Yes, they had a mad case of lust-at-first-sight, but there was no love here. The optimist in her liked to think there might have been something more between them if circumstances were different, but this farce had ended any possibility of that. And she wasn't quite sure where that left them.

Reece set the bottle aside and finally met her gaze. "We need to figure out the rules for this…marriage."

She resisted the urge to roll her eyes. Of course he'd want rules. He liked black and white. No shades of gray. And definitely no spontaneous bursts of color. What a boring life he must lead. "Oh, I don't know. I thought we'd wing it."

He narrowed his eyes at her. "I don't *wing* anything."

"You did a good job of it today." She held up her ring finger, wiggled it for emphasis. "Unless you planned to put a ring on it when you got up this morning?"

Groaning, he pinched the bridge of his nose like he had a headache. "Fuck me. What have I done?"

She would *not* let those words hurt. Nope. Not at all. Rubber and glue and all that bouncing. "Hey, if you're having second thoughts, we can go get it annulled right now. Claim temporary insanity. I bet it will go down as the shortest marriage in history. Even by Vegas standards."

"No." He dropped his hands to his lap. "We'll see this through. We have sixty days to get an annulment. That's time enough to solve both of our problems."

"What if you don't catch your blackmailer by then?"

His jaw hardened. "I will." He left no room for argument in his tone. It was as if a conversational wall had dropped around the subject with a big sign that read, "Off fucking limits."

O-kay then. Reece was so buttoned-up and reserved she sometimes forgot he was a Wilde. None of those brothers were soft, weak men. Even the family geek had the blood of a warrior pumping through his veins, and the glimpse of that side of him discomforted her. She'd never before lumped Reece in the same mental category with his cavemen brothers, but she'd be sure not to make that mistake in the future. He was just as dangerous as the rest of them, and it'd serve her well to remember that.

For the first time since this insanity started, she began having second thoughts. It seemed like such a good idea a few hours ago, a way to solve a whole host of problems, some of which she hadn't told Reece about. But her worst fails always seemed like good ideas at first. Like The Bean Gallery, for example. And…other things.

A sudden case of nerves ate at her. She fidgeted—couldn't seem to stop—and smoothed out the fabric of her skirt. "Um. What kind of rules?"

Leaning forward, he linked his hands between his knees. "If we are going to do this, we have to go all out and play it like a real marriage, like we're madly in love, or it won't be convincing."

"Even with family?"

He winced, showing a chink in the armor he seemed to have drawn around himself since leaving the chapel. "I'm not looking forward to that."

"They'll know we didn't magically fall in love in the past six hours and decide to elope."

"Agreed. But we will have to make them understand our reasoning so they'll play along. Though I'd rather not divulge the details about the blackmail. My brothers will go into fight mode, and this situation requires a more delicate touch than their slash-bang-boom method of dealing with problems."

She laughed. Her sister really was the perfect fit for the Wilde family. That was exactly Eva's method of dealing, too, which only highlighted how very different Shelby was from them all. She preferred to laugh away her problems and, if that didn't work, she ran away and remade herself. Still, she could play the part of a Wilde woman for two months.

Maybe.

She also leaned forward. "If you don't want to tell them about the blackmail, then I'd prefer they not know I borrowed money to buy The Bean Gallery."

He scowled. "With the arson investigation, it's going to come out whether we tell them or not."

"The same can be said for your blackmail." When the scowl only deepened, she sighed. "I know, okay? Just…not yet. Please."

"Fine. I won't say a word."

She held up her hand, pinky outstretched. "No talk of your blackmail or my money issues. Pinky swear."

He stared at her, unblinking. "You're not serious."

"Yes I am." She wiggled her hand in the air. "In my world, pinky swears are as binding as a legal contract."

"You and Jude must be from the same world," he muttered, but hooked his pinky through hers. "Okay?"

She nodded, satisfied, and relaxed into her seat again. "Any other rules, Oh Great Rule-maker?"

And there was the scowl again. "When we return home, you'll take my name. Doesn't have to be a legal change, but in public you'll be Shelby Wilde. You'll also have to move in."

"Whoa, hold up. The name thing? Whatever. A rose by any other name and all that. But moving in? You do know I'm a package deal, right? I have a parrot, and he lives where I live."

"A parrot?" Reece sighed heavily. "Loud. Colorful. Somehow that doesn't surprise me."

"He's an African gray, for your information, and a good bird. Very affectionate."

"Fine. We'll make it work, but I can't guarantee the cat won't try to eat him."

Of course he'd have a cat. They were a match made

in pet-owner heaven. "Aloof, cold. Somehow that doesn't surprise me."

He didn't acknowledge her mocking tone. "You can keep your bird in the guest room where you'll be sleeping."

"Wow. Okay. That was about as subtle as an anvil falling from the sky."

"You're my wife in name only and we won't be, uh…" He cleared his throat. "Consummating this marriage."

"I didn't know anyone used the word 'consummating' anymore."

"I was trying to be polite, but if you'd rather I put it in terms you understand, then fine. No fucking."

"What about oral?"

"We will not be sharing a bed. Period."

She was getting under his skin. She could tell by the tick in the muscle just below his temple as he tried to hang on to his temper. And maybe she was suicidal, but she had to keep poking at him. She wanted to see him lose that mighty control, same as he had earlier in the evening when she'd tied him to the bed. "You don't have to do it in a bed. I mean, you should know that since you worshiped quite thoroughly at my altar in the hotel's hallway."

His teeth ground together. "I've never paid for sex in my life, and I'm not starting now."

The words hit her like a slap, and every drop of amusement drained away. If they had sex, and he gave her money to pay back her debt, that would essentially make her a prostitute, wouldn't it? Her stomach knotted. "Oh."

"Yeah," was all Reece said, his tone heavy with scorn.

"Oh my God. You think I've done it before? Traded my body for money?"

"What you've done in the past is none of my business. Just know it's not happening with me."

"Anyone ever tell you that you're a complete asshole?" Tears blurred her vision as the car came to a stop. She didn't wait for the driver to let her out, but gathered her poufy skirts in one hand and shoved open the door, because she was about five seconds from a sobbing fit, and she wasn't going to let him see how much he'd hurt her. The hotel entrance was busy with people, and a few stopped to stare as she stalked across the pavement and pushed into the front lobby.

Her intention was to go up to her room, pour herself a glass of wine, and have a good long sulk, maybe make use of the Jacuzzi tub, but that idea was dashed when she turned the corner into the elevator bank and literally ran into her sister and Cam, both still dressed in their wedding clothes. And, crap, there were Vaughn and Greer getting out of one of the elevators. And Jude and his wife Libby. The whole fam damily.

"Shelby!" Eva grabbed her in a hard hug, then set her back at arm's length. "Jesus. Where have you been? And... what the hell are you wearing?"

She sensed Reece approaching behind her and told herself to suck it up when his hand landed on her shoulder. She had a role to play. The sulking would have to wait until later.

Eva narrowed her eyes at Reece and then her gaze zeroed in on his hand—his left hand—and her eyes bulged. The expression would have been comical if Shelby could work up the energy to be amused. As it was, she just felt... used up.

Why did they all have to be standing right here, right now?

"What. The. Fuck?" Eva said, and that was the only warning she gave before winding up and sending her fist into Reece's jaw. His knees buckled, and he collapsed right there on the hotel's marble floor.

The brothers all burst into motion. Greer stepped between them, using his big body as a blockade, and Vaughn yanked Shelby out of the way. Cam locked his arms around Eva and all but lifted his wife off her feet to keep her from going at Reece again. Jude hurried to Reece's side and propped a shoulder under his arm to help him up.

"Motherfucker!" Eva spat. "How dare you take advantage of my baby sister!"

"You assume I'm the one taking advantage." Reece swayed a little on his feet and touched his quickly bruising jaw. "It was a mutually agreed upon marriage."

"What?" Several of the guys said at the same time, and their heads all swiveled in Reece's direction.

"Dude. You *married* Shelby?" Jude said, and burst out laughing. He grabbed his phone from his pocket and started snapping pictures. "Oh yeah. This is going in the family album for sure."

Everyone ignored him.

"I assume this is your doing, because she doesn't know any better," Eva said, jabbing a finger in Shelby's direction.

All right. Enough of this.

Shelby crossed to Reece's side and slid an arm around his waist since he still seemed a bit unsteady on his feet. "Evie, I'm almost thirty. Stop treating me like a child."

Eva whirled on her. "Then stop acting like one! Jesus,

Shelby. In what world is marrying a man you hardly know adult-like behavior? This isn't a fucking Disney movie."

"I know what I'm doing."

Eva snorted. "That'd be a first."

Shelby flinched. Ouch. To her surprise, Reece's armed curled around her shoulders and tightened, pulling her against his side.

He glared at Eva. "Apologize."

Eva crossed her arms. "No. She needs to hear it."

Their argument was starting to draw a crowd, and Greer made a cutting motion with his hand, ending all discussion. "All of you. Upstairs. Now."

Chapter Nine

"What the hell were you thinking?" Greer demanded and whirled on Reece as soon as the suite's door shut behind them. Everyone thought it best to keep Eva away from him, so the women had broken off and gone to Cam's suite, leaving the brothers to duke it out in Reece's.

They should have let Eva have another go at him. Getting his ass handed to him by her would be easier than the upcoming conversation. "I was thinking...it's none of your fucking business."

"Goddammit, Reece." Greer dragged a hand across his jaw, scrubbed it over his military-short hair. "I told you to stay away from her, not go and fucking marry her."

Exhausted, his jaw aching, Reece dropped to the couch and stretched out on his back, resting his arm over his eyes. "It's a business arrangement. Nothing more."

Vaughn entered the suite carrying a bag of ice from the machine down the hall. "For your jaw. She whacked you good." He tossed the bag at Reece's gut, then smirked over at the rest of their brothers. "And you all thought *I* had issues."

"You do," Cam said to his twin. "But that's a discussion for another day." He squared off in front of the couch and crossed his arms. "What kind of business can you possibly have with Shelby? I mean...*Shelby*? Really, bro? I get that you had a thing for her, but Jesus Christ."

"He must have knocked her up. That's the only explanation," Jude said cheerfully and helped himself to a beer from the fridge.

The suggestion set them all off again like a match to a bomb's fuse. Reece closed his eyes, pressed the ice to his jaw, and let them rage around him. Was Shelby having any better luck with Eva and Libby?

Probably not.

"Holy fuck," Cam said as he paced back and forth across the room. "Please tell me that's not the case. Eva will kill you."

Vaughn nodded his agreement. "Oh, hell yeah. And slowly."

Cam groaned. "Yeah and then she'll ask me to help her hide the body. I don't want to make that choice between my wife and my brother."

Reece sat up. "Shelby's not pregnant." At least, as far as he knew. Damn. Maybe that was the reason she pushed for marriage? "Or if she is, it's not mine."

Cam scowled. "You're gonna play it like that? I've never known you to shuck your responsibility."

"And I'm not now. I'm telling you she can't be pregnant because we've never fucked, all right?"

"What about earlier tonight?" Greer asked softly, finally breaking his silence.

Jesus. Could this conversation get any more uncomfortable? "It was a blow job. Now can we drop this?"

A murmur of awkward agreement went around the room, and the five of them sat in brooding silence for several minutes.

Cam scrubbed his hands over his head. "Just…why?"

Now came the tricky part. How did he explain the marriage without divulging the blackmail and the potential for Wilde Security's financial ruin?

Reece met his brother's gaze. "Cam, you know me. You know I always have a reason, and you just have to trust that I know exactly what I'm doing. Like I said, it's a business arrangement, and when I can tell you the whys of it, I will. But until then, I need you all to play it like we're really married."

"You are legally married?" Greer asked.

"Yes, we are. But for the sake of appearances, it needs to look like more than the business arrangement it is. It needs to look real."

Cam paced away. "This is so fucked up." He stood in front of the windows for a moment. Then with a shake of his head, he spun back to face the group. He held up a finger in warning. "Don't hurt her, Reece. You hurt her, you'll hurt Eva, and then we're gonna have problems."

If anyone was going to get hurt in this whole fucked up situation, he had a feeling it'd be him—but he wasn't about to say that to his brothers. "I'm not going to hurt her."

The room settled into another uneasy silence.

Finally, Jude held up the beer in a mock toast. "Let's all just take a moment here to appreciate the fact that I am no longer the family fuckup."

A chorus of groans rang out, and Vaughn smacked him upside the head.

Even Greer cracked a small smile. "Nobody can take that hard-won title from you, little brother."

Jude shrugged. "But you gotta admit, Reece is doing a damn fine job of trying. And Vaughn's not far behind. Hell, Greer, even you've been in the running lately. A distant third, but still third place. I should have trophies made up."

More groans. And just like that, everything was normal again. Reece had to admire Jude's ability to break the tension in any situation. For the longest time he'd thought his youngest brother was little more than the family clown—annoying, somewhat scatterbrained, and all but useless during a crisis. He'd been wrong. Jude wasn't an idiot, and he wielded his sharp wit like a weapon, but also knew how to use humor as a kind of glue to bring the five of them back together after a fight. It was a respectable talent, one not many people had.

Shelby had that same talent, he realized with a jolt of surprise. But somehow he doubted she was using it now over in Cam and Eva's suite. If anything, Libby was playing the peacemaker between the sisters. And for some idiotic reason, he wanted to walk over there and stand in front of Shelby, use himself like a human shield to keep away all the hurtful things Eva was probably saying. The kinds of things he knew too well because he'd said them enough times to Jude over the years.

He watched his youngest brother mercilessly poke fun at Greer, who sat there and took it with a half amused, half exasperated expression on his hard face. It was like watching a grizzly bear patiently enduring the antics of a rambunctious cub.

Reece had never been patient when it came to Jude. Still wasn't, although he was working on it. And he'd already apologized for it, but…

Suddenly, it didn't seem enough.

"I'm sorry," he said. "Jude's right. I fucked up."

And there went the moment of levity. If Jude's superpower was humor, then he must be the villain of this story, the anti-Jude, sucking the funny out of everything.

The room went silent again.

"Well," Cam said after an uncomfortable amount of time. "I'd better go make sure the girls aren't killing one another. Reece, you should probably stay out of Eva's way for…ah, the next decade or so."

"Unless you want to be KO'd again," Jude said. "She knocked you flat."

"Yeah, man, what happened to all those black belts you have?" Vaughn asked.

"I don't hit women." Unless it was his open hand on Shelby's gorgeously heart-shaped ass.

And, fuck, that was not an appropriate thought, given the circumstances.

Vaughn grunted. "You could have subdued her."

Yes, he could have, but he'd deserved the punch for the way he'd spoken to Shelby in the limo. He *was* an asshole.

And he owed her an apology.

Reece knew when he was being avoided, and Shelby had gone into full-blown avoidance mode since the disastrous announcement of their marriage to the family. He'd tried to corner her in the casino, and again during a tense dinner with the family, but she always managed to escape before he could talk to her.

This marriage scheme wasn't going to work if she kept avoiding him.

But now, as they boarded the plane back to D.C., she wasn't going to have a choice but to talk to him.

He boarded first and waited, watching the line of passengers until she finally appeared. She spotted him, too, but then pretended to concentrate on looking for her seat.

He caught her arm before she passed. "Where are you going?"

She didn't even glance at him, stared straight ahead. "To my seat, if that's okay with you."

He motioned to the empty spot beside him. "This *is* your seat."

"No, it's not. It's in coach—" She glanced down at her boarding pass, then up at the number over the empty seat. Scowling, she plopped down. "You changed my ticket. I know I didn't buy a first class seat."

"Yeah, I did." He lowered his voice. "We're married now, and we need to act it in case someone's watching."

"I really doubt anyone is."

"Someone was in the hallway at the hotel."

She opened her mouth but pressed her lips together a second later without uttering a sound. She dragged her bag up onto her lap and started digging through it.

Shit. That had been the wrong thing to say. He scrambled

for another conversational thread. If he could just get her talking…

"Uh, how did it go with Eva?"

"It didn't. She was already pissed about Mom and then we sprung this marriage on her and… Well, she's not speaking to me." She pulled an iPod and large set of pink earphones from her bag. "And I don't want to talk to you."

Damn. Tiptoeing around the ugly words still hanging in the air between them wasn't getting him anywhere. He should've known it wouldn't. Shelby was nothing if not direct.

"Hey." He stopped her from putting the earphones on and blocking him out. "Will you let me apologize?"

She heaved a sigh and finally looked at him, one eyebrow arched.

And now that he had her attention, the nice little speech he'd composed in his mind flew away, leaving him grasping for whatever words he could find. "Uh, what I said to you in the limo was wrong. I'd had a lot to drink and was overwhelmed—and-and that's not an excuse. I've never thought of you as the type of woman to sell your body, and I'm sorry for insinuating that you are."

"It's okay." She lifted a shoulder in a shrug meant to be dismissive, but he saw through it. He'd hurt her deeply with his careless remark, and he had no idea how to make it up to her.

"No." He reached out, covered her hands with his. "It's not okay. I was an ass."

"Yeah, but you're also not that far off from the truth. I mean, you're paying me to be married to you." She released a humorless laugh. "New low for me. It feels…sleazy. I really don't want it. It seemed like a good idea at the time, but I don't want your money, so let's get the annulment when we get home, and I'll figure something else out."

His heart sank. Surprising, since he'd been conflicted about this plan from the get-go. "No."

Her eyes popped wide. "What?"

"We've taken it this far already. Might as well see it through. I need your help with this blackmail problem."

She huffed out a breath and leaned back in her seat. "I can't—"

"Please." He squeezed her hand. "And if you're not comfortable accepting money from me, then at least take the protection of my name for the next sixty days. I don't know much about The Headhunters, except that they've been around for decades, and I doubt they've outlasted their competition by being stupid." Even though the motorcycle club was a criminal organization, they were also a business. And if Reece knew anything for sure, it was business. "They're not going to attack a well-known businessman's wife. Too much risk with not enough payout."

Shelby said nothing in response until the plane pushed away from the gate and the flight attendants started their safety spiel. She glanced away from him, but not before he saw a glimmer in her eyes, something dangerously close to fear. "I don't want my past hurting you. I've…done a lot of things I'm not proud of."

"Shelby." He waited until she lifted her gaze to his. Then he gave her the truth, point-blank. "Wilde Security is not going to survive if I don't get this contract. We're operating in the red, and it's dragging DMW Systems down with it. And I can guarantee my deal with Irving James will not happen if that video or those photos leak. I need your help with this."

She plucked at the cord of her headphones. "Okay," she said. "I'll help, but I'm warning you, it's going to get messy and chaotic, and I know how much you hate that." Without another word, she put on her headphones, closed her eyes, and leaned her head back against the seat, blocking him out.

He sat back and turned his gaze to the window, watched the ground drop out from under them as the plane took flight.

She was right. He did hate mess. He hated chaos. And his life had been nothing but since she flounced into it.

Jesus. He hoped he was making the right call here.

Chapter Ten

Reece's apartment was...sterile. It was the only word Shelby could think of when she stepped through the door. He'd done nothing to the plain white walls. His furniture was black leather, and the end tables were all glass and metal and sharp angles. A huge island with a breakfast bar separated the kitchen and living room, and the space off the kitchen meant for a formal dining room was empty. The floor-to-ceiling windows in the living room offered breathtaking views of the city, which was about the only thing this apartment had going for it.

She looked as Reece. "It's cold in here."

"I'll turn up the heat."

"No, not temperature-wise. Just...unloved. It's not a comfortable space."

His brow wrinkled and he opened his mouth, no doubt

to ask what the fuck she was talking about. She waved a hand, cutting him off before he made a sound. "Never mind. Where am I staying?"

He motioned to the hallway off the living room. "First door on the right. This apartment has top-of-the-line security, so you're perfectly safe here."

Maybe physically safe, but emotionally? Oh, she was in so much danger.

Adjusting her grip on Poe's cage, she followed the instructions and found the bedroom was just as industrial as the rest of the apartment. The bed had no headboard, and there was no other furniture in the room—not even a dresser. But there was a massive walk-in closet and a small en suite with a shower. Good. At least she wouldn't have to share a bathroom with Reece. That would be way too… intimate.

But if she was going to live here for the next two months, she had to make some changes.

She set down Poe's cage and took the cover off. His gray feathers were fluffed up; the drive had made him anxious. She reached through the bars and rubbed his head to calm him. Best to give him time to adjust to his new surroundings before letting him out to explore, she decided. Traveling always ruffled his feathers.

As she straightened away from the cage, she spotted a bushy orange tail under the bed and squatted down. Reece's cat reminded her of Garfield, fat and orange with big green eyes that blinked at her when she held out a hand to him.

"What's his name?" she asked. Reece had followed her and now loitered just outside the door.

"The Cat."

She gazed up at him in disbelief. "You didn't give him a name?"

He shrugged. "It's the one he came with. Sam the Cat."

"So he's Sam?"

"The Cat suits him better."

She shook her head and peeked under the bed again. "Hi, Sam. You're going to be a good kitty and not try to eat my bird, right?"

Sam inched out from under the bed until Poe let out a squawk from his cage. The cat's tail poofed up and he hissed, then scampered between Reece's legs and disappeared up the hallway.

"Sam the Scaredy-Cat is more like it." She stood. "Is he always so jumpy?"

"I don't know."

"How can you not know? He's your cat."

"He's only mine by default," Reece said and walked away as if they weren't in the middle of a conversation.

Shelby stared at the empty doorway for a second, then chased him down the hall to the master bedroom. He'd done a bit more decorating—if it could be called that—in this space, adding a large dresser and some nightstands on either side of the king-size bed. But it was still all very austere. "Hold up. You can't have a pet by default."

"Yes, you can." He disappeared into a closet the size of her bedroom at the house she shared with Eva. And now Cam. Which reminded her she still had to find a new place to live because once this thing with Reece was over, she didn't want to be the proverbial third wheel, stuck in a house with the newlyweds.

She shook her head to dislodge the depressing thought

and walked over to the closet. Suits lined the bars in tidy rows, all pressed and neat. So different from her closet, which spewed a rainbow onto her bedroom floor. What would Reece do if she pulled one of his ties off those anal-retentive hangers and tossed it on the floor? Her fingers tingled with the urge, and she crossed her arms over her chest to keep herself from doing it.

Reece was shirtless and halfway through pulling off the slacks he'd traveled in. "Jesus, Shelby. A little privacy?"

She leaned a shoulder against the jamb and admired the view. He looked damn fine in a suit, but it was a shame he had to cover up all that lean muscle. "It's nothing I haven't already seen. I'm not understanding this whole pet-by-default thing."

He heaved out a sigh and finished pulling off his pants. She'd always been a boxers kind of girl, but the formfitting briefs he was wearing made her belly jitter.

"Jude fell in love with the cat and brought him home from Key West," Reece said and chose a fresh dress shirt. "Except he and Libby can't have animals in their apartment. Cam and Vaughn took the cat for a while, but turns out, the twins are both allergic. And Greer's not home enough to take care of an animal, so that left me until Jude and Libby's lease is up."

"You took in a cat for your brother?"

He stepped into a pair of slacks and looped a tie over his shoulders. "Wouldn't you, for your sister?"

"Well, yeah. But—" He looked over at her and she closed her mouth without finishing the thought. She hadn't expected that kind of commitment from a workaholic like him. Instead, she asked, "Where are you going?"

"I need to check in at DMW, then go to the Wilde Security office."

"You know, most people take the evening off when they've been traveling all day."

"Most people don't have a blackmailer to find."

"Touché." She sketched a point in the air. "Reece, one. Shelby, zero."

He scowled and buttoned his shirt. "This isn't a game."

"Sure it is. Life's one big game. Everyone's playing, but few realize that it's rigged. None of us ever win—we all end up in the same place—so why not have fun with it?"

"You sound like Jude," he muttered.

"I'll take that as a compliment. Jude's got his shit together."

"Are we talking about the same Jude? Captain Annoying: the First Fuckup, champion of loudmouth little brothers everywhere?"

She gaped at him. "Did you just make a comic book joke?"

His face went blank. "No."

"You did so!"

He turned to the door. "There's a dinner party tomorrow night, and I plan to use it as our official debut as husband and wife. It should take the heat off the blackmail threat, and then we can work on clearing up your money issues. A stylist will be here at eight a.m. to fix your hair."

"Uh, whoa." She held up her hands. "I can do my own hair."

He glanced back, his gaze assessing, almost cold. "It needs to be a normal color."

Self-conscious, she tugged on a purple strand. "I know that."

"We'll keep the stylist appointment, then Libby will take you shopping tomorrow afternoon. She has a good eye for fashion and will help you find something appropriate."

Shelby resisted the urge to tug on the hem of her skirt. The fact she even wanted to pissed her off. She'd never before been uncomfortable with herself, and she wasn't about to let him make her feel that way. "If you think you get to order me around just because we're temporarily married, you have another think coming. I'll do my own hair and choose my own clothes, fuck you very much."

His eyes flashed, but not in anger. Something darker, hotter, and her panties dampened. She caught her breath at the unexpected throb of lust and reached for him, but he abruptly turned on his heel and stalked out.

A moment later, she heard the front door click shut.

She blew out a breath and staggered backward a step until the bed touched the back of her thighs. She sank to the mattress and told her libido to calm down. But when he got all commanding like that… Whew. And the heat between the two of them? Holy hell. It put a volcano to shame, and she'd never experienced anything like it before, with anyone. How could she want to throttle the man and at the same time, want to jump his bones and ride him until they were both screaming?

Shelby groaned and dropped her head into her hands. She was used to getting herself in and out of trouble, but this time, she just might have stepped in over her head.

"Reece. I didn't expect to see you in." Reece glanced up from his computer at his vice president's surprised voice. "Didn't expect to see you here, either, Dylan."

Dylan Porter smiled in his charming, too-slick way and sidled into the office. "No rest for the wicked." He sat down in one of the leather chairs opposite Reece's desk and leaned forward. "So I've been hearing this crazy rumor going around about you..."

Fuck. Did he know about the blackmail? But how could he? Unless...he was the blackmailer. The idea sent a ripple of hot betrayal through Reece's gut. Dylan was the closest thing he had to a friend, but yeah, the guy couldn't be ruled out just because of that. A computer genius in his own right, Dylan certainly had the skills for blackmail. Not to mention, he was ambitious, and his vision for the future of DMW didn't always line up with Reece's. He didn't want help from Irving James, and they had gotten into more than one argument over it.

Reece's heart kicked against his ribs, but he kept his face firmly impassive. "You know better than to believe rumors."

"I do," Dylan agreed, his eyes crinkling with humor. "But judging by the ring on your finger, I'm guessing this one's true. You really went and got yourself hitched?"

Reece gazed down at the band. Oh, right. That. Not the blackmail then. "Yeah, it's true."

A grin broke across Dylan's face. "Congrats, man. You sure play things close to the chest. I didn't even know you were seeing anyone."

"It's..." He thought about lying, saying the relationship had been going on for a while, but made a split-second decision against it. For one thing, he and Shelby would never be able to pull off faking a long-term engagement. And lying to Dylan sat like a lump of lead in his gut, so he settled on a half-truth. "It was a bit of a whirlwind."

Whirlwind. Hah. Wasn't that a fitting description of Shelby?

Dylan laughed. "Sweep you off your feet, did she?"

"Something like that."

"Well, when you know, you know. I knew Alicia was it for me after our first date. 'Course, it took me three years to convince her of it. What's her name?"

"Shelby."

"You do realize Alicia is going to want to meet her? And she'll probably want to drag us all out on double dates to the opera."

Reece internally winced at the mention of opera. He wasn't a fan, but Dylan and Alicia were and somehow, attending with the power couple had become part of his public persona. He was expected to go and mingle and pretend he gave a fuck, so he did, even though he was out of fucks to give at this point.

But the thought of Shelby at the opera was so ridiculous, a snort of laughter escaped before he could stop it. Shelby would give that lot of uptight pricks coronaries.

Dylan raised an eyebrow at him and Reece coughed to hide the laugh. "I, uh, don't think Shelby's the type to appreciate opera."

"Really?" Dylan frowned. "What does she do?"

"She's a small business owner." Which was the truth, but it still boggled his mind. "She owns The Bean Gallery."

"The place you like that serves horrible coffee?"

It could be pretty horrible, he had to admit, but come

to think of it, the coffee had improved considerably in the last few months. Starting right around the time Shelby had bought out the previous owners. Maybe she knew what she was doing after all. "It's not that bad, Dyl."

"Uh-huh. Just like I don't tell Alicia her cooking sucks, but I'll defend it until my dying breath if anyone else says so. Welcome to married life." Dylan levered his gym-honed body out of the chair. "When will we get to meet her?"

"She'll be at the party tomorrow night."

Dylan scowled. "I still say we don't need to impress that old blowhard James. We just need to lose the dead weight of your brothers' security company. Cut them loose and then we can take DMW public—"

Sighing heavily, Reece sat back in his chair. "We've had this discussion. We're not ready to go public."

"Maybe not, but we'd be a hell of a lot closer to ready if you quit playing Dick Tracy. You're not a private investigator, Reece. We're computer geeks and number crunchers. Stick to what we're good at, and DMW will flourish."

"I'm not abandoning my brothers. You know I can't do that."

"I know." Dylan walked to the door, but paused before leaving and glanced back. "But, Reece, if it came down to it, would you choose your brothers over all the people who rely on us for their paychecks? Would you really give our employees their pink slips to save your brothers' struggling business?"

The answer felt like a betrayal and clogged his throat. It took a hard swallow before he was able to give it voice. "No. I wouldn't. But it doesn't matter because I'm going to secure this deal with James. It will keep DMW in the black and give Wilde Security the time it needs to get its legs back under it."

"I don't know about that, buddy." Dylan shook his head. "I'm a gambling man…but Wilde Security is a risk even I wouldn't take."

Same old discussion, different day. Reece turned to his computer, signaling the end of the conversation. "I'll see you tomorrow night."

"All right." Dylan tapped his fist lightly against the doorjamb a couple times. "I look forward to meeting your bride. Don't look forward to kissing James's saggy ass."

Reece stared at the door for a long time after it shut behind his VP. Dylan was 100 percent against this deal with James, but would he actually stoop to blackmail to sabotage it and force the choice between DMW and Wilde Security?

Reece's heart said no, but he still pulled up the spreadsheet he'd started and added Dylan's name under the column labeled "suspects" then took a minute to fill in the other columns, including "motive" and "opportunity" with the information he had. Then he studied the mostly empty sheet. Yes, Dylan had a motive, but where was his opportunity? He hadn't been in Vegas, but it was possible he had hired someone. He couldn't be eliminated.

And that hurt.

Dammit.

Reece sat back and pinched the bridge of his nose.

Dylan was right about one thing. He was no Dick Tracy. In fact, he was so out of his element with this, he was at a loss as to where to start. He usually let his brothers handle the investigating part of Wilde Security while he dealt with the finances and the occasional home security installation.

But he couldn't very well hand this problem over to them. There was something going on with Greer, and Reece feared the big guy was silently falling apart. Vaughn was obsessed with finding Lark. Cam was a newlywed, and Reece wasn't about to dump a problem like this in his lap so soon after the wedding. And Jude...

Well, Reece could admit to himself in the quiet sanctity of his office it was pride keeping him from asking Jude for help. Last summer they'd taken the first steps toward mending the rift that formed between them after their parents were killed, but they still had a ways to go yet. He wasn't comfortable enough to take a problem as personal as blackmail to Jude.

He closed the spreadsheet and sat back in his chair. Dick Tracy or not, he was on his own with this investigation.

Chapter Eleven

Shelby had heard the front door open an hour ago, but continued unpacking without so much as peeking out into the living room. She figured she wasn't Reece's wife—legally, yes, but not really, not at heart, where it counted—so she didn't have to meet him at the door with a drink and dinner in the oven.

Right?

Crap. She had no clue. The only thing she knew about marriage was what she'd seen on TV. Her mother had been married on and off throughout the years, but those relationships had been toxic, more like a how-not-to-do-marriage guidebook than a good template.

Not that this was a real marriage, she reminded herself as enticing scents started drifting under her door. Her stomach rumbled, and she pressed a hand to it to quiet it.

Speaking of having dinner in the oven, she hadn't eaten all day.

All right. She couldn't hide in her room forever.

Sucking in a breath, she pulled the door open and followed the yummy scents to the kitchen.

Reece had a bowl tucked in the crook of his arm and was in the process of whisking the hell out of the mixture inside. His sleeves were rolled up to his elbows, exposing his muscled forearms sprinkled lightly with dark hair, and his shirt was partially unbuttoned, the light smattering of hair on his chest peeking out. He was wearing glasses—funny, she hadn't known he needed them before now—and looked more relaxed than she'd ever seen him. All calm and...

Sexy as sin.

And she was staring. She shook herself and walked toward him. "You're...cooking?"

"You sound surprised," he said, barely glancing up at her.

"I guess I am." She wandered around the island to take a peek into the oven. She had no idea what was in there, but it smelled spicy and delicious and made her mouth water for a taste. "Most of the bachelors I know can't even boil water."

He returned his attention to his task, pouring the mixture from the bowl into a saucepan. He grabbed a bottle of wine from the counter and splashed some in, then reached for a pair of glasses in a cupboard overhead and poured them each a healthy dose.

He handed one glass to her, clinked the rims, and tasted his wine before setting it aside. "Technically I'm not a bachelor anymore."

She smiled and tasted her wine. "For the next two months at least."

This situation wasn't so bad, after all. Not the least bit

awkward like she feared it would be. With all of the angst and uncertainty of the past few days, she had forgotten how truly easy Reece was to get along with. They had always just…clicked, right from the beginning.

And, let's be honest, it didn't hurt he was a gorgeous specimen of a man who apparently knew how to cook.

Nursing her wine, she leaned against the fridge to watch him. She had no idea what he was doing, but he moved like a man confident in his skills.

"Seriously," she said after a moment, "I'm impressed. To tell the truth, *I* can barely boil water."

"Yeah, well. My brothers and I…we were five teenage boys basically living on our own. Someone had to learn or we were going to starve." He took down a couple plates and started scooping portions of a veggie mix onto each. Then he opened the oven and used a towel to pull out the main entree. Chicken, she noted as he forked a portion onto each plate and slathered the breasts in the sauce he'd just finished.

"It's done. We can sit here at the breakfast bar." He brought the plates over and she chose one of the four high-backed chairs pushed in under the bar. He set one plate in front of her, opened a nearby drawer, and produced a pair of forks.

When he handed one to her and their hands brushed, she tried not to think about the sizzle of pure lust that flared at the contact. Yeah, they'd always just clicked. That was, when they weren't sparking off each other like fireworks.

She cleared her throat. "Thank you."

And there was the awkwardness again.

They both ate in silence for the first few minutes. The food was really good, and she thought she should tell him, but every time she opened her mouth to say so, she shoved in another bite of chicken instead.

Man, she didn't like this tension, or how she was hyper-aware of his every move. There was no denying the intense sexual attraction, and even though he'd laid down the no consummation rule—well, wouldn't it be easier to just jump each other's bones and get it out of their systems? They weren't going to fool anybody into believing they were husband and wife when they shied away from touching each other.

Shelby drew a breath and took a sip of her wine for courage. "So…" She twirled the stem of her glass between her fingers. "I've been thinking. Since the money thing wasn't working for either of us, maybe we can also reconsider the no-sex rule?"

Reece fumbled his glass, and wine sloshed down the front of his shirt. "No."

Okay, that sounded final. She watched him blot at the stain, then finally give up and pull the shirt off. Underneath he wore a tank top that showed off his carved biceps and broad chest, which did nothing to help calm her libido. He had such a drool-worthy body, with a slim waist and washboard abs dipping into a sharp V at his hips, and she desperately wanted to tie him up and make him beg again. Or he could tie her up.

Either way, they'd have a fun time together.

"Why not?" she asked.

Without looking at her, he stood and grabbed some paper towels to clean up the spill on the counter, then picked up his plate and took it around to the sink on the other side of the island. "Because."

"Because you're the boss and you said so? That doesn't work with me and you know it."

He rinsed his plate and placed it in the dishwasher, but he still avoided facing her. "I don't want—"

She pointed her fork at him. "You better not say you don't want me, mister. I'll know for a fact you're lying."

"I do want you." He braced his hands on each side of the sink. His shoulders slumped, his head dropped forward, and he sighed. "But I don't have the experience to…uh, I mean I've never…"

He trailed off. Seconds ticked by in silence. Then a few more. His shoulder muscles knotted tighter with each passing beat, and realization struck her with all the shock of a lightning bolt.

No. No way. He couldn't be.

She left her seat and circled the island to stand beside him. "Are you telling me you've never had sex?"

His spine straightened, and he met her gaze. "Yes."

Whoa. For a solid half minute, her brain fizzled out, and she couldn't find two words to put together. Her mouth worked soundlessly. "You mean, at the hotel in Vegas…? The oral sex? Was that your first time?"

"No." Shrugging off the hand she'd set on his forearm, he turned away, but not before she caught the stain of color filling his cheeks. "I'm not a monk, but I've never gone beyond oral."

"How is that even…? You're a handsome, successful, healthy, thirty-something-year-old male, and you've never gotten past third base? With anyone?"

He winced. "Not because I didn't want to."

"But…" Crap, she was approaching this all wrong. She

shook her head, hoping to clear it. "I'm sorry. I'm not bashing your lifestyle choice. I-I'm just…stunned."

"Remaining celibate wasn't a conscious decision," he said in a carefully modulated tone, as if they were discussing a business matter over a boardroom table. She could almost see him building his walls up, surrounding himself with the supercilious attitude he had down to an art.

That attitude was a shield.

How had she not realized it before? He acted all uptight as a way to protect himself. As someone who was well versed in internal shields, she should have made the connection sooner.

"Okay," she said. "So if it wasn't a conscious decision on your part, then why didn't you find yourself a willing high-society lady and do the dirty?"

"I…" He cleared his throat. "I merely felt there were more important ways to spend my time than pursuing a bedmate."

"A bedmate?" She snorted a laugh, hoping to break down his wall again. She hadn't meant to goad him into re-building it in the first place, and she preferred relaxed Reece over this uptight version. "Oh, Hershey, you were born in the wrong century, pal."

"Fine," he snapped and, yes, that was more like it. "I had more important things to do than look for a fuck."

"That's better." She waited a beat, but when he said nothing more, she prompted, "More important things like…?"

"Like making enough money to take care of my family."

Not the answer she'd expected. "But your brothers all had their own careers. You didn't have to provide for them."

"Yes, I did. I do." He paced away from her, did a lap

around the kitchen. When he circled back, his expression was serious, and was that sorrow lurking in the depths of his eyes? "You have to understand, Greer could have let the foster care system sweep us up, separate us, but he worked his ass off to make sure we stayed together in our own home. He gave up his childhood to take care of us, and he didn't have to."

"So you gave up your adulthood." Her heart cracked, just a bit. She went to him, circled her arms around his waist, and pressed her check against his spine. He was tense, all knotted, and her hug only tightened his muscles more. Wasn't that always the way? Whenever she tried to help, she only made things worse. But she wasn't letting go. This time, she knew exactly how to help.

"I didn't give up anything," Reece said, again using that restrained tone.

"What about college?"

"I went to college."

"No, I mean…the whole college experience. Frat parties and questionable one-night stands. You didn't do any of that?"

He lifted a shoulder. "I was ROTC and worked full time in the school's IT department for money to send home to the twins and Jude. My free time I spent setting up DMW Systems."

She huffed out a breath in disbelief. "You really are a workaholic."

"Yes, I am." He finally turned and faced her, jaw set. "I promised Greer years ago that I'd make damn sure we never had to scramble to survive again, and I've worked my ass off to keep that promise."

Scrambling to survive. God, she knew how that felt. Their childhood experiences had been vastly different and yet surprisingly the same. And she got it. She got him. Understood why he'd ignored his own wants and needs all these years. It was equal parts dedication to his family and guilt.

But she wasn't going to let him cast himself aside. Not anymore. She'd simply have to ease him into it. "I want an ice cream sundae for dessert."

Reece just stared at her. "What?"

"Ice cream. It sounds good." She walked over to the freezer and found the carton of vanilla she'd bought during her grocery run earlier in the day. She held it up, wiggled it side to side. "Want some?"

He blinked several times. "Uh…that's it?"

"Well, no. Duh. We need hot fudge, peanuts, sprinkles…" She opened a cupboard and gathered the ingredients. "Oh, and Reddi-wip."

His jaw dropped. "I just told you something nobody else knows and your only response is…ice cream?"

"What did you expect?" She had to fight to keep from grinning as she dug the scoop into the carton. He was making this too easy. "You said sex is off the table. And although I'd rather have sex on the table—literally—and I think your self-imposed celibacy is kinda martyr-ish—and not in a good way—I'll still respect your decision. I'm all about alternative lifestyles. Live and let live."

He looked completely baffled. "That's…mature of you."

"It is, isn't it?" She grabbed the canister of Reddi-wip, shook it, and aimed at him. "But this isn't." She pressed her finger on the tip.

"Shelby!" He sputtered in disbelief as the cream

splattered his face. "What the hell?"

"Hey, you said no sex, but that doesn't mean we can't still have fun." She hit him with another spray from the can. "You need to learn about fun and spontaneity."

"Give me that." He tried to swipe it and got another face full of whipped cream for his trouble. He growled and lunged. She dodged. They circled the island, her grinning, him scowling, until he feigned right and caught her around the waist when she darted to the left. He swept her up off her feet, but lost his footing on the now slippery tile, and they tumbled to the floor in a knot of limbs.

Reece took the brunt of the fall, but it didn't slow him down. He snatched the can from her and constructed a neat pile of cream on top of her head. "You are trouble."

"Yeah, I am." She scooped up some of the cream and smeared it over his face and chin, down his neck and chest.

And like that, the mood changed, just as she hoped it would. His heart pounded under her palm, and his breathing quickened, became choppier. She moved her hand up his chest, around the back of his neck, and tangled her fingers in the hair at his nape.

He tensed. "I know when I'm being manipulated."

"And you like it." Obviously, judging by the action going on below his belt. She continued skimming her hand down his back, over his ass, then circled around to cup the growing bulge of his cock. "Still so sure you want sex off the table?"

He shuddered. "If we do this, it doesn't change anything."

"Of course it doesn't. It's just sex." As soon as the words left her lips, she knew she was wrong. For a man who had put aside his physical needs for years, it wouldn't be just sex.

Still she wanted it. Wanted him. Wanted to be his first.

His fingers trembled as he traced the line of her jaw, the caress light and soft. He leaned down, and she thought for sure he was about to kiss her, but he stopped at the last second before their lips touched. "Shelby…there's something else."

"What?" she breathed. For the love of all things sexy, what else could there be?

"I didn't deny myself for only the reasons I told you." His breath fanned her cheek as he nuzzled her just under the ear before giving the lobe a quick little nip. "I've… there's a darkness in me, and it's always frightened me. Like I'm not normal."

Her pulse fluttered. "What kind of darkness?"

"The first time we met, I wanted to put my handprint…" He skimmed a palm up her leg and squeezed her ass. "Right there."

She shivered and wetness pooled between her thighs. "I want it there, too."

"And I thought I'd want to tie you up, blindfold you, and maybe I still will, but the way you had me splayed out on that bed in Vegas was so fucking hot, I want you to do it to me again."

She speared her fingers into his hair and tugged until he met her gaze. "If you think you're turning me off right now, you have another think coming." She was so hot she was about to internally combust. "Touch me, Reece. See for yourself." She guided his hand between her legs.

He growled and traced the seam of her jeans. "Let's take this to the bedroom and get these off you."

"No." She pulled him back when he tried to get up. "Here. Right here."

She expected a protest. Instead, he scooped her up,

stood, and laid her on the island. His hands shook as he fumbled the button on her jeans, slid them and her panties down her legs. Whether from nerves or desire, she didn't know. Maybe a bit of both.

Her hands weren't all that steady either when she reached to unfasten his belt. He stepped back and pulled off his shirt, his muscles bunching with the movement. His belt hissed as he whipped it off. He trailed the end of the leather strap over her stomach. "Next time, I plan to tie you up with this."

She caught her breath. "There'll be a next time?"

"I'm not going to kid myself. I won't be able to keep my hands off of you after this." A smile quirked his lips. "I can barely do it now."

"I don't mind." She captured his hands, guided them to her aching breasts. He massaged her through her shirt, then tugged the fabric off over her head. She wasn't wearing a bra and basked in the appreciative sound he made before he dipped his head and sucked one nipple into his mouth.

For a virgin, he had the mouth of a sex god. Especially when he worked his way down her stomach and licked her slit in one long motion.

She moaned and worked her hips against his mouth. She was close. So close. All she needed was…

His tongue left her and he walked away.

Shelby lay there on the island counter, confused and panting, right up to the edge and vibrating with the need for release. Where had he…?

But then he was back, tearing open a small package.

Condom.

He'd gone to get a condom.

Thank God.

She propped herself on her elbows and watched him roll it on. Their eyes met and his flared hot before he took himself in hand and stepped into the V of her parted legs. She watched as his cock nudged into her opening, inch by inch. It was erotic, feeling the slow friction of his intrusion, seeing him disappear inside of her, and knowing he'd never done this with anyone before.

He froze, trembling. "You're tight."

"You're big," she gasped and couldn't force herself to hold still for a second longer. She lifted her hips. "God, Reece. Move."

It took him a moment to find his rhythm, then another to keep her counter-thrusts from throwing him off. But once he got it…dear God. He fucked her mercilessly, driving her toward orgasm with an exuberant, single-minded focus.

"Fuck," he gasped. "I need to go deeper. Lift your legs."

She did as commanded, and he shackled her ankles with his hands, holding her still as he drove harder into her. Her sex opened wider to him, and he watched with hooded eyes as their bodies slammed together.

"Look at you taking all of me." He punctuated each word with a merciless thrust. "You like it, don't you? Nod."

She nodded and managed a gasped "Yes!" which faded into a moan when he hit a spot deep inside her that made her convulse. He was so wonderfully rough, demanding, and yes, now she could see that bit of darkness, the edge in him he'd been so afraid of.

And, holy God, she couldn't wait to explore that further.

An orgasm exploded through her, taking her by surprise, and her body locked down on his. Reece shouted and jerked through his own climax, then released his grip on her ankles. He'd left red handprints there, but she didn't mind one bit.

Gasping, he collapsed forward, his damp forehead pressed to her belly. "You tightened up like a fist. I wasn't ready for it. Jesus."

She laughed and combed her fingers into his hair. "Want to try again? Practice makes perfect."

"Hell yes. Except this time..." He straightened and climbed up on the counter beside her. Wrapping his hands around her waist, he lifted her easily, setting her down over his hips. "You're going to ride me, and you're not going to come until I tell you to."

Chapter Twelve

Shelby floated through the morning, all nerves about her upcoming shopping trip with Libby buried by memories of excellent sex. Reece had proved to be a fast learner. A fast, *enthusiastic* learner. And, holy hell, he liked to be in control. He about killed her by not letting her orgasm until he was good and ready for her to. And when he finally let her…

Boom.

She'd detonated. She still wasn't entirely sure she had all of her pieces put back together again.

After spending several hours the night before fucking on every flat surface they could find, they had worked themselves into exhaustion and parted ways, each going to sleep in their own beds. It was a really good arrangement. One she had to be careful not to get used to, she reminded herself as she dressed comfortably for a daylong shopping marathon. This situation was only temporary.

Still, nothing would be able to ruin her mood today.

Or…so she thought. Then she spotted Jason Mallory loitering by the mall entrance where she was supposed to meet Libby.

She stalked over to him. "What are you doing here? You need to leave! Now."

When she turned away, he grabbed her arm. "You fucking *married* him?"

She tried to jerk free, but Jason was too big, too strong. "You wanted me to get closer to him, so I did. I've done everything you've asked. What more do you want?" She again tried to free her arm with one hard tug.

He let her go. "How about thinking with your head instead of your hormones? After all these years, haven't you learned? Sex only gets you into trouble. Remember Steven Moore?"

She flinched. Direct blow. Her sister had even said something similar to her in Vegas, and Eva was right. They both were right. She always let her hormones cloud rational thought. She was no better than her mother that way, and her ex-boyfriend Steven had died because she got too involved.

"It's not like that this time."

"Are you willing to wager your future on that? Because that's exactly what you're doing, Shelby. Giving up your freedom for an easy lay."

"No." Heat gathered behind her eyes, and her vision started to blur. "I promise, I'm only doing what you asked. Please, believe me. But it's not going to work if you keep approaching me like this."

Jason said nothing for a long moment. "You have a week. Next time we talk, you'd better have something good for me."

She slumped against the wall as he walked away and willed herself not to cry. Oh, God, she didn't want this duplicitous life anymore. She hated Jason with every fiber of her being. Hated the things she'd been forced to do for him. The things he was still forcing her to do. She'd thought The Bean Gallery would be her ticket out from under his thumb, but now that was gone, and she was right back to where she started.

Maybe she should come clean about everything to Reece. Except if Jason found out, she'd never escape him. The thought turned her stomach.

"Shelby, are you okay?"

She started and looked up into Libby Wilde's concerned face. She'd been so busy wallowing, she hadn't heard her approach. "Yeah. Sorry." She swiped a hand under her nose and forced a smile. "Allergies."

Libby glanced in the direction Jason had disappeared. Yeah, she didn't buy that excuse for a moment.

Shelby kept the smile firmly in place and pulled open the store's outer door. "So, dresses?" She walked straight toward the dress department, putting a bit too much bounce in her step. "You're here to help me look like a passable Mrs. Reece Wilde, so work your magic."

Libby followed, a frown drawing her perfectly sculpted brows together. "Are you sure this is what you want to do?"

Shelby gazed over the rack of clothes at the woman who was technically her sister-in-law. How strange to have another sister, even if only for a little while—well, she did have several other blood related sisters, but she didn't know any of them except Eva. And this was different somehow.

Libby couldn't be more her opposite — a lawyer with a level head and calm disposition — and yet, in the short time they'd spent together, Shelby already felt a strong bond with her. "What do you mean?"

Libby chewed her muted pink lipstick off her lower lip as she browsed through the dresses, then shook her head. "It's none of my business. Forget it."

"No, tell me. I want to know."

She said nothing for several seconds, obviously waging an internal debate. Then she stopped fiddling with the dresses and met Shelby's gaze. "Changing who you are to please someone else never works. Just ask my husband. He'll tell you. Jude did it for years, and he hurt us in the process. We missed out on eight years together because he wasn't true to himself."

"Really? Jude always seems so...comfortable with himself."

"Well, he is now. But you have no idea how much misery we went through to get to that point." Libby gave a little laugh and returned to browsing through the rack. "And the thing is, Reece is a great guy, but he has a tendency to steamroll over the people around him when they don't conform to his standards and...I guess I'm saying I don't want to see you lose yourself."

Libby was worried about her? A sweet ache bloomed in her chest. So close on the heels of Jason's surprise visit, the emotion nearly overwhelmed her. She found herself blinking back tears for the second time in less than ten minutes. It would be so easy to open her mouth and tell Libby everything, such a relief to have someone to confide in...

But, no, she couldn't. Libby would feel obligated to tell her husband, and Jude would tell his brothers. Cam would tell Eva. Reece would find out…

And it'd all blow up in her face.

"I'm not changing for Reece." She turned away from Libby's searching gaze and picked up a black dress with long lace sleeves. "Will this one work?"

Libby regarded her with knowing eyes but, thank God, let the matter drop. She adjusted her stylish glasses on her nose, then turned her attention to the dress. "Modest, but with just the right amount of edge. It suits you. I approve. But what about this one?" She held up a long, sleek black number with a plunging V in the back held together by delicate chains. It was gorgeous, something Shelby would totally wear, but…

She winced. "It'll take too much makeup to cover my tattoos."

Libby frowned, obviously still not 100 percent on board with this whole ugly duckling transformation thing, and thrust the dress into her arms. "Well, try it on anyway. And the lace one, too."

Shelby accepted the silky gown and grinned. Here Reece had wanted Libby to go shopping with her to help tone down her style, but Libby was doing just the opposite. The curvy blonde was no wilting flower, and Shelby decided in that moment she'd still count Libby as a sister even after she and Reece annulled their marriage.

She found the nearest fitting room and wiggled into the lace dress first. It fell to mid-thigh, and the sleeves were soft rather than itchy like she'd expected. There was a bit of sparkle in the lace, too, that caught and threw light in subtle ways when she moved. The dress fit like it was tailor-made for her, which was so hard to find straight off the rack since she was petite. She usually had to hem everything. "Oh, Libby. I think I'm in love."

"Are you going to let me see it?"

She smiled at her reflection before unlocking the door and stepping out for Libby's inspection. Having someone to shop with was fun, a nice change of pace from Eva, who would only set foot in a mall if she were forced at gunpoint.

Libby twirled a finger in the air, indicating Shelby should spin. She complied, and Libby clapped her hands, gave a little squee of excitement. "It's perfect. I wish I could be there to see Reece's reaction. He's going to swallow his tongue. And probably want to peel you out of it first chance he gets."

"You think?" Warmth gathered in her belly and spread downward as she studied her reflection again in the three-way mirror. She pictured his long, graceful fingers pulling down the side zipper, his lips tracing the line of flesh he uncovered. Oh, the man was a god with those lips but, despite last night, he was still too restrained. He was still holding back from that darkness she so desperately wanted to see him unleash.

She smoothed a hand down the front of the dress. Would this be the thing to finally snap his control?

Libby laughed. "You're thinking dirty thoughts."

"What?" Her cheeks were hot, and not from embarrassment. She fanned them, told herself to chill with the X-rated fantasies of Reece. "No. I'm not looking for a dress to impress him."

"Oh, c'mon. Fess up. You so are." A dreamy look crossed Libby's pretty features. "And when your man sees you for the first time in a dress you picked out just for him...whew."

"Now who's thinking dirty thoughts?"

Libby shrugged, unapologetic. "You've seen my husband. The long hair, pretty blue eyes, roguish smile, and that body of his...mmm. How could I not have dirty thoughts?"

Shelby laughed and shook her head. "Reece is not my man."

"Uh, you're married to him. That pretty much means he's yours and you're his."

"Yes, but it's not the same. It's not like you and Jude or Cam and Eva. It's...complicated." She turned back to the mirror and pouted. She really liked this dress. "I'm not going to get it."

"No, no, no, no. I'm here as your personal style consultant and I'm telling you it's perfect. You're getting it. Now march your thin self back in there and try on the other one."

An hour later, Shelby had the lace cocktail dress and the long black gown because, after trying it on, she hadn't been able to pass that one up, either, although it needed hemming. She also had several pairs of slacks, a few modest pencil skirts, sweaters, and blouses. Except for the dresses, none of it was her style, but it fit the persona of the new Mrs. Wilde, wife of a successful businessman. And Libby did have good taste, so even if it wasn't anything she'd normally wear, she wasn't going to look matronly or frumpy.

She cringed when the cashier rattled off the total. Oh, that hurt, but she refused to take a cent from Reece and by-passed the card he gave her in favor of her own credit card. She gathered her bags and waited while Libby paid for the two dresses she'd found. Then, together, buzzing from the shopping high, they headed for the door.

"This was fun—" As Shelby turned to thank Libby for all

of her help, she realized she'd lost her shopping companion somewhere between the register and door. She backtracked and found Libby standing in front of the infant section, staring longingly at a display of tiny shoes.

Shelby glanced from Libby's face to the booties and back. That was the look of a woman with a secret. "Libby, are you…?"

She shook her head. "No," she said, her voice cracking. "I thought I was for about a week, but no."

"You want to be, don't you?"

"So much." She picked up one pair of booties and caressed them in the tender way only a woman desperately wanting a child could. "Jude and I both want a baby. We've been trying since our wedding night."

"It's only been a few months."

Libby sighed. "I know. I just thought it'd happen right away." She started to put the booties down, but Shelby stopped her.

"No. You're going to buy them."

Her eyes widened. "Why?"

"They'll be your good luck charm for next month. Like a self-fulfilling prophecy. If you have the booties, you'll have to have a baby to wear them."

"You know what? You're right." Libby hugged the booties to her chest. "I'm buying them."

Shelby waited with her while she bought the booties, then they walked out of the store together. Before they parted ways in the parking lot, Libby pulled her in for a quick hug. "Welcome to the family, Shelby."

Chapter Thirteen

Reece was exhausted. He wanted to go home after leaving DMW for the day, but he'd promised Vaughn he'd look into Lark Warren's financials, and he had several hours before the dinner party tonight. Might as well spend them helping his brother.

And, he decided as he drove by the burned-out husk of The Bean Gallery, he wanted his brothers investigating the arson. Something about it sat like coal in his gut. It didn't add up and, as a numbers guy, he hated when things didn't add up.

He pulled the Escalade into his usual spot in front of the Wilde Security building and took a moment to stroll over to the opposite end of the empty strip mall, where their office used to be before the bomb that nearly killed Vaughn had damaged it. He owned the whole building and had dreamed of fixing up the other empty stores to rent out.

Maybe it was time. It'd generate some income that

would take the pressure off him until Wilde Security started operating in the black.

Problem was, he didn't know what he wanted to do with the building. They'd moved the Wilde Security office and he liked the new spot better, but these other empty stores? Did he want to rent them out as stores again or offices?

Hands stuffed in the pockets of his wool coat, Reece studied the blackened facade of the building. It was still structurally sound according to the contractors he'd hired shortly after the blast, but it needed some work inside, and the front was a total loss. The rest of the old mall had been tagged with graffiti back when this had been a bad part of the city, and the paint was chipping off the concrete block walls. The whole thing needed a facelift before he could think about renting to anyone. But he'd only be able to afford the work needed if he could secure this deal with Irving James.

Damn.

Always came back to that.

As he strode back toward the office, wind whipped up a small dervish of snow near his feet, reminding him he needed to call the snow removal people to plow the lot before they got the forecasted four more inches tomorrow. Great. More money flying out the window. Maybe he should see about taking on a home security job soon. They were usually out-of-town gigs, and leaving right now would be a headache, but the paycheck would be a godsend for Wilde Security, and it'd take some of the strain off DMW Systems, which would make Dylan happy. He'd follow up with some of the people who had shown an interest in his home security system in the past. Maybe one of them would bite.

In the office, he found Cam talking to a dark-haired man.

A potential client? One could only hope. Both Vaughn and Jude were absorbed with whatever they were doing on their computers, so Reece didn't bother any of them and continued to his small office. He peeked into Greer's office next door to his, but the desk sat empty and looked untouched from the last time he was here before the Vegas trip.

Jesus. Where was Greer now? This vanishing act of his was getting fucking old. Starting Wilde Security had been his idea in the first place and now, out of all of them, he spent the least amount of time here.

They were going to have a heart-to-heart about that. Soon.

Reece sat down at his desk and before the computer even booted up, Vaughn darkened his doorway. He didn't knock, but closed the door behind him and strode forward with a handful of printouts. "I found something."

"About...?"

"Lark."

Reece resisted the urge to sigh. Barely. He accepted the papers, still warm from the printer, but didn't look at them. "Vaughn. Man, you can't be doing this on company time."

Vaughn crossed his massive arms over his chest. "What else am I supposed to be doing? That guy out there with Cam is the first client we've had in days."

True. This time, he did sigh. "Have you seen Greer?"

"Nope. Not since we left Vegas."

"Figures."

"He's up to something."

"You think?" Reece snapped, but then took a breath. Told himself to rein in his frustration. "All right. I was just about to snoop into Lark's financials anyway, so you might as well tell me what you've found."

Vaughn grabbed a folding chair from against the wall and dragged it over. He was still in a walking cast and, although he didn't say it, his leg had to be hurting him. "First thing, I talked to Libby. Lark was her bridesmaid, so I figured Libs had to know something about her. She said Lark started working at the district attorney's office as a secretary two years ago and, although they were good friends at work, Libby didn't know anything about her personal life. She played her cards close and put on this dumb bimbo act, but Libby saw through it. *I* saw through it at Libby and Jude's wedding. Lark's smarter than she pretended to be."

"Okay," Reece said and made a get-on-with-it rolling motion with his hand.

"So, knowing that about her, and knowing she must have passed a background check to work at the D.A.'s office, I started digging. She took the real Lark Warren—the sixty-some-year-old dead woman—and stole her entire life. To do that and pass an extensive background check tells me she's done it before. And she has." He took the papers back and spread them out on the desk. "Before she was Lark Warren, she was a maid named Robin Jones in Baltimore for just over a year. And before that, Autumn Clark, a waitress in Richmond, Virginia for a year. I'm thinking there are even more names I haven't found yet."

Intrigued, Reece picked up the paper nearest him that showed a driver's license photo for Autumn Clark. It was definitely the woman they had known as Lark Warren, but with a shorter haircut. "She's running."

Vaughn straightened. "What makes you say that? She's a thief. She's stealing people's lives."

"Dead people."

"Still, she's hopping around the east coast committing acts of fraud, and we're the only ones who know about it as far as I can tell. She needs to be caught."

Yeah, if that wasn't hurt pride talking, Reece would eat his tie. Vaughn could try to make it into a quest for justice, but it was a case of plain old bruised ego. Vaughn was the runner in all of his past relationships, and it was eating him up that for once, the woman had not only run from him, but all-out disappeared.

Reece rubbed his chin and then at the knots in the back of his neck. Vaughn wasn't going to let this drop, especially now that he felt justified in his pursuit, but someone had to rein him in before he went into self-destruct mode.

And Reece knew just how to do it.

"All right." He sat up straight again and met Vaughn's gaze. "Here's the thing. I need you working a case that's not this."

"Reece—"

"No. Listen. I need you to look into the arson at The Bean Gallery. I'm fairly certain someone was trying to kill Shelby that night, and I want to know who. You look into that for me, and I'll dig up what I can on Lark's previous identities for you. Deal?"

Vaughn's jaw slid to one side as he thought it through. Finally, he gave a short nod. "Okay. But only because I like Shelby and the thought of someone trying to hurt her pisses me off."

"You and me both, bro," Reece muttered as Vaughn stalked out. "You and me both."

Something was different.

Reece paused just inside his front door and scanned the apartment's open layout. Something was…off, but damn if he could put his finger on what it was. He walked in slowly, his senses humming. After the whipped cream fight last night, he wouldn't be surprised if Shelby launched some kind of sneak attack with silly string or some shit, but she wasn't in the living room or kitchen.

He made it halfway across the living room before he spotted the two colorful pillows now decorating his sofa. He picked one up. It looked like it had been sewn together using multiple strips of leftover fabric, a clash of colors and patterns. He frowned over at the other one. It was shaped like a sugar skull.

What the…?

"Shelby!"

No answer, but he heard the first strings of music coming from her bedroom and scooped up both pillows before following the sound.

"Shelby?" He tried knocking on her door, but got no response. The music—Jesus, it was reggae—wasn't overly loud, but unless he pounded on the door, she wasn't going to hear him. He sucked in a fortifying breath, because who the hell knew what he'd find on the other side, and tried the knob.

Shelby was standing barefoot on a mat, her back to him, one knee bent, the other straight, and her arms out at her sides. Warrior II pose. She was doing yoga.

Okay, that was not what he expected.

Somehow, every time he thought he had her figured out, she managed to throw a curve ball at him. It was thrilling—kind of like a puzzle that changed the moment he had it put together. *She* was thrilling and until he saw her standing there, deep in her own thoughts, he hadn't realized how much he'd been itching all day to get home and see her again.

She turned to repeat the pose on the other side and spotted him there in the doorway. She smiled. "Oh. Hey. I see you found the pillows. I saw them while shopping with Libby today and couldn't resist."

He looked down at the pillows still in his hand. He'd completely forgotten about the damn things and couldn't remember what it was about them that had bothered him. He set them aside on her dresser. "You also picked up some of your things, I see."

A bright paisley-print bedspread and more colorful pillows now covered the mattress and several boxes lined one wall, spilling clothes onto the floor. Her bird sat inside a bigger cage than the one it had traveled in, its head bopping to the beat of the music. Sam the Cat squatted on the end of her bed, eyeing the bird like he was considering a snack.

"Yes. Just enough to get by for a few months." She sank deeper into Warrior II and closed her eyes, breathing slow and deep.

"How was your shopping trip?" he asked, unwilling to let the conversational ball drop.

"Successful." She opened her eyes, and the corners crinkled with a smile. "I have clothes that won't scare away your friends now. I also dyed my hair. Hope the red's not too much."

Hell, he was already so used to all of her bright colors and he'd been so focused on her lithe body, he hadn't even noticed the change, but he studied her hair now. She wore it pulled back in a sloppy bun. It wasn't an in-your-face kind of red, but soft and natural. It suited her while still being within an acceptable spectrum for hair color. "I approve."

"Libby picked it out. She's great. We had so much fun together. It's nice having a sister who actually enjoys shopping." Shelby smoothly shifted positions into the reverse warrior, raising one arm and bending backward, thrusting her breasts toward the ceiling. His mouth went dry at the memory of having her bare breasts under his tongue. He'd love to strip her out of her tight-fitting yoga outfit and drive into her while she held the downward dog pose until he allowed her to move…

And she shifted into downward dog.

Reece turned on his heel. "We need to leave for the party in an hour."

Shelby straightened and propped her hands on her hips. That man. She'd been about done with her daily yoga routine when he walked in, and she purposely chose poses that highlighted her assets. And still, he walked away. Here she thought last night had changed something between them.

Poe let out an alarmed squawk, and she spun in time to see Sam the Cat lunge for the cage from the bed. He didn't make it, falling to the carpet with a muffled plop. "No! Bad cat!"

"Bad cat. Bad cat," Poe echoed and if she wasn't mistaken there was a note of triumph in his tone. They had been going at each other all day and, for all she knew, Poe had been baiting Sam this whole time.

"Oh, what am I going to do with the two of you? Might as well start calling you Sylvester and Tweety." She shooed Sam from the room. He sulked out then turned in the hallway and gave her a look of abject feline betrayal. She shook her head. "Sorry, pal. You can't eat my birdie."

She shut the door, leaned her back against it, and scanned the room while Poe continued to chatter from his cage. It was all still sterile, even with her belongings scattered throughout, and she suddenly felt like an unwelcome stranger in a bizarre land. She wished she had more time to unpack, get comfortable.

Her gaze landed on the black lace dress she planned to wear tonight, hanging on the back of her bathroom door.

Okay, if Reece wanted to play it like nothing happened between them, she could do that. Just like she could go to this stuffy dinner party, learn the things she needed to know about his company, and not completely embarrass him.

She hoped.

"Oh God." She banged her head against the door a few times. "What have I gotten myself into?"

Fifty-five minutes later, Reece paced the living room and alternated between checking his watch and glancing toward Shelby's door. Had she heard him say they needed to go in an hour? He'd been in a hurry to leave her room to keep himself from doing something stupid, so maybe she misheard him or…

Another minute ticked by.

Damn. He really didn't want to go knock on her door, but this was not the kind of party to be fashionably late for. He took two steps in the direction of her room, and the door opened. His breath of relief snagged somewhere around his Adam's apple. Shelby looked…like a completely different woman. Red hair fell in loose ringlets around her shoulders. Her black dress was cocktail length and flared at the hips in a striking silhouette. Underneath the long lace sleeves, he saw no hint of her colorful ink and honestly, he wasn't sure what to make of that.

She smirked. "Roll up that tongue and put it back in your mouth, Hershey."

"Uh, sorry." He re-hinged his jaw. "You look…"

"Like a good little housewife?" she suggested at the same time he said, "Different."

"Well of course I look different. That's the point, right?" She held out her arms and twirled. "Do I pass inspection, Mr. Wilde?"

No. It was the first answer to pop to mind and he bit it back. This was wrong. This wasn't Shelby, and asking her to change was wrong. He should call the whole thing off right now and figure something else out, but when he opened his mouth, all that emerged was a strangled, "We need to go."

She nodded and disappeared back into her room for a second. When she returned, she wore a knee-length coat that tied at her waist and was in the process of putting in pearl earrings. He grabbed his own coat and held open the door for her.

Neither of them said anything during the nearly forty minute car ride to Irving James's home, but when Reece pulled up to the gate, he couldn't take the silence any longer. He turned in his seat to face her. "Are you sure you want to do this? It's not too late to call it off."

Smiling slightly, she reached over and cupped his cheek with her left hand. Light flashed off her wedding ring. "I'll be okay. I won't embarrass you. Promise."

"It's not that." His gaze traveled out the windshield to the looming mansion. All that glitz and glam might look like a fairy tale from the outside, but he knew what lay waiting within. "Shelby, these people are —"

"Bunnies compared to the people I'm used to dealing with. The Headhunters are after my head, remember? Doesn't get much worse than that."

Another problem he needed to deal with. She didn't want his money, but he had to do something to help smooth the waters there until her insurance paid up. "That's not a fact I'm soon to forget, but you're wrong. Maybe these socialites won't gun you down, but they'll stab you in the back if you give them the slightest opening. Don't give them one. Don't trust anybody."

"It's only paranoia if they're not out to get you, right?" When he didn't smile back at her, she nudged his shoulder. "Relax, Hershey. I'll watch your six if you watch mine. Now let's go in before whoever is manning the security cameras wonders why we're just sitting here."

Yeah, she was right. He rolled down his window and hit the buzzer for the gate, waited a moment for a response, and stated his name. The gate slid open soundlessly a moment later, and he guided the Escalade toward the valet waiting in front of the house. "If you get cornered at any point during the night, your best bet is to play the dumb trophy wife. It'll be what they expect from you, anyway."

"Oh, dream come true! I've always wanted to be a trophy wife," she said with mock excitement then rolled her eyes. "Not."

He winced. Jesus, this was so wrong. If his mother were alive, she'd slap him silly for putting Shelby through this farce. "I'm sorry."

"Reece." She tugged on his jacket sleeve until he looked at her again. "I wouldn't be here if I didn't want to be, okay? This is about more than me needing the protection of your name. I'm the reason you're being blackmailed and I want to help. If I have to play the dumb trophy wife, then I'll be the dumbest trophy wife around. Now deep breath and *woosah*. We got this."

Impossibly, a smile tugged at the corner of his mouth as he climbed out of the SUV and walked around the hood to open Shelby's door for her. She hooked her arm through his and smiled up at him like the smitten wife she was supposed to be. Damn, she was good. He had to give her that— as adaptable as a chameleon.

And if he didn't relax, he'd be the one to blow up their little charade, not her.

Chapter Fourteen

The evening passed in a whirl of fake air kisses and small talk, and Shelby lost interest about halfway through cocktail hour. She'd played up the dumb trophy wife, but now as she sipped at her glass of champagne, she wondered if she'd done too good of a job. The women she found herself surrounded with gossiped endlessly about people she didn't know and frankly, didn't care about. But one of them was Irving James's wife, Charlotte, and so she made all the appropriate noises at all the appropriate times.

Reece had been right. These people had teeth, and navigating the room was like swimming through a shark tank with an open wound. Honestly, she'd be more comfortable mingling at The Headhunter's bar, but then, she'd been born into that world. A different universe, really, full of guns and drugs and the roughest of rough men. This whole entitled, born-with-a-silver-spoon life was so far beyond her, she could see why Reece had suggested the dumb act. There was no way she'd fit in with these people as herself. At least you always knew where you stood with The Headhunters.

And how interesting that Irving James, a man with such strict expectations of proper behavior, had a wife who was less than half his age. Hypocritical much?

Shelby was just about to make up an excuse to leave the group when a gorgeous brunette in a sapphire dress sauntered up and gracefully cut in to the conversation. She handled herself like she was used to swimming these dangerous waters. "Oh, I'm so sorry to interrupt, Charlotte, but is this Reece's new bride?"

Charlotte tittered. There was no other word for the delighted sound she made. Yup, their wedding was already providing fodder for the rumor mill. "Alicia, this is Shelby. Shelby, Alicia Porter. I'm surprised you two haven't met before now."

"We haven't had the pleasure," Alicia said and smiled at Shelby. "But I was hoping to see you here tonight. Dylan has talked about you nonstop since Reece told him about you yesterday."

Dylan? Shelby froze, her mind drawing a complete blank. On the way to the party, Reece had briefed her on the names she'd hear tonight, but she didn't remember a Dylan. Probably because she'd only been half listening at the time, too distracted by nerves.

Okay, process of elimination. Reece had only gone two places yesterday that she knew of—the Wilde Security office, and nobody but his brothers would have been there, and DMW. So this Dylan guy must work at DMW and, if he and his wife were here tonight, he must be high up in the company. Maybe even Reece's second-in-command.

She turned on the slightly vacant smile she'd been sporting all night. "I haven't had a chance to meet Dylan yet. It's all been a bit of a whirlwind."

"It's so romantic," Charlotte said. "You *have* to tell us how you landed confirmed bachelor Reece Wilde. I honestly never thought I'd see the day he married."

"He was never interested in anyone before," another of the women—Lena?—scoffed and plucked the olive out of her third martini. Probably pretty at one time, she was starting to show some wear and trying to hide behind a spray tan, bleach blond hair, and plastic surgery. She sucked the last olive off the swizzle stick. "Tell us, what makes you so special?"

"Actually," Alicia cut in, "I was hoping to steal Shelby for a little chat before dinner."

Several of the women frowned disapprovingly at Lena, who snagged another martini from a passing waiter.

"Ignore Lena," Alicia whispered as she guided Shelby away from the group. "Before she married her husband, she had a thing with Reece that went nowhere fast, and she's been bitter about it ever since. But can you blame her?" She motioned to an elderly man already seated at the table for dinner. "That's her husband. She's been drowning herself in martinis waiting for him to die, but he knows it, and he's stubborn. At the rate she's going, he'll outlast her."

"Oh my God. She's such a stereotypical desperate housewife, she practically breaks the cliché—oh." Realizing she'd said her thoughts out loud, Shelby winced. "And I probably shouldn't have said that. I promised Reece I'd behave."

Alicia laughed. "No worries. I'm glad you're not as cardboard as the rest of those ladies. I've known Reece since college, and it didn't make sense to me that he'd fall for an airhead."

Shelby decided in that moment, she liked this woman. "He...might have told me to play up the dumb trophy wife act," she admitted.

"Oh, Reece, you knucklehead." Alicia rolled her eyes toward the ceiling, then laughed. "He means well."

A waiter stopped to offer them glasses of bubbly. Alicia accepted and passed one to Shelby, then clinked their rims.

"I know he does," Shelby said after a sip, then sought Reece with her gaze. He stood on the other side of the room with a handful of other men in suits. Who knew what they were so intently discussing, but he was in his element here. Poised and confident, so different from the man who bumbled every time she made a pass at him.

"That's my husband, Dylan." Alicia motioned to the handsome blond man standing beside Reece. "And that Jeff Bridges look-alike is Irving James. The third."

So that was the man Reece wanted to impress. Not what she'd pictured. Come to think of it, she wasn't quite sure what she pictured, but it hadn't been a distinguished, slightly grizzled gentleman with crinkles around his eyes and a bright white smile behind his graying beard.

Belatedly, she picked up the note of disdain in Alicia's voice and turned back to the woman. "You don't like him?"

"I don't like his politics. He has a very antiquated view of women in the workplace. Or, for that matter, women in general. I honestly don't understand why Reece feels this deal is so important, but he's the boss."

"You work for DMW, too?" Shelby asked. Alicia gave her an odd look and for a heart-stopping moment, she wondered if she'd tipped her hand. She hurried to add, "Reece doesn't talk about work much at home."

"He doesn't?" Genuine surprise colored her voice. "I didn't know Reece ever talks about anything but work."

Crap. That was true. She'd pushed the lie a bit too hard. Time to back off. She tried on her best sheepish expression. "Uh, it's actually a rule I came up with. Between DMW and Wilde Security, he gets so wrapped up, you know? If I don't force him to put it aside, take a break, he never would."

Alicia eyed her as if seeing her for the very first time, and a certain amount of respect filled her eyes. "Good for you. Yes, I think you'll be good for him."

Pleasure warmed Shelby's belly at the words, even though she knew they weren't the truth. She wasn't good for Reece. But, still, hearing someone say so... She wanted to hug Alicia for it. Nobody had ever thought her good for anything or anyone.

Alicia took a sip of her drink. "Dylan and I are both workaholics. Just as bad as Reece. We never stop. And, yes, I work for DMW. I'm the chief financial officer, but I also help Dylan with marketing and operations."

"Oh. Now I feel stupid for not knowing that."

"Nah. Don't worry about it. Your no-work-at-home rule is a good one. Don't let Reece break it."

"Believe me, I won't." She scanned the room again. "Are there any other DMW employees here I should know?"

"Hmm." Alicia followed her gaze. "Over there." She tilted her chin in the direction of a skinny man with a slicked-back ponytail of thinning brown hair. "Cliff McWilliam. He took over as head of development after the company started getting too big for Reece to handle both development and his duties as CEO. I'm actually a little surprised to see him here. He and Reece haven't been seeing eye-to-eye lately."

Interesting. "About the merger with Irving James?"

"No, no. Cliff is all about technology and could care less about the business side of things as long as he can keep tinkering with his computers. I'm not quite sure what happened, but from what I gathered through the company's gossip mill, Reece caught Cliff doing things in development that Reece hadn't given his okay for."

Shelby made a mental note of the name for later. She should probably change the subject now before she aroused any suspicion, but Alicia was definitely a little tipsy. Alcohol was great for loosening lips, and she was afraid she'd never get this chance again. "Who else do I need to know about?"

"Oh, well. Lena. She was the head of sales until her drinking got to be too much. Reece let her go about three weeks ago—with a more than generous severance package if you ask me—but it did nothing to lessen the grudge she's been holding against him since he turned her down." Alicia leaned in, lowered her voice. "Word of advice. Avoid Lena if you can. She's not above starting cat fights."

Shelby glanced in the woman's direction, only to find Lena scowling at her. Wow. That was more than a grudge. That was pure hatred.

Yeah, definitely better to avoid her.

Another mental note.

"Well, look at this," Dylan said as he and Reece joined them. "Our wives are bonding. We're doomed."

"You were doomed the second you married me." Alicia leaned in to kiss her husband, then smiled over at Reece. "And you, mister, have no idea what you've gotten yourself into."

"I have a pretty good idea." He slid his arm around Shelby's waist. It was the first time he'd touched her since last night. He'd been avoiding her as if she were combustible and he'd burst into flames at even the smallest contact but—surprise—he didn't.

Sure, he was only touching her now as part of his husband act, but she took full advantage. She leaned in to his side as they followed the other couple toward the dinner table, played up the whole crazy-in-love newlywed thing. But instead of making him uncomfortable, he went with the flow, again surprising her. The man could act. Nobody looking at the two of them would see anything other than happy newlyweds and it made her...well, a little sad. Deep down, she admitted to herself that she wouldn't mind if it was more than an act. Wouldn't ever happen, but still. That didn't stop her from wanting it.

Reece nuzzled her ear. "Are you okay?"

No. No, she wasn't because she'd been lying to him from the start, and she hated it. Hated that she'd just given his slightly tipsy financial officer the third degree to get info on his company. But she didn't dare tell him the truth about Jason's investigation into DMW Systems, especially not while he was already worried about the blackmail, so she shoved the guilt aside. Besides, maybe her snooping would uncover something to help him because the more she thought about it, the more her instincts called foul at the oh-so-coincidental timing of Jason's investigation and Reece's blackmail.

Were they connected? Something to think about.

Reece pulled her to a stop, searched her eyes. The crease of a frown formed between his brows. "Shelby?"

Realizing she'd gone too long without answering his question, she plastered on a smile and nodded. "I'm fine, but I could do without Cruella De Vil over there staring holes into us."

He lifted his head, spotted Lena, and his frown deepened. "I didn't know she was here. I'm sorry. I should have warned you about her."

"That's okay. Alicia saved me." And was then interrogated for her trouble. Dammit. She wished she didn't like Alicia so much, because now guilt gnawed at her insides for using the woman as an unwitting source of information.

At the dinner table, Reece held out a chair for her before taking his own seat. Irving James sat at the head of the table to Reece's left and the moment his butt hit the chair, the waiters appeared with the first course. Like a well-rehearsed play. Or maybe a dance. All of the waitstaff moved with graceful efficiency, setting plates in front of the guests and keeping glasses filled. Shelby had never seen anything like it.

James ignored his staff and picked up his drink. "So, Reece, this the little wife?"

The little wife?

She glanced over at Reece to see his reaction. His lips tightened slightly, but he nodded. "Yes, this is Shelby. Shelby, Mr. James."

"A word of friendly advice, from one married man to another…" James smiled in a slimy wink, wink, nudge, nudge kind of way. "Keep her on a short leash. You know what they say about redheads."

A short leash? Was this guy for real?

Shelby stared across the table at Charlotte James, expecting the woman to say something chiding to her husband about the inappropriateness of the comment. At the very least, she could apologize, woman-to-woman. But Charlotte wasn't even paying attention, too wrapped up in a conversation with one of her friends. And, that, more than the comment itself, boiled Shelby's blood. Charlotte wasn't unaware of her husband's sexism—she was choosing to ignore it and setting women's lib back sixty years in the process.

Shelby opened her mouth, but Reece's hand landed on her thigh under the table and squeezed hard in warning.

Oh, come on. Not him, too. She glanced over, saw his lips pressed together in a tight, disapproving line. He gave a slight shake of the head.

He was mad at *her*? But for once, she hadn't done anything wrong. Sure, she'd wanted to tear that chauvinist a new one, but she wouldn't risk the future of Reece's businesses just because she was offended. And in the long run, James's opinion meant nothing to her. Months from now, he'd be little more than a blip on her radar.

So she was going to keep her trap shut, which didn't explain why Reece was looking at her like *she* had said something offensive. She'd put up with James being a jackass if she had to, but Reece? Hell no.

There would be consequences for this.

Smiling to herself, she picked up her glass, took a sip. And she knew exactly how to get under his skin.

Chapter Fifteen

What a chauvinistic, entitled jackass.

Reece had a few choice things to say to Irving James. Oh, how he wanted to rip the guy a new one and feared he wasn't doing a very good job of keeping his thoughts off his face. One wrong word and he might as well kiss Wilde Security good-bye. His brothers would be out of jobs, and he refused to let that happen, even if it meant biting his tongue.

He'd apologize to Shelby later. Make it up to her somehow. He hadn't expected James to take cheap shots at her, though he probably should have. Should have prepared Shelby for the abuse. Or better yet, shouldn't have subjected her to it in the first place.

He was a jerk.

And his hand was still on her thigh. He didn't realize it until she parted her legs and his fingers slipped toward her inner thigh. Heat gathered in his stomach, and his cock perked to attention.

Shit.

He removed his hand and focused on Irving James again. "I was hoping we'd have some time to talk business."

James waved a hand. "No, not tonight. Tonight is about getting acquainted."

Something landed on his leg under the table. He reached down, thinking his napkin had slipped, and found a tiny scrap of lace, damp in the middle. His mouth went dry, and he grabbed for his drink with his free hand. Shelby innocently picked at her salad as if she hadn't just handed him her underwear.

Jesus. Was she trying to ruin him? She had to know by now his brain didn't fire on all cylinders when she did stuff like this. Wasn't last night proof?

James was talking to him, but all he could concentrate on was that damp spot on the lace. He rubbed the fabric between his fingers, fantasized about having his mouth on her sex again…

No. No, no, no. Fuck, he needed a minute alone to get his head on straight or he wasn't going to make it through dinner. He stuffed the panties in his pocket and stood, murmuring an excuse, not even entirely sure what he said. He strode out of the room, intending to head for the front door. The winter air should cool his jets and allow him to think again.

Only he didn't make it. He got as far as the front hallway when he heard the click of heels following him across the tile and turned.

Shelby.

That dress was sin. He'd done his best to avoid touching her tonight because ever since she stepped out of her bedroom wearing the dress, the only thoughts in his head had involved peeling her out of it.

Sex had never been a distraction before, probably because he hadn't known what he was missing. This was new territory for him, way off his normal beaten path, completely uncharted. And that pissed him off. He liked neat and tidy and carefully calculated plans.

Shelby was none of that. If there was one thing you could count on from her, it was that she'd throw a wrench into the works. It was exasperating as hell. And fucking hot. Her unpredictability turned him on like nothing else.

He was insane. Had to be.

He didn't realize he'd stalked forward and caged her against the wall with his hands on either side of her head until she sucked in a deep breath and her breasts scraped against the front of his shirt.

"Are you trying to sabotage me?"

She reached down and squeezed him through his pants. "I'm punishing you."

A tremble shook through his arms and legs, and he bit back a groan. "Why?"

"Because you scowled at me like I'd done something wrong when James was the jackass."

That cleared some of the lust-fog from his brain. He backed away far enough to meet her gaze. "Shelby, I wasn't angry with you. I was trying not to reach over the table and throttle James."

She blinked. "Really?"

"Yes, really. Insulting you like that was out of line and—" Voices nearby caught his attention, and he glanced up.

Shit.

They couldn't be seen by James or his staff like this, both vibrating with so much sexual tension they could light a fire with the heat between them.

He grabbed for the nearest door. Closet. Figures. But it was large, the size of some people's bathrooms, with a center island of drawers meant to hold who knew what.

Shelby snorted as he pushed her inside. "What is this, seven minutes in heaven? I feel like I'm back in high school."

"Just—stop." He pulled the door shut, plunging the room into darkness.

"You've probably never played, huh?"

He heard her move, the air stirring with her scent in the moment before she wrapped her arms around him from behind. Her hand flattened on his stomach and slid lower, fingers dipping below his belt. She just brushed the tip of his cock and every muscle in his body tensed in response.

"Shelby." His voice sounded hoarse. "We're not doing this here."

"Why not?" she whispered and her breath fanned over his ear. "You don't like Irving James any more than I do, so let's give him a big middle finger and fuck in his closet."

A thrill shot through him. He should not be turned on by the suggestion but, holy fuck, he was. His cock was so hard, he had to undo his belt or risk permanent damage. "I don't have a condom."

"I do." She trailed the edge of a foil packet across the back of his neck and he shivered.

"Where did that come from?" His mind ran wild with all of the possibilities.

"My bra."

"Jesus." He spun and crushed her mouth with his. All

demand and no finesse. He lost all sense of reason when it came to this woman. It was liberating and maybe that was why he couldn't keep his hands off her. With her, he found freedom.

When they parted for air, Shelby laughed softly. "You only have seven minutes. That's how the game works." She nipped his bottom lip. "So make me scream."

His heart thumped hard in his chest. He held out a hand for the condom. "Bend over."

"Ooh. Makes me hot when you get all demanding." She slapped the package into his palm and turned around. His eyes had adjusted to the darkness, and he could just make out the outline of her leaning in to the island, parting her legs and thrusting her ass toward him.

She was just begging for a spanking.

He found her thigh with his hand, skimmed his palm up the smooth flesh of her bare ass. He'd wanted his handprint there since the very first time he saw her, so he hauled back and gave her firm cheek a solid slap. "You are trouble."

Her gasp slipped into a moan as he traced her cleft until he found her opening, then dipped his fingers inside. He loved the way her inner walls clamped down to keep his fingers from withdrawing. How something so soft could grip so hard was a wonder to him, and he wanted more time to explore her body. He hadn't gotten the chance last night and couldn't take the time now. But soon he would. Very soon.

He withdrew his fingers and fumbled around until he found her clit. Last night, he'd figured out how to tell when he touched the right spot, because her knees would go weak and he had to wrap an arm around her waist to keep her up. He caged her against the island, felt the trembles racing through her body. He circled her clit with his thumb, applied more pressure, and her body seized up, breath rushing out in a squeak.

Triumph roared through him with a burst of pure testosterone. He needed inside her. Hard and fast and claiming and right fucking now.

Reece tore open the condom, unzipped his pants, and sheathed himself in the rubber. He gripped her hips, found her entrance, and slammed home, closing his eyes at the exquisite pleasure of her body giving in to his. Shelby moaned and arched her back, pressed against his thrusts.

Jesus. She took all of him, right to his base. Good thing she only gave him seven minutes, because he wasn't going to last. He pounded into her, hard, fast, urgent, the only sounds slapping flesh and ragged breathing and the throaty little noises she made as she urged him on with her body.

He was so lost in her, he nearly missed the footsteps outside the closet. Voices followed.

"Where the hell is he?" Dylan asked.

"It's not like him to just get up and leave," Alicia said, worry in her voice. "I hope everything is all right."

"I'll call him."

Shit, Dylan and Alicia had stopped right in front of the closet. All they had to do was open the door and they'd get an eyeful of his ass pumping away.

Reece froze and clamped a hand over Shelby's mouth to keep her silent. He felt her lips curve into a smile before the warm pad of her tongue caressed his palm. She tightened her inner muscles around him, milking him, and he shook with the restraint it took to remain still. Adrenaline poured through his system and, impossibly, the thought of getting caught only hardened him more, to the point of pain.

He couldn't do it. He couldn't stay still.

Even as his cell phone vibrated against his leg, he thrust into her again, the strokes short and fast. He kept his hand over her mouth because he didn't trust that she wouldn't make one of those sexy as hell sounds and give them away.

With his free hand, he released his hold on her hip and reached between their bodies. He needed her to come. Now. His orgasm was clawing down his spine and was going to rip him in half if he didn't finish soon. He found her clit, rubbed in tight, fast circles, and her body locked down. She shuddered through the climax, his hand muffling her moans.

Outside the closet, Dylan said, "Reece, it's Dylan. Where'd you go? Everything okay? Call me when you get this."

"No answer?" Alicia asked, and their voices faded as they finally moved away.

Reece removed his hand from Shelby's mouth, gripped her hips, and hammered into her as hard and deep as he could get until he found bliss in his own explosive release. He collapsed forward, resting his head on her back. Under his ear, her breath rushed in and out, and her heart thundered.

Playing with fire.

Yeah, he was, and Shelby was burning him alive.

He groaned. "Your sister was right."

She laughed softly. "About what?"

"You are a very bad influence." He straightened and gave her ass one last smack before withdrawing from her heat and dealing with the condom. He put it back in the wrapper, then dropped the bundle in his pocket for later disposal. It wouldn't do to have Irving James's butler stumble across it when he retrieved everyone's coats at the end of the night.

Still breathing hard, Shelby turned to face him and smoothed down the skirt of her dress. "You need a bit of bad influence in your life, Skittles." She stood on her toes and lightly brushed her lips over his before returning his ass smack with one of her own. "You're too uptight without it."

He wanted to be annoyed. He even tried to conjure up some irritation with her, but all he managed was exasperated amusement. Even her candy-themed nicknames were starting to grow on him.

Before he fully realized what he was doing, he cupped her upturned face in his hands and pressed his lips to hers.

It wasn't the kind of kiss she was used to from Reece. Wasn't the usual crush of mouths, the demand of tongue, the war for superiority. It was soft. Gentle. Somehow even more intimate than the sex they'd just had. Her belly jittered with unwanted emotions too painfully sweet to name.

Oh, this was trouble.

If she knew anything, it was mistakes, and falling for Reece Wilde was the kind of mistake everyone walked away from broken.

She drew away, but only by inches, and stared up into his eyes. In the dimness of the closet, they were little more than black pools, which was for the better. She didn't know if she wanted to see his emotions.

Reece tucked a strand of hair behind her ear and opened his mouth. Oh God. He was going to say something she both dreaded and desperately wanted to hear.

Someone pounded on the closet door.

Reece jolted as if he'd been poked in the ass with a hot brand.

"I know you're in there," Dylan said. "I lured Alicia away and she's entertaining everyone with a story about our trip to Venice, so it's safe to come out. If you're dressed," he added with amusement after a beat.

Shelby giggled but stifled it behind her hand when Reece glared at her.

He cleared his throat and hit the light switch. "Give us a minute."

"Take your time," Dylan said, obviously enjoying the whole thing.

Reece shut his eyes for a moment and sucked in a breath through his nose, letting it out slowly. If she didn't know any better, she'd think... "Are you embarrassed?"

Color filled his cheeks and, okay, that was adorable. "You are! Big, bad, Mr. Gazillionaire is embarrassed. And blushing!"

"I'm not fond of getting caught with my pants down."

She couldn't help it—she pinched his butt when he turned to find their coats. He sent her his patented *I am not amused* glare and handed over her coat. Grinning, she swung it on and opened the door.

"Hi, Dylan."

He tipped his head slightly in greeting and didn't bother hiding his grin. "Shelby." Then he gazed past her and burst out laughing. "You both look like you just had energetic closet sex."

"We did."

Reece growled. "Shelby..."

She shrugged. "He already knows."

Dylan just laughed harder, until tears rolled down his cheeks. "Oh man," he said finally, gasping for breath. "I never thought I'd see the day. I like you, Shelby. A lot. You're good for him."

"I like you, too, Dylan." And she did. He seemed like a nice guy, a little on the nerdy side and not nearly as stuffy as the rest of the dinner guests.

Reece grumbled again and Dylan straightened, knuckling away his tears. "It's okay, buddy. I remember what it was like to be a newlywed. But…you might want to beg off the rest of the night. You can't go back in there looking like that or everyone will know. I'll make all the proper excuses for you."

Leaving now was an irresponsible thing to do. Then again, staying was probably even more irresponsible at this point. Either way, if he offended James, he was putting his employees and brothers at risk of losing their jobs.

He needed to learn how to control himself around Shelby. Maintaining control had never been an issue in the past, but now? All he had to do was touch her and he was lost, and it was causing him to make bad decisions.

A quickie in the closet wasn't worth losing everything he'd worked for. And it wasn't going to happen again.

Too many beats of silence passed as he mentally berated himself for losing control.

Finally, Shelby looped her arm through his. "I already told everyone you weren't feeling well when I left the table to come looking for you. Dylan can elaborate on that, and tomorrow you can call James and apologize. Tell him you had some sort of twenty-four hour thing."

Dylan was nodding. "Listen to your wife, man. Go home."

Reece swore under his breath. "All right. But if he starts talking about the merger—"

"He won't," Dylan insisted. "He already said tonight wasn't about business. Go. I think I hear Alicia coming this way."

Shelby pulled him toward the door, and he gave up protesting. They were right. Even before Shelby's distraction, he hadn't been in top form tonight.

This was for the better.

The valet retrieved his SUV, and he held the door for Shelby before circling around the hood and climbing behind the wheel. He didn't say anything more to her—didn't know what to say. He put the Escalade in gear and drove away from the mansion.

"So." Shelby said after the silence between them started getting heavy. "That was fun."

"It was stupid."

"Ouch." She was silent for another moment. "I'm sorry. I really thought you were mad at me, and it...hurt. I just wanted to make you as uncomfortable in that situation as I was, but I swear I had no intention of letting it go as far as it did. It's just...we were suddenly in the closet, and things were coming out of my mouth I shouldn't have been saying, and all I could think of was how much I wanted you again."

Some of the knots in his shoulders loosened. He stopped the SUV at a red light and glanced over at her. "I'm sorry I let James make you uncomfortable. I should have spoken up, but—"

"You're afraid of what will happen to your companies if you do. At least your motives were altruistic. Mine were just childish. As usual." Sighing heavily, she leaned the side of her head against the window. The streetlamps cast a soft yellow glow over her face, making her look years younger, very much like the lost little girl she once was. "Sometimes I wonder what's wrong with me, why it's so hard to act like a normal, responsible adult. Why am I so different?"

"I know how that feels."

She turned enough in her seat to look at him. "No, you don't. You're Mr. Responsible."

"Yeah, but I know what *different* feels like." The light turned green, but he didn't hit the gas. He tapped his fingers thoughtfully on the steering wheel for a moment. Easier to show her what he meant than to explain. "Are you in a hurry to get home?"

"No. Why?"

"I want to show you something."

Chapter Sixteen

Shelby had no clue where he was taking her. They left the city and ended up in Arlington, but he still wouldn't answer any of her questions about their destination.

Okay, then. Top secret.

She tried to fill the silence with small talk and, when that didn't work, decided to go for something with a little more shock value. "I think I know who your blackmailer is."

That caught his attention. His gaze zeroed in on her. "What?"

"You and Lena Schilling had a thing, right?"

"Who told you that?"

"Alicia."

"Jesus." He shook his head. Pushed out a sigh. "No. It was one date, years ago. Afterward, she very insistently tried to invite me back to her place, and I turned her down. That was the end of it."

"Oh, you silly man. That wasn't the end of it. She's still

bitter."

"Because that woman is bitter about everything. There's a reason it was only one date. She's a vile person."

"You turned her down, hurt her pride." She ticked off each point on her fingers. "Then you fired her. And, you know, hell hath no fury and all that."

"One has nothing to do with the other. I fired her because she wasn't doing her job. She hadn't been for a long time, and the only reason I kept her as long as I did was out of loyalty. She's been with DMW since the beginning."

"And I bet she feels entitled to the company because of it."

Reece opened his mouth but snapped it shut again without uttering a sound. "Shit," he said after a moment. "You're right. I'll add her to my spreadsheet."

Oh God. He was trying to find his blackmailer with a spreadsheet? That was adorable, but Shelby had lived with her sister and Cam long enough to know that crime wasn't solved by spreadsheets. The poor guy was doomed. "You should tell your brothers what's going on, Reece. At this point, it's silly to keep it from them. They already know we've been together, so the pictures aren't going to faze them. They're trained investigators. They can help."

He said nothing for so long, she didn't think he was going to answer. "I know," he finally admitted softly. "But I'd rather handle it myself. Greer's gone MIA again and Vaughn's obsessing over the disappearance of Lark Warren. Cam and your sister just got married, and it's only courteous to wait at least a month before dumping my shit on them. And Jude…something's going on with him, too. He's been moping lately."

"Oh, I know why. He and Libby want a baby."

He jumped like she'd poked him in the side with a knife. "They what?"

"Yeah, Libby said they've been trying for a few months now, since their wedding, but keep getting disappointed. They're both pretty bummed about it."

He stared at her for a solid ten seconds until the light they were sitting at turned green. "How do you know all this?"

She lifted a shoulder. "People talk to me. It's a gift." And a curse, but she wasn't ready to open that can of worms with him yet. If she didn't have the unique ability to get people to open up to her, she wouldn't be trapped under Jason Mallory's thumb now.

"A baby?" Reece said, shell-shocked. "They want a *baby*?"

"That's usually how it works. First comes love, then comes marriage, then the baby carriage."

"B-but—" He actually stuttered. "No. That's... I can't picture Jude as a father."

"Really? I think he'll make a great one. He has a good sense of humor, which I've heard is essential for parenting. Have you ever wanted kids?" The question slipped out without her permission, and she silently cursed herself for it. None of her business. Nope. His answer was not even a little bit her business.

"No," he said with absolutely no inflection in his voice.

"Yeah." A small ache throbbed in the center of her chest. She resisted the urge to rub at it. "Me neither."

They rode the last bit of their trip in silence until Reece guided the SUV into the driveway of a gorgeous brick colonial that looked like something out of a magazine.

"We're here," he said, shutting off the engine.

"Where?"

"The house I grew up in."

She looked at the house again and, yes, she could so easily picture that childhood, one so far removed from her own she'd often wondered if that kind of life was even real. But she could picture Christmas lights under the eaves of the pointed roof and a wreath on the front door welcoming visitors. Could see the five Wilde boys running around in the large, sloped front yard, starting snowball wars and building forts. During the spring and summer, they probably climbed that big maple tree and swung in the tire still hanging from the lowest branch. They had probably run through that front door with all kinds of bumps and bruises and scrapes, hoping for their mother to kiss the boo-boos better. Maybe there had even been a broken arm or two and a few rushed trips to the nearest emergency room.

It was the kind of house she and Eva had dreamed about growing up in, the kind they'd seen on TV shows featuring happy families.

Shelby blinked hard, appalled that her vision had started to blur. "Why did you bring me here?"

"You didn't believe me when I said I know how different feels." He pushed open his door, and cold air rushed inside. "Come on."

Like the driveway, the path to the door had been cleared of snow recently. She knew none of the brothers lived here, so they must have hired someone to plow.

No, not "they," she realized, watching as Reece found the right key and slid it into the lock. This was all his doing. He paid for the upkeep of his empty childhood home. There was something tragic about that, and her heart melted a little.

Inside, the house wasn't dusty, but it did smell unused. It was like a time capsule, transporting her twenty years into the past, as if the brothers couldn't bear to change anything from the way it was the day their parents died.

Reece moved around the living room, turning on lamps, upping the temperature on the thermostat until the heat kicked on. Then he just stood there in the middle of the room, seemingly at a loss.

She wasn't sure what he expected her to say, so she said nothing and wandered. The stairs to the second floor were positioned at the back of the living room and shared a wall with the dining room, which had a table big enough to fit the entire Wilde family—dad, mom, and all five boys. She imagined dinnertime at that table had been a loud, exasperating, and entertaining family affair.

Colorful marks on the narrow strip of wall between the stairs and the dining room caught her attention, and she moved in for a closer look. A height chart, indicating the Wilde boys' growth from toddlers to young men. She could track Reece from the time he was a year old, all the way up to the last mark, dated several months before his parents died. He would have been thirteen at the time and looked to have hit a growth spurt, shooting up over his younger brothers, though Greer was still taller than him by quite a bit. Made sense because Greer was a huge guy. Like, intimidatingly big.

She touched that last mark, imagined the two older boys groaning and rolling their eyes as their mother corralled them for the measuring. "You were happy."

Reece moved up behind her, close enough that the subtle scent of his cologne wrapped around her like a comforting hug. She smiled back at him. "I can tell. You were all happy here."

His Adam's apple bobbed, and he also reached out, dragged his fingers along the marks. "We were."

"I'm sorry that ended."

"Yeah. Me too." After another moment, he shook his head and grasped her hand, pulling her up the stairs. On the second floor, he opened the first door they came to and flipped on the light. "This was Greer's room."

Like the living room, it looked untouched, as if teenage Greer would be home from football practice at any moment. There were posters of sports icons, and one of Pamela Anderson from her *Baywatch* days. Several trophies and awards lined the dresser—baseball, football, wrestling. He had pictures of his friends on his desk and nightstand, including several of a pretty blonde girl who must have been his high school sweetheart.

Reece continued on down the hall and opened the next door. "This was the twins' room."

Fascinated, she stepped inside and immediately knew which side of the large room was Vaughn's and which was Cam's. Cam's more laid-back attitude showed in every nuance of his side of the room, and he was the kind of teenager who was interested in music and pop culture. Vaughn's side of the room had a definite counterculture vibe to it with darker colors and Goth-rock band posters decorating the walls.

She picked up a photo of the twins from Cam's dresser. Teenage Cam was in his usual jeans and T-shirt combo—

though the jeans were baggy, more in line with the style of the mid-90s. Teenage Vaughn was dressed head-to-toe in black, wearing a lip ring, spiky black hair, and a bad attitude.

"Vaughn went through a Goth phase," Reece said from the doorway.

"So did I." She set down the photo and grinned over at him. "And, you know, I'm not surprised. I can see why the culture would have appealed to him. Vaughn has this natural…intensity. As a teenager, he must have been a hormonal wreck trying to get control of it."

"He was, but he got over it when he joined the navy. Ended up funneling all that intensity, as you put it, into SEAL training. Probably the only thing that got him through." He tilted his head to indicate the corner of the room where a pile of hockey gear sat. "But even at his angstiest in high school, he never stopped playing hockey. Both of the twins lived for the game. They were good, too. Dad always fantasized about one or both of them going pro."

"But they both went into the military instead?"

"Greer's orders." He shut off the light and waited for her to join him in the hallway again. "After we lost our parents, the military was the only way we were all going to college. Jude and I both chose college first and enrolled in ROTC— NROTC for Jude since he chose the marines. Greer and the twins went directly into the military and studied for their degrees while serving."

The next door he opened led to Jude's old room. Typical teenage boy, the walls lined with late 90s pop culture and *Sports Illustrated Swimsuit Edition* covers, but there was color here, a playfulness that was lacking from his brothers' spaces. A handful of old board games sat on a bookshelf, along with some comics and video games. He had a few trophies as well, appeared to have played football and baseball, like his oldest brother had. There were also pictures of him hiking, rock climbing, kayaking, surfing—he'd been more outdoorsy than the rest of his brothers.

"It looks like Jude," she said and backed out of the room. "But I don't get why you're showing me all this."

He motioned to the final room at the end of the hall. "My old room." She waited for a moment, but he didn't move, so she walked over and opened the door herself, surprised to find a set of stairs leading up to the attic.

"They kept you in the attic?" She meant it as a joke, but couldn't quite hide the sudden horror that gripped her by the throat. Had their family not been as picture-perfect as it first appeared? Oh God. For his sake, she hoped they had been.

He gave a small snort of laughter and shook his head. "Relax. They didn't lock me away. I chose it. More room up there."

Curious now, she climbed the stairs. His room took up the entire attic, and he had computers everywhere, in all states of disassembly. Instead of posters of a favorite band, he had one featuring the cast of *Stargate* and pencil drawings of fantastical creatures. His shelves were stacked with books and comics. All neat and categorized, demonstrating his OCD.

It was all so different from his brothers' rooms, she stopped short and blinked in stunned surprised.

This was what his apartment should look like.

This was Reece.

He had a bunch of gaming systems pulled apart,

including some newer ones. While his brothers' rooms had been frozen in time the year they each left for college or the military, Reece's room had life.

She turned to him. "You still come here."

"Sometimes. I do my best thinking here. It's where I came up with the military simulations that started DMW Systems." He walked out in front of her toward the desk, pushed aside a plastic crate of computer parts, and gathered up several of the notebooks stacked there.

"What are those?"

He rubbed at the back of his neck. "Just...something I've been meaning to pick up."

Okay, he didn't want her to know. She could live with that. He was already sharing so much more with her than she ever thought he would.

She turned in a slow circle, then walked to the other side of the attic, where his bed sat between two dormer windows.

"So this is it," she said and sat down on the bed. He should have looked silly standing there in his expensive suit, but he appeared more at home here than he ever had in his upscale apartment. She patted the mattress next to her. "This is what you wanted to show me?"

He set his notebooks by the staircase and crossed to her in several long strides. The mattress sank with his weight, and she slid toward him. Their thighs touched, but he didn't draw away from her, and she wasn't about to draw his attention to it.

"I've always been different from my brothers," he said. "They've never understood me. Dad..." He sighed heavily. "He didn't understand me, either. He tried, but we had nothing in common, and he didn't know what to make of me. I can't throw a ball to save my life, and even though I'm great on ice skates, I hurt myself every time I pick up a hockey stick."

She smiled at the mental image—could totally picture that—and leaned her head on his shoulder, lacing their fingers together. "Did your dad ostracize you for it?"

"No. Not on purpose at least. He'd take my brothers out to hockey games, football, baseball. I just wasn't ever interested, so I never went. He tried taking me to science fairs and things like that, but he was always bored out of his mind. Finally, when I was about ten, Mom was exasperated enough with the two of us circling each other that she signed us both up for karate lessons. And that was it. Our common ground. It was the perfect blend of physical for him and mental for me. I even continued studying after he died. I wanted to make at least second level black belt, so it'd kind of be like getting two. One for me and one for him." His voice cracked a little on the last word, and he glanced away.

God, what would it feel like to love a parent so much that twenty years after they were gone, you still grieved?

Bittersweet, Shelby imagined, but she'd never know for sure. She'd never feel for her mother what Reece felt for his parents. If Katrina died tomorrow, the shock of it would hurt, yeah, but the loss of the possibility of a good relationship with her mother would hurt worse. And in her heart, she knew she'd be mostly…relieved.

"I wish I could have met your parents, Reece. They sound like good people."

"They were." He gave a small smile, a sexy uptick at the corner of his mouth. "Mom would have loved you. Dad…he wouldn't have known what to make of you, either."

She nudged him with her shoulder. "We're two peas in a pod."

He laughed. "Hardly."

"You should laugh more often."

"Yeah?" He glanced over at her, a mischievous glint in his eyes as he lowered his head, closing the distance between their mouths. "Does it turn you on?"

"Oh yeah," she breathed, in the moment before his lips touched hers.

Reece took his time with the kiss, a slow caress with no sense of urgency. Just like that last kiss in the closet before Dylan interrupted them. She trembled at the sweetness behind it and fisted her hands in his jacket, intending to push him away, but instead drawing him in closer. She didn't want this tenderness from him, though. Hard, dirty, lust-slaking sex? Yes, absolutely. But anything more than that, no matter how much she secretly yearned for it, would only end in broken hearts. It was too much.

For once, she broke the kiss first.

He drew away slightly, confusion in his eyes. "Is everything okay?"

"Yeah." She didn't sound very convincing, even to her own ears, so she made herself smile despite her heartbeat thundering nervously. "Yeah, everything's fine. But we should go. It's getting late, and I'm supposed to meet with the arson investigators tomorrow to talk about The Bean Gallery."

The confusion morphed into concern. "Did you tell them you're the owner?"

"Yes. They weren't happy with me for withholding the information."

And the concern nosedived into alarm. He stood. "They don't think—are you a suspect?"

"No. No," she added more firmly when he started to pace.

He stopped in front of her. "I'm going with you tomorrow. I want to tell them I was there."

"That's up to you, but I don't think it's necessary."

"I do." He held out a hand to help her up. "Let's go home."

Chapter Seventeen

On the way downstairs, Shelby paused and studied the framed photos hanging in the stairway. She hadn't noticed them earlier, but now that she knew more about his family, she had to stop and look. Some candid shots, some posed, some obviously from school. She studied those first because school photos were always a riot. They appeared to have been taken the school year before their parents died — Reece was about twelve in his.

"Oh, man. You *were* a nerd!" An adorable nerd, yes, with his unruly dark hair and clunky glasses.

"What do you mean, *were*?" he said from the bottom of the stairs. "I still am."

"You said it, not me." She traced the frame of the photo. "Were you picked on a lot in school?" In her experience, high schoolers mercilessly teased anyone not like them. She'd certainly wanted to go all *Carrie* on more than one "cool" kid during those endless four years.

She turned to find him watching her with those unnervingly intense eyes of his. She sometimes wondered if he could see through her to the scared little girl she kept locked away inside.

"Were you?" Her voice wobbled, and she cleared her throat, infusing her words with as much cheer as she could muster. "Picked on, I mean?"

"No." He came back up the stairs and tapped Greer's picture on the wall next to his. It showed the same square jaw, hard mouth, and wide shoulders, but fewer shadows hid in the eldest Wilde brother's dark eyes.

"Nobody ever wanted to piss off Greer. He was always big for his age. Takes after Dad that way."

Shelby spotted a wedding photo farther down the stairs and moved closer to get a better look. "What were your parents' names?"

"David Wilde, Sr. and Mom was Meredith."

The groom in the wedding picture looked shockingly like Greer—or, more accurately, Greer looked like him. "He was a senior?"

"Greer's the junior. David Greer Wilde."

"Oh. Never knew Greer goes by his middle name." She went back to studying the picture. The senior David Greer Wilde was a hulk of a man, all hard lines, with coal-dark eyes that should have been intimidating as hell, but beamed nothing but joy and love as he held his bride in a permanent spin, her white dress flaring out around her.

Exactly how Shelby had pictured him from Reece's stories.

Shelby took a step down to see another photo, one showing Meredith Wilde in a hospital bed holding two swaddled bundles—the twins—and beaming at the camera with toddler-sized versions of Greer and Reece at each arm. Unlike the other brothers, who all strongly resembled their father, Reece took after his mother. He had her hazel eyes, her aquiline nose. And while he was by no means a small man, he was the smallest of his brothers, having inherited Meredith's long, lean form rather than David's bulk.

Another photo—Meredith holding a baby with a tuft of dark hair. The twins were still toddlers in diapers and sitting on their father's lap. Greer would have been six when this photo was taken and Reece, already wearing glasses, would have been about three. He appeared utterly fascinated by his new baby brother, Jude.

They were all so happy. So...complete. A real family.

An ache Shelby didn't want to explore lodged in her belly, and she spun away from the wall of memories and stalked down the stairs. She didn't know the whys of her sudden burst of anger, but she embraced it. "Why bring me here, Reece? The *real* reason."

Reece glanced away. "I'm not sure. I don't often come here myself."

"I'd like to go now." The walls were closing in on her, all of the happy smiles like a mockery of her pathetic childhood. And if the hot pressure kept growing behind her eyes, she was going to embarrass herself and ugly-cry all over him.

"Okay." Reece picked up her coat and held it out to her. As soon as she accepted it, he grabbed the notebooks he'd set down on a table and strode toward the front door like he was in just as much of a hurry to leave as she was.

But she didn't move. Her boots stayed glued to the floor, and she found her gaze tracing over all of those photos once more.

Eva wanted this. She'd never understood her sister's drive to find a man and start a family—until now. Staring at the Wilde family photos, she got it. She felt like an unwelcome stranger from the wrong side of the tracks, but she totally got it.

And, goddammit, she wanted it, too.

She just couldn't have it with Reece.

Reece waited on the front porch for Shelby, but she barely looked at him as she strode from the house. She'd been rattled ever since that kiss upstairs in his bedroom, though he couldn't put his finger on why.

Had he done something wrong?

The car door slammed shut behind him, and he winced. He must have. Why else would she be angry with him?

And this was exactly why he'd avoided relationships. Women were just too damn confusing.

Sighing, he took one last look around the living room of his childhood home.

Why had he brought her here? He didn't know, except that he'd wanted to show her…himself. The real Reece and not the one he projected to the world. He kept expecting time to dull the pain, but the hurt never went away. Every time he came here the grief slapped him again. Because his parents should still be here, excited that Jude and Libby were trying to give them grandbabies, happy that Cam had finally married Eva, whom they'd have loved. They should still be here, dancing in the kitchen together.

But they weren't.

Maybe it was time to pack everything up and sell the old house…

But his heart lurched at the thought. As painful as the bad memories were—he'd been standing right over there at the bottom of the stairs when Greer answered the door to the cops the night their parents were killed—there were far more good memories here, and he wasn't ready to let them go. Not yet. Maybe not ever.

Reece shook his head and started to close the door, but a strange smell stopped him.

Smoke?

At first it was only a drifting curl of scent in the air, and if it had been summertime, he might have brushed it off as a nearby bonfire. But it was the middle of winter, with temps hovering in the low twenties, and nobody would be having a bonfire now. And it was close, the scent of burning wood becoming heavier, acrid.

No.

Heart dropping like a stone, he stared at the house. No, no, no. Not this house. Please, not this house.

"Fire!" he yelled to Shelby over his shoulder. "Call 911!"

He dropped his notebooks and raced back inside, through the living room, toward the kitchen, where there was a fire extinguisher under the sink. Flames danced across the back porch, casting orange shadows over the kitchen floor where his parents used to dance together after dinner. The dead ivy vines clinging to the side of the house—the ones he'd been meaning to pull down since summer—went up like kindling in a flash of heat and light, climbing toward the roof.

Holy shit. It shouldn't be spreading this fast. Already it was too big, and his little fire extinguisher wasn't going to do a damn thing, but he had to try.

He had to try.

If the fire reached the roof, the house was done.

He grabbed the extinguisher and ran to the sliding glass doors, but the wood frame was charring, warping, and he couldn't get the door open. He slammed the end of the extinguisher into the glass with every ounce of strength he possessed, and it shattered. He couldn't step out onto the porch because of the heat, so he aimed the extinguisher hose at the door. White powder doused the flames climbing up the frame, but it wasn't enough. The kitchen started filling with thick black smoke, and his eyes burned. The extinguisher sputtered and died in his hands.

"Fuck!" He threw it aside and tried to remember where there was another one stashed. Laundry room? Yeah, there was one next to the washer.

"Reece?"

Shelby's voice. Had she come inside? Jesus. What was she thinking?

His heart stuttered, and he gave up on finding a second fire extinguisher. He had to get her out of here, away from the heat and smoke. She needed to be safe.

Coughing hard, he spun and ran toward the front of the house, moving entirely by memory now because he couldn't see shit. Overhead, the roof groaned.

Oh shit.

He inhaled to yell for her to get outside, he was right behind her, but smoke rushed into his lungs. He gagged and choked, nearly doubling over from the pain of it.

A small hand gripped his arm and tugged. Shelby. She *was* in the house, damn her. And the fire continued chewing away at the roof. It was going to collapse at any moment, and they'd be trapped.

Straightening, he scooped her into his arms and ran. Through the living room, stumbling over the coffee table, and finally, out the still-open front door.

Cold air poured into his heated lungs, making him cough harder. He staggered and dropped Shelby into the snow in the front yard. His legs didn't want to hold him any longer, and he collapsed on his ass beside her.

Shelby coughed, and tears streamed down her soot-smeared cheeks. "Oh my God," she whispered. "Reece. Your house…"

He lay back in the snow and watched flames reach toward the sky, coloring the underbellies of the low-hanging clouds a dull yellow. Then, biting back a sob, he closed his eyes so he didn't have to watch the only place he'd ever considered home burn.

Sometime later, Reece realized he was no longer lying in the snow but in the back of an ambulance, breathing into an oxygen mask.

How did he get here?

Must have passed out, because he didn't even remember the firefighters and medics arriving. He yanked off the mask and sat up. Jude and the twins stood in a loose circle around the back end of the ambulance, their gazes all focused on the still-burning house. He saw his own anger and heartache reflected in each of their expressions, and a lump of sorrow clogged his throat.

He scanned for Shelby but didn't see her, and that sorrow took on the sour note of dread. He stood and—he was dizzy as fuck. His lungs and throat were raw.

Cam glanced over, noticed him swaying on his feet. "Hey, whoa." He climbed into the ambulance and made Reece sit down again. "Take it easy, bro. You inhaled a lot of smoke. They're just getting ready to transport you to the hospital."

"No hospital." Holy shit, was that his voice? It sounded like broken glass. He tried to clear his throat. "Shelby?"

"You're going to the hospital," Cam said. "And, yeah, she's fine. She's with Eva and Libby, and she's talking to the police, but she doesn't know what happened."

"Someone set fire to the back porch. Pretty sure accelerant was used. It got big fast." His gaze traveled past Cam to Vaughn and Jude. "Where's Greer?"

"We don't know," Jude said. "None of us can get ahold of him."

"This Houdini act of his has to stop," Vaughn said. "He should be here."

"We're not arguing that," Cam said. "And we plan to corner him as soon as he shows up again, but he's not our top concern right now. Reece—"

"I'm fine." Reece pushed to his feet and stumbled past Cam, out onto the sidewalk. When he saw what was left of the house—bricks blackened, roof completely caved in—his knees threatened to buckle.

Oh. Fuck.

Vaughn propped a shoulder under his arm to keep him upright. "Jude, help me get him back into the ambulance."

"I'm not going to the fucking hospital." He shook them both off and walked to the edge of the property. Stared up. Even the tree with the tire swing his dad had hung was now nothing more than a blackened skeleton of its former self.

"It's gone." He sensed his brothers joining him but didn't look away from the smoking ruins. "Just...gone."

"Reece," Jude said softly. "It was just a house."

"It wasn't—" He stopped short, sucked in a calming breath. "Everything we had of Mom and Dad was in that house. Every-fucking-thing. Wasn't it enough that we lost them?"

"I don't know about you guys," Vaughn muttered, "but I'm tired of being the butt of the universe's sick cosmic jokes."

"I don't think this is the universe's doing," Cam said, and his gaze tracked to Shelby.

A blast of heat flashed through Reece, and his fingers folded into fists at his sides. He stared, unblinking, at his brother. If Cam was suggesting Shelby was some kind of pyromaniac, he'd pummel him. Plain and simple. He may be the nerd of the family, the odd man out, but he'd grown up with four brothers who liked to fight and could brawl with the best of them. "Shelby didn't do this. She was with me the entire time."

Cam crossed his arms over his chest. "I love Shelby like a little sister, and I don't want to think she's capable of this any more than you do, but we have to look at the facts. This is the second fire she's been involved in—"

"Second fire I've been in, too," Reece interrupted. "I was with her the night The Bean Gallery burned down. You want to question me for arson, too?"

Cam opened his mouth, then closed it again. Shook his head. "I *knew* I saw your car that night," he grumbled. "Still, two fires in as many weeks? Actually, three if we count the fire at a neighbor's house a few years ago."

That…was news to him and chilled his anger from inferno to low boil. "What fire?"

"A five-alarm fire at the house across the street from Eva's," Cam said. "Nobody was hurt, but the house was a complete loss. Eva was out of town at the time and, ever since, she's been afraid to leave Shelby home alone. Told me once she thinks her sister is a walking jinx, a magnet for bad luck. So even if Shelby's not setting the fires—"

"She's not, and I will punch you if you say it again. Don't test me."

Cam held up his hands in surrender. "Just saying it's a big ass coincidence. Too big. So something's going on with her, and you need to find out what it is, because she won't tell Eva."

"And you think she'll tell me?"

"You're married to her."

"It's a business arrangement."

"That's bullshit." Cam took a step forward, got in his face. "What are you really doing with her, Reece? Huh? Because you say it's a business thing, but you're obviously fucking her every chance you get, *and* you brought her to Mom and Dad's—"

"I had to pick up something I left here. That's all."

"No. That's not all. I know you, bro. I know you wouldn't have brought her here if this thing between you is as superficial as you claim it is. But I'm telling you now, you need to end this."

Reece's molars hurt and he realized he was grinding his teeth. He worked his jaw to loosen it. "Back off, Cam. We'll end it when and if we're ready to."

"Uh, guys," Jude said and stepped between them, pressing a palm into each of their chests. "How about we take this somewhere…I don't know…less public?"

"Nah," Vaughn said, "let 'em duke it out. It'll be good for them both."

Cam ignored them, stepped around Jude, and jabbed a finger at Reece's shoulder. "I can't believe I'm saying this to *you*, of all people, but get your head out of your dick. Remember the night Shelby and Eva's mother attacked them? You ducked out and didn't see Shelby break down like I did. You didn't watch her cry herself into exhaustion or have to carry her to her bed. She's…fragile. So much more than she lets people know, and you're not gonna just hurt her when things go sour between you. You're gonna break her."

Not unless she breaks me first. But he kept his mouth shut, because saying that out loud would be like ripping open his chest and offering up his heart to his brothers for dissection.

"She won't bounce back from it," Cam continued. "And Eva will worry herself sick if Shelby goes into another nosedive. I can't let that happen."

"Are you more worried about Shelby or your wife?" Reece asked softly.

"Both. I knew going into this marriage they're a package deal, so don't make me choose between my wife and my brother. It's not a road I want to walk. Get your shit together, and do the right thing."

With that, he stalked away. Several beats of silence

passed.

"Wow," Jude said finally. "I've never seen Cam get that angry."

"I have," Vaughn said. "And he has a point about Shelby. There's something we need to talk about later, concerning the fire at The Bean Gallery."

Jesus. He really couldn't deal with anything more tonight. Not after the emotional sucker punch of watching his memories go up in flames, followed by that little sparring match with Cam. "Can we do it tomorrow?"

Vaughn gave one sharp nod, clapped Reece on the shoulder, and chased after his twin as fast as his walking cast allowed.

"What a fucking mess." Reece coughed again and dragged his hands over his head. Soot rained down around him, falling loose from the strands. He stared at his hands. He was covered head-to-toe.

Jude stuffed his hands in the pockets of his leather coat and rocked back and forth on his feet. "Uh, dude. I don't wanna make a bad situation worse, but..." He titled his head toward the road, where several media vans had gathered. "Looks like you're going to be headlining the news tomorrow morning."

Reece groaned. "Fuck me. That's the last thing I need."

"Hey, listen. I'm usually the last person to cast stones. People who live in glass houses and all that jazz." He looked at their childhood home and winced, rubbing the heel of his palm against his chest. A bone-deep sorrow showed on his face for an instant before he smoothed out his features and glanced back at Reece. "But this whole sitch is seriously fucked up. Whatever your end game is—and I know you have one, because you always do—just make sure Shelby's using the same playbook, all right?" And then Jude walked away, too, leaving Reece standing there on the sidewalk alone, watching the firefighters douse the last little bit of the blaze.

Chapter Eighteen

"All right. What the fuck is going on?"

Shelby flinched at the edge of anger in her sister's voice. "Nothing."

"This." Eva waved at the burning house. "*This* is not nothing. This is so not nothing. Do you have *any* idea how much this is going to hurt the guys?"

Shelby glanced away from her, but her gaze landed on the four Wilde brothers standing on the sidewalk, bathed in the orangey light of their childhoods burning to the ground in front of them. She focused on Reece. The rush of relief that he was up and moving around was a fleeting thing, replaced by a gut-aching sorrow for him. She didn't know about the rest of the Wildes, but he was hurting. That house had been his heart. His home.

And it was her fault it was gone. Her breath lodged in her throat. "This shouldn't have happened."

"Why did it happen?"

She looked into her sister's face. A war of anger and worry and sorrow raged over Eva's expression. Hurt, too, and when she glanced over at Libby, she saw the same battle. Both women were hurting because their husbands were. That was love, wasn't it? A form of pain?

She rubbed at the heavy ache in her own chest and for one sluggish heartbeat, she considered spilling the truth, laying all her mistakes out there for the world—and her sister—to scrutinize. Could she do it? Could she finally tell Eva that years ago, she'd dated a pyromaniac who had set the neighbors' house on fire, and her father had intervened in the worst way possible? Could she detail all the things she'd done for her father out of love, and then the things she'd done to him later out of fear? The things she'd done— and was still doing—to keep herself out of prison?

No. Eva would hate her. Likely turn her into the police— hell, maybe even arrest her herself. She'd lose her sister and the friendship she was building with Libby. Worst of all, she'd lose Reece. He'd never speak to her again, and she honestly didn't know if she could stand rejection from him.

"Shelby," Eva said softly when the silence dragged on too long, a note of concern in her tone. "What's going on?"

"You can tell us," Libby added. "We're not here to judge you. Whatever it is, we want to help."

But they would judge her. People had been judging her one way or another her entire life, to the point that she finally said *fuck it* and did what she wanted, wore what she wanted, and ignored the things whispered about her. So why would anyone stop judging her now?

Tears burned in her eyes, spilled down her cheeks. She let them fall, unable to muster the strength to hem them in.

"You can't help. I don't know what's happening."

Eva stared at her for a long time. "Goddammit. You're lying. You're fucking lying to me. I thought we were past this. I thought—no, forget it. You're the same as Mom. You're never going to change." Her voice cracked and she shook her head. Walked away without another word.

"Eva," Libby called after her, but received no response. She sighed and spun on Shelby, a spark of anger lighting her blue eyes behind her glasses. "You're hurting her—and the rest of us—by lying. But worse than that, you're hurting yourself." She started to walk away. Stopped. Whirled around in a burst of indignation. "Like it or not, you married into a big family, and families take care of each other. Once you get that through your head, you'll know where to find us."

Shelby watched her go to her husband and fold her arms around him in a move meant to comfort. Jude tucked her in against his chest, held her tight. In the moment before he buried his face in Libby's hair, his expression crumpled with grief. Nearby, the twins were leaning on the hood of a police cruiser, arms and legs crossed in identical positions as they watched the house burn. Their body language was all but screaming "keep the fuck away from us if you want to live." But when Eva approached, they scooted over and made room. She touched Vaughn's arm in a gesture of solidarity, then sat between them, circled her arm through Cam's, and rested her head on his shoulder. Cam kissed the top of her head.

Family.

They were family.

And Reece…

She scanned the crowd of firefighters until she found him

again. He hadn't moved, still stared up at the house, covered in soot. Alone. Did he realize he was only alone because he separated himself from his brothers?

She wanted to go to him, the urge to soothe him nearly overpowering, which was precisely why she walked in the opposite direction. Legally, yes, she had married into the family. Emotionally, she was a complete outsider. Even her sister was distancing herself from the hot mess that was Shelby's life. Not that she blamed Eva for it. If it was possible to distance herself from her own life, she would do it in a heartbeat.

But that was impossible and, family or not, the Wilde brothers and their wives couldn't help her. There was only one person who could, and she hated that fact.

She needed some privacy, so she climbed into the passenger seat of Reece's car, which had been backed out of the driveway to allow the fire trucks better access to the house. What she really wanted to do was jump behind the wheel and put the pedal to the metal until she left all of her problems in the rearview mirror. But adding grand theft auto to her list of misdeeds seemed like a very bad idea, so passenger seat it was. Besides, Reece still had the keys.

She locked the door and sat in the cold, silent darkness for several minutes. Working up the courage. Or, no, more like biting back the surge of intense disgust. The one person who could help her now was the last person on earth she wanted to talk to, and the idea of asking him for anything turned her stomach into an acid pit.

But what choice did she have?

She found her cell phone in the glove box where she'd left it during the cocktail party. Didn't give herself time to rethink it and dialed Jason Mallory's number. He answered almost immediately, and she didn't waste time with pleasantries. "There was another fire."

She heard some shuffling on his end, and a door shut quietly. "Where?"

"Reece's parents' house."

"I thought his parents are dead."

"They are. He owns the house now. Or at least, I think he owns it. Or maybe all five of the brothers do, I'm not sure." And she was rambling. It didn't matter who had owned it. It had been more precious to them than anything, and now it was gone. Because of her.

She sucked in a deep, slow breath to calm herself and got to the point. "I thought Steven was gone."

"I thought so, too," Jason said after a moment. "Honestly, I thought he was dead. Figured they had killed him."

Oh God. She'd thought so, too, and had carried the guilt of her ex-boyfriend's death as a stain on her soul ever since. Steven hadn't always been on the right side of the law, and her relationship with him had started out as another info-gathering job for Jason, but she'd stupidly fallen in love with him. Jason had been furious, had demanded she end the relationship or face consequences for reneging on their arrangement. So she had broken up with Steven. That night, the neighbor's house went up in flames, and Steven had been the number one suspect. Her father had vowed to kill Steven for trying to hurt her and when her father made vows like that, he kept them.

Sure enough, Steven hadn't been seen since.

And she'd been so angry, so afraid of what her father was capable of, she turned over every bit of damning information she knew about him.

"Except if Steven is dead," she said into the phone, "who else is setting these fires?"

Another beat of silence on Jason's end stretched into two, then three. She stiffened in her seat. "What aren't you telling me?"

Jason hesitated. "Shelby." More silence. "Is it possible you've been made?"

"You think they know I'm a snitch? Great." She laughed bitterly. What else could she do? "Just great. I wish I could say it's been awesome knowing you, but fuck that. I hate your guts."

But, no, that didn't make sense. If she'd been revealed as the snitch who put their leader and several other members behind bars, The Headhunters would kill her. Wouldn't matter what her last name was or whose blood she had in her veins, they'd roll up to her house and put a bullet in her without a second thought. They wouldn't set fires to the buildings she was inside of and hope for the best. That was a coward's crime, and The Headhunters were not cowards.

"Shelby, listen. You're doing great work. If you can just get the information we need about DMW Systems, we can protect you. We can see about relocation, maybe witness protection."

She lifted her head and stared out the windshield, but she was so numb with disbelief, she didn't see anything beyond the glass. "Are you serious?"

"Of course I am."

"Protect *me*? What about *Reece*? He could've been killed tonight. He lost his childhood home, and it's all my fault." She'd known it, but hearing herself say it out loud was a devastating blow, and it took all of the air out of her lungs. "I have to tell him the truth."

"You can't," Jason said with no remorse in his tone. "You know what will happen if you do. You need to play your part, and I'll make sure you stay safe. You're right. This *is* your fault. Your poor life choices led you here, so suck it up and deal."

"You're a bastard. How do you sleep at night?"

"Quite well. The law is on my side here, Shelby, not yours. Now," he said, a whole lot of *end-of-discussion* ringing in his tone, "you had that cocktail party tonight. What did you learn?"

She shut her eyes. She wasn't going to win this. She never did. And, although her stomach twisted, she was going to tell him. She always did. "If there's dirty money coming into DMW, Reece has no idea. If he did, he wouldn't be so worried about securing the partnership with Irving James. He'd just turn to the dirty money to keep his companies afloat."

"All right," Jason conceded, "you have a point. What else? Have you noticed anything suspicious going on?"

She decided not to tell him about Reece's blackmailer. He didn't need to know. "No. These people aren't going to spill their guts to me—"

"People always do. You know how to read people, how to weasel your way into their good graces. That's what makes you the best informant I've ever had. That was a compliment," he added when she didn't reply.

"I don't want it."

He laughed.

Shelby had to work to unlock her jaw. "I'm the woman their boss married on a whim. For all I know, they see me as a gold digger and nothing more."

"Then you need to get in good with that circle. Show them you're one of them."

"But I'm not."

"You seem to be doing a fine job of convincing Reece Wilde that you are."

But Reece isn't like them, either.

Except she wasn't about to say that. Jason didn't need to know how emotionally invested she had become, but she had to give him something, or he wasn't going to leave her alone. "There is this woman, Lena Schilling. She was in charge of marketing until Reece fired her a few weeks ago, and she's been extremely bitter about it ever since. She might be one to look at. And the head of development, Cliff McWilliam, was recently caught doing something that Reece didn't approve of. I don't know any more details than that, but could be something there, too."

"See?" Jason's smugness wafted like a noxious fume through the phone line. "I knew you'd already worked your magic. Don't bullshit me like that again, Shelby. I'll call back in three days. Have something more for me."

And the line disconnected.

She pressed her head into the headrest and let loose the sob working its way up her throat. No sense in holding it in, since she was alone. It sounded unnaturally loud, bouncing around inside the vehicle.

She'd really screwed the pooch this time. And she couldn't see an out that ended this nightmare happily.

She spotted Reece walking toward the Escalade and bit back another sob. She unlocked the door, closed her eyes, slowed her breathing. Feigned sleep because that seemed so much easier than talking to him right now. The driver's side door opened and his pants rasped across the leather seat as he climbed in. The key slid into the ignition, but he didn't turn the car on.

He sat there, unmoving, just breathing.

She'd gone nose blind to the smell of soot and smoke on her own clothes, but he brought the scent roaring back, stronger than ever. It clogged the air around them, somehow made the silence heavier.

"I know you're not sleeping," he said eventually.

"I'm trying to." Oh God, her voice sounded like broken glass had scoured her throat. She hoped he thought that was from the smoke inhalation and not from a suppressed sobbing fit.

He still didn't look at her. "Cam wants me to break off this thing between us. He's worried we'll hurt each other."

A knot tightened in her belly, and she sat up straighter, finally facing him. He stroked his hands over the leather of the steering wheel in an up-down pattern of three. The tic was subtle, not anything anyone would notice unless they lived with him, but he often did things in three-peat patterns when he was upset or nervous or just thinking hard about something. A little touch of OCD rising to the surface, and she'd thought it was adorable.

Until now.

Now, that kind of intimate knowledge had the knot in her belly twisting into cramps that were equal parts guilt and panic. She didn't want to fall for him and his silly tics. She had a horrible track record when it came to men and relationships and, although he was different from anyone she'd ever dated, he was also the first man she'd ever blatantly lied to. A relationship with Steven the pyromaniac had had a better shot at working than anything with Reece, and look how that had turned out.

A disaster. As usual.

Eva was right. She was a walking jinx.

"Do you want to end it?" she asked, throat so tight she was barely able to squeak the words out.

"No," he said without even a hint of hesitancy. "Do you?"

"I…" Her heart fluttered. Stupid thing. "I want to see this through. Help you catch your blackmailer."

He said nothing for a long moment, then gave a sharp nod as if she'd confirmed something for him, and cranked the ignition. "Yeah. Right. It's a business arrangement."

R eece said nothing more for the entire drive home. At first, she'd welcomed the silence because her heart was too heavy with guilt to carry on a normal conversation. Besides, what was there for them to talk about?

But when he parked in his building's garage and they got out of the car, the silence became grating. Strained. He was hurting and she was a bitch for not breaking the silence sooner.

She waited until their apartment door closed behind them. "Are you all right?"

"No."

Stupid question. Of course he wasn't okay. He'd just lost something invaluable and there was no way to ever get it back. "I'm sorry."

"You keep saying that like it's your fault." He turned,

met her gaze. "Is it?"

"I don't know," she admitted. "It could be. Indirectly."

"How?"

She wanted to tell him. God, did she want to tell him, but Jason's warning still rang in her ears.

You know what will happen if you do…

She shook her head.

Reece studied her for several long seconds, then pushed out a sigh. "I wish you'd tell me, but I know you won't. For whatever reason."

"I'm sorry."

"Stop." He held up a hand. "Shelby, just…stop apologizing. You're pissing me off."

"It's not because I don't trust you—"

"Doesn't matter," he muttered and strode into the kitchen. He snagged a bottle of Scotch on his way and splashed some into a tumbler without ice. "This is a business arrangement, nothing more."

Head thrown back, he downed it in one gulp and smacked the glass down on the counter, the sound like a gunshot. She flinched. He had every right to his anger. The night had gone straight to hell without the hand basket, and here she was being all evasive and shit. In his shoes, she'd be pissed off at her too.

Across the room on the coffee table, Reece's laptop signaled a new email. He snarled at it. Honest to God *snarled* like he wanted to rip its motherboard out with his teeth. Bottle still in hand, he stalked over.

Ignore it, she wanted to say. Whatever it was, it could wait. He'd already dealt with enough tonight. But she wasn't really his wife and it wasn't her place to tell him what to do, so she slid off her shoes, gathered them up in one hand, and started toward her bedroom with the intention of taking a long, hot shower. She needed to wash off the makeup covering her tattoos. Wash off the grime and lingering stink of the fire. The heat would go a long way toward relaxing the knots of tension in her neck and along her spine. Maybe she'd even stay in until the water ran cold—

Glass shattered behind her, and she yelped in surprise. She whirled, heart hammering in her throat, and spotted the scotch splattered across the living room wall, the bottle in pieces on the hardwood under it. She stared at the mess for a long time, uncomprehending.

He'd thrown the bottle.

Mr. Always-in-Control Reece Wilde had thrown. The. Bottle.

She turned her gaze to Reece as he sank to the floor beside the couch as if his legs no longer had the ability to hold him. He propped his elbows on his drawn-up knees, shoved his hands into his hair. He looked like a man who had reached his limit and then been forcibly shoved over.

She couldn't leave him sitting there, hurting and alone. She set her shoes down by her bedroom door, then tiptoed toward him, careful of the broken glass. "Reece." She knelt down, laid a hand on his forearm and squeezed until he lowered his hands and looked up. She expected to see anguish, but he'd pulled on an expressionless mask, devoid of all emotion.

"The blackmailer emailed me again. He knows about your past."

Her breath snagged in her throat and her chest constricted around her heart. "What?"

He flopped a hand in the general direction of his laptop, still on the coffee table. Oh, no. She didn't want to see whatever was in that email and stared hard at the glowing Apple logo on the back of the machine, willing the thing to blow up.

No such luck.

Swallowing down the sour taste of dread, she made herself reach for it and turn the screen around. Pictures of her in her wilder days, none of them painting a very flattering portrait of her character. But there was nothing about Steven or her association with The Headhunters or Jason Mallory. She released the breath she'd been holding. The blackmailer didn't know her entire past. Bits and pieces, maybe, but nothing that was going to get her killed.

The text accompanying the pictures was short and to the point.

Pay up or these photos would be emailed to Irving James.

Shit. Marrying Reece was supposed to protect him from the blackmailer, not make the situation worse. But of course the blackmailer had the ability to find dirt on her. Not like there was a shortage of it out there to find.

And the rest would come out. If he or she had found this much, the rest would follow.

She glanced up at Reece and opened her mouth to—what? Apologize? That would only piss him off more. "Um, are you going to pay?"

He stared back with exhausted eyes. "What choice do I have?"

"Reece—" The words snagged in her throat. "Let's get the annulment. First thing tomorrow. Then you can just stop paying the blackmailer and if the photos leak…well, make the end of our marriage my fault. Tell James I tricked you. I'm a gold digger and—"

"And you think that will give him the confidence to enter into a business deal with me?" he interrupted with a snort. "In James's mind, if I'm stupid enough to let a woman get the better of me, I'm not fit to do business with. Whatever I do, I'm fucked. I'm—" He shook his head and lumbered to his feet, moving like a sleepwalker. "I can't handle this. Not tonight. I'm going to bed."

Chapter Nineteen

Reece woke up the following morning feeling like he had the flu. He'd only had it once before, when he was twelve, but distinctly remembered the pounding head, the allover body aches, the blasts of brain-melting heat followed by bone-numbing cold.

Yeah, he was reliving it now.

For the first time in his adult life, he considered ignoring his alarm, rolling over, and going back to sleep for the rest of the day. Except he was scheduled to man the Wilde Security office for a few hours this morning, and he needed to see about scraping up a home security contract. He should also spend some time on Vaughn's search for Lark Warren since Vaughn had held up his end of the deal and looked into the fire at The Bean Gallery.

He couldn't sleep in. Too many people were counting on him.

Moving required more energy than he possessed, but he

still managed to push himself upright. He smacked his lips—his mouth tasted like ash and felt as dry. Had he remembered to brush his teeth before falling into bed last night? Or, for that matter, shower?

Nope. One look down at himself confirmed he was still in his soot-smeared clothes. Apparently, he'd mentally checked out of the real world at some point last night.

Or, wait. It hadn't been *at some point*. It had been after the newest blackmail threat hit his inbox. Right. He was fucked good and hard last night, and not in the fun way.

Reece shoved to his feet and plodded to the bathroom to clean up. Twenty minutes later, feeling almost human again, he walked out to the kitchen to brew a pot of coffee, half expecting to see Shelby had beaten him to it like she had the last few mornings. He'd been surprised by her early bird tendencies and when he commented on it, she'd said owning The Bean Gallery had revised her night-owlishness.

But this morning, the apartment was quiet. Her door was still shut, and he didn't even hear Poe squawking on the other side. Still asleep.

Probably for the better. He wasn't ready to face her again after the embarrassment of his actions last night.

He'd *thrown* the scotch. The memory of it heated up the back of his neck. He'd had a fucking temper tantrum. What was he, thirteen? Jesus.

As his coffee brewed, he studied the living room, searched for the stain on the wall, the broken glass, and found nothing. Guilt and shame hit him square in the gut in a one-two punch. Shelby had cleaned it up.

Yeah, he definitely wasn't ready to face her yet. As soon as the coffee finished, he poured some into a travel mug, then left the rest on to warm until she woke up. He thought about leaving a note, decided against it, got to the door, and changed his mind. Back in the kitchen, he found a pen and paper…and stalled out.

What should he write?

Something short. Simple. Maybe…*I'm sorry*? No, that had a ring of finality to it, like the start of a Dear John letter. How about, *Your past doesn't matter because I'm pretty sure I'm falling in love with you*? Yeah, that wouldn't send her running like her ass was on fire.

He finally settled on: *Went to the WS office. Left the coffee on warm for you. Be home later.*

Good enough.

Since it was a Saturday, the drive to the office was peaceful. He didn't have to battle traffic, and he was grateful for it. He made it in twenty minutes instead of the usual forty and opened the office early even though he doubted he'd have a stampede of clients in that extra half hour. Business had been abysmally slow lately.

Maybe he should look into advertising. Of course, he'd need money for advertisements, and Wilde Security was already operating on a shoestring budget as it was.

He could sell the Escalade and drive his Scion FR-S full time. He actually preferred the scrappy, budget-friendly sports car, but the Escalade made for a better appearance, which was why he drove it more often. All for show. And if he started selling things off now, people would take notice, eyebrows would raise, and Irving James might get cold feet.

Always came back to that, didn't it? Irving Fucking James.

Reece was starting to hate the man. Did he really want

to align his company with the James name? No. But did he have a choice? Nope. James owned half the damn world, and it wasn't like other investors were exactly beating down the doors at DMW Systems right now since the economy was still tanked and simulations were such a niche product.

Maybe it was time to talk to Cliff about the artificial intelligence he'd been tinkering with on company time. Reece hadn't been happy about the side project at first, but the more he thought about it, the more he wondered if Cliff might be on to something.

Man, he missed the good old days when he would sit around late into the night with Dylan and Cliff, guzzling Red Bull and talking technology. How had they all gotten so far away from their computer geek roots? Well, actually, Cliff hadn't. The guy was still down in DMW's basement, playing with his toys, tinkering with artificial intelligence.

Reece wanted that part of his life back. So much. But he wasn't going to get it, so he needed to stop throwing himself a pity party and get to work.

On his way back to his office, he started another pot of coffee. He had a feeling he was going to need it. Then he booted up his computer and made a few follow-up calls, checking on the home security systems he'd installed for clients and nudging a few people who had previously voiced an interest in the system. He managed to secure two installation jobs, both neighbors of a previous client in Virginia Beach. He'd have to leave town for a long weekend to do the work, but it made him feel better about Wilde Security's financial situation.

After a quick trip to the coffee maker for a refill, he dove into Vaughn's problem. A deal was a deal. By the time the twins showed up that afternoon, both looking as ragged as he felt, he'd uncovered two more of Lark Warren's previous identities and thought he had a lead on the very first alias she'd ever used—Violet Smith. She'd gone through her first several identities fast, as if afraid to stay one person for too long. In fact, it looked like she'd been Lark Warren the longest at nearly two years.

She was definitely running. But from what?

And wasn't it interesting that she always chose nature-themed names? Made him suspect her real name was something similar, except nobody matching her description with a nature-themed name had been reported missing five years ago, which was when "Violet Smith" miraculously rose from the dead and got a job waitressing at a topless bar in New York City. And he was positive Violet had been her first alias, because he couldn't trace her beyond that.

As far as her financials, he came up empty. She never used bank accounts, even when she was settled into her life as Lark Warren. If she was smart—and he thought she was—she probably kept her money close at hand for an easy getaway. She didn't have any loans or credit cards, and her twelve-year-old car had been sold to a chop shop before she left town.

Brick wall.

Reece was so wrapped up in the puzzle of Lark Warren, he didn't hear Vaughn enter his office until his brother sat down in the creaky chair next to his desk.

"Lark?" Vaughn asked, picking up the printouts of the new identities he'd uncovered.

"Yeah." He pushed back from his desk and rolled his head around, cracking his neck. He'd been hunched over the computer for too long. "Vaughn, man, she doesn't want to be found. Maybe it's time to drop it."

"No." Vaughn folded the printouts and slid them into his pocket.

"All right. It's your call, but I really think you should let her go." When he only received a dark scowl in reply, he shook his head and changed topics. "You wanted to talk to me about the fire at The Bean Gallery?"

Vaughn settled back in his seat and folded his hands over his abs. "I looked into it like you wanted. I assume you've known all along that Shelby owned the place?"

"Yeah, I knew."

"Blows my fucking mind, but figured as much. It went down about like the arson investigator said. Molotov cocktail through the front window. There might have been a little something extra in the mix to give it some oomph, because the place barbecued fast. But of course you already know that because you were there, you sneaky bastard. Here's the weird thing. Security cameras monitored the store, and the fire never reached the back office so the computers were salvageable. Everything was there, employee schedules, financial information—and surprisingly Shelby was making a solid profit—but the security footage was missing."

"But Shelby and I were the only two people there before the fire and neither of us touched the computer." A ripple chased down Reece's spine. Excitement, dread. Probably both. His blackmailer had sent him the security footage with the first email. Was it possible Shelby's fires and his blackmail problem were connected?

"Except," Vaughn continued, "the footage didn't disappear until *after* the computer was collected into evidence.

The investigators hadn't even looked at it yet and were all shocked that it was gone."

"Who would have access besides law enforcement?"

"Nobody."

Reece sat back in his chair and rubbed at the unshaved stubble on his chin. Why would a cop blackmail him? It didn't make sense. None of it made sense and he was so fucking tired of having more questions than answers.

"There's something else," Vaughn said.

Reece groaned. "There always is."

"Cam told you about the fire at the house across the street from Eva's a few years back? I looked into that too. Eva was out of town, and Shelby had just moved in after breaking up with a boyfriend. The guy, Steven Moore, was the number one suspect in that fire. The going theory is he wanted to get back at Shelby for ending things, but flambéed the wrong house. He disappeared shortly afterward and hasn't been seen since."

"So he could be behind the Molotov cocktail at The Bean Gallery. And…" His parents' house, the last link he'd had to them, was gone. His stomach lurched at the reminder and he cleared his throat. "And last night."

Vaughn inclined his head. "It's a possibility, if Moore's back in town."

"We need to find him."

Vaughn said nothing for a beat. "I'm not dropping my search for Lark."

"I didn't say you have to. But, man, I seriously need your help right now. If there's a firebug gunning for Shelby, we need to stop him. She's escaped two fires already. Odds are not on her side that she'll escape another."

Another stretch of silence. Finally, Vaughn nodded and shoved out of his chair. "I'll see what I can do."

"Thank you."

Vaughn paused at the door and glanced back. "Have you heard from Greer?"

"Nothing. You?"

"Nope." He scratched at his chin. "I know it's not the first time he's pulled a Houdini on us, but…this time feels different. Should we be worried?"

It did feel different. And, yes, his gut told him something was wrong. "I'll go over to his place when I leave here, look around."

Vaughn grunted. "I'm going to kick his ass when he turns up."

"I'd pay to see that. Especially given your recent fashion accessory."

Vaughn scowled down at his walking cast. "Fucking thing comes off in a week, and then I'm burning it."

Since the twins had the office covered, Reece decided to pack it up and go get some work done at DMW Systems. But, first, a trip to Greer's place.

Greer lived on the other side of a postage-stamp-sized park out behind the Wilde Security office. It was usually faster to walk over, but the wind had bite today and Reece opted to drive around the block. He pulled into the complex's parking lot and scanned for Greer's ten-year-old Jeep Cherokee, but didn't see it.

Inside, the apartment building was light-years away

from his in terms of style. Where his looked like a swanky hotel, Greer's building opened into a drab corridor with mailboxes on one wall, elevators on another, and stairs in the back. There was also an empty desk, presumably for a security guard, but in all the years Greer had lived in the building, Reece had never seen anyone manning that desk.

Greer lived on the second floor, so Reece didn't bother waiting for the elevator, which was notoriously slow, and pushed through into the stairwell. He took the steps two at a time and strode to apartment 211, a man on a mission.

His knock received no reply. He waited a moment. Pounded on the door again, harder. Still nothing. Or at least nothing from Greer's silent apartment. The door across the hall opened, though, and a pretty woman with short dark hair peeked out.

"Sorry to disturb you," he said gently, not wanting to scare her. "I'm looking for my brother. He lives here. Have you seen him?"

"No," she said after the briefest of hesitations. "I picked up a package that was left by his door after it had sat there for a week. I thought you were him returning home, was going to give it to you."

"So he hasn't been around for a while?"

"I'm not sure. I mean, I usually pass him on the stairs or see him at the mailboxes, but it's been almost two weeks since the last time I saw him."

"I'd better take a look around his place." Reece dug in his coat pocket, found his keys, and searched for the extra Greer had given him. The door opened easily, and he flipped on the light. Nothing moved. The apartment smelled abandoned even though Greer's few possessions were exactly where they should be. There was food in the cupboards and some leftover Chinese still in the fridge, but he'd bet it was past its best-by date since the milk was also outdated by a few days. The sink was empty, the dishwasher full, but it looked like the dishes inside were clean, so it had been run. There was a blanket wadded up on one end of the couch and a pillow at the other, as if Greer had taken a nap there before he pulled his vanishing act. The bed in the bedroom was made with military precision, and his suitcase from Vegas sat next to the dresser, still packed. A quick scan through the closet didn't tell Reece much. Greer didn't have a lot of clothes, but it was impossible to tell if anything was missing when he had no idea how much had been there to start. Only things he didn't find were Greer's cell phone and wallet.

He returned to the living room and stood there for a second, at a complete loss. The whole place looked as if Greer would return at any moment. And maybe he would. He had before.

A sound from the door caught his attention and he turned to find Greer's neighbor standing there. "I brought the package over." She nodded to the box on the floor just inside the door that appeared to be from an online retailer.

Yet another clue that wherever Greer had gone, he had expected to be back in time to receive whatever he'd ordered online. "Thanks."

"No problem." She was wearing a huge sweater over leggings and the material swallowed her thin frame as she folded her arms over her chest. "Is he okay?"

"I hope so." He grabbed his wallet and picked out a business card for her. "If you see him, I'd appreciate a call. My name is Reece."

"Natalie." She accepted the card, backed out into the hall, and waited for him to shut and lock the door. "I'll keep an eye out for him."

"Thanks, Natalie. And if you happen to talk to him, tell him his brothers are worried."

Back in the Escalade, he called the office to tell the twins—and Jude, who must have arrived shortly after he left—what he'd found at Greer's place. Cam suggested they file a missing person's report, while Jude said they should wait. After all, Greer was a thirty-five-year-old man and could drop off the face of the earth if he wanted to—and he'd done so before. Multiple times. He'd eventually turn up again, just like the last few times he'd disappeared, and act like he hadn't been gone. Vaughn agreed with Jude, and it was decided they'd give him a week—the same amount of time he'd been gone before—to show up. If he didn't, then they'd reevaluate the situation.

Goddamn Greer. None of them needed this stress right now. And from *him* of all people? What the fuck was going on?

Reece barely made it into DMW's office before he was cornered by Alicia. "What happened to you last night?"

"I wasn't feeling well—"

"You were caught in a fire?" She all but shrieked it. "It's all over the news! Are you okay?"

"Uh, yeah. I'm fine."

"And Shelby?"

"She's fine. We're both…fine." And let's see how many more times he could use the word "fine" in a sentence. He edged past Alicia and hit the button to call the elevator. "Is Cliff here?"

Her brow wrinkled. "I don't think so. He doesn't usually come in on Saturdays. Why?"

He'd have to call him later, then. The elevator arrived and he stepped inside, pushing the button for the top floor. "Nothing. Where's Dylan?"

"In your office."

Reece shot out an arm to catch the door before it closed. "Why?"

She bit her lip. "Irving James is here."

"On a Saturday? Why didn't you call me?"

"I was about to. He just got here maybe five, ten minutes ago."

"Fuck," he muttered and let the doors slide shut. He hardly recognized the man he saw in the reflection on the polished steel doors. He looked like he'd been dragged through hell. He rubbed his hands over his unshaven face and through his hair, trying to tame it.

Jesus, he wasn't even wearing a tie. How could he have forgotten a tie?

He found Dylan and James seated in the leather chairs in his office, deep in discussion. Dylan did a double take when he spotted him.

"Reece! I wasn't expecting you in today. You should be home."

"I'm fine." And there was that word again. He needed to come up with a better adjective. He plastered on a smile and strode toward James, hand outstretched. "I'm sorry I had to leave the party early last night. I wasn't feeling well."

He must have looked the part of an ill man, because James used a small bottle of sanitizer after the handshake. "I heard you were also caught in a fire last night?"

He nodded and kept his face calm and pleasant, even as his insides jumped around in complete panic. "At my parents' house."

A frown pulled James's brows into a crease over his eyes. "And didn't your wife's coffee shop burn down recently? I seem to remember reading something about it."

"It did," he admitted, wincing internally. "But I can assure you, I've not let my recent troubles affect DMW Systems."

"I was just assuring Mr. James as much," Dylan said smoothly. "We're still operating full steam ahead, and our profits have never been better."

James's lips twisted in distaste. "And as I was telling Mr. Porter, I'd like to have my accountants look through your books before we finalize anything."

"Absolutely," Reece said, a spark of hope flaring deep in his chest. He'd been expecting this request, so maybe everything hadn't been fubar'd yet. "I'll make it happen."

"Good." James relaxed and even smiled. "Now that business is out of the way, I'm attending a charity gala for the Washington National Opera tomorrow night. I've heard you're both WNO patrons. Are you feeling well enough to attend another event? I'd like to introduce you to some of my business partners. The invitation extends to your wives as well."

Shelby at the opera. That was exactly the situation he'd hoped to avoid putting her in. Damn. But what other choice did he have?

He again forced a smile. "We accept. Gladly."

Chapter Twenty

Shelby woke to an empty apartment, shocked that Reece was already gone for the day. Was the man a machine? Because he'd taken a category five emotional wallop last night, and no average human withstood that kind of heartache and got up for work the following day. Just wasn't natural. It hadn't even been her house and she was sick about its loss, maybe even more so than when she'd lost The Bean Gallery.

Which reminded her. She was going to be late for her meeting with the arson investigators if she didn't get moving.

The meeting went about as well as she expected, given the fire last night. They told her the security footage had gone missing before anyone had the chance to view it. She told them about Steven and her suspicions that he might have come back to terrorize her, but left off the part about thinking he was dead because The Headhunters had killed him.

By the time the meeting was over, she was exhausted and starving. She'd turned off her phone out of courtesy, but while waiting for the elevator, she turned it back on. It vibrated with an incoming text message from Reece. They'd been invited by Irving James to an opera gala tomorrow night.

Wow. That sounded fun.

Not.

She sent him a quick text back, then called Libby to apologize for last night and see if she wanted to meet for a late lunch. She did, and they ended the day with a shopping trip. Turned out, some quality girl-time was exactly what Shelby had needed to brighten her spirits.

She got back to the apartment around eight that night, fully expecting to see Reece— nope. Still not home.

Was he avoiding her?

That didn't seem like him. Maybe he was just dealing with…things. Libby had mentioned the guys were all worried about Greer. Maybe they were out looking for him. And no doubt Reece had a ton of paperwork to fill out about his parents' house. She'd had reams of it after the fire at The Bean Gallery.

God, she missed that place. Up until The Bean Gallery, she'd always hated her jobs. But, thing was, running the coffee shop had never felt like a job to her. She'd loved her workers and the customers. She'd loved ordering inventory and the ever-changing puzzle of scheduling. She'd loved the badly painted "masterpieces" on each table. Loved jumping behind the counter and whipping up a latte when it got too busy for the baristas to handle it on their own.

Maybe when the arson investigation ended and her

insurance paid out, she'd buy a new place. *If* the arson investigation ever ended. They didn't seem to be getting very far with it.

With the apartment so silent, she needed a distraction from her thoughts, so she found a Japanese monster movie on Netflix and huddled down on the couch to watch it. Sam the Cat snuggled up next to her, apparently having decided to completely ignore her bird's existence. A step in the right direction, she supposed. At least Sam didn't view Poe as lunch anymore.

She'd taken Poe out of his cage when she got home, and he now sat on his perch by the window, happily imitating the sound effects on the movie—one of his favorite pastimes. And with the background noise of her bird's mimicry and the cat's purring, she didn't stand a chance of staying awake and drifted off long before the movie ended.

She wasn't sure what woke her, but Shelby opened her eyes sometime later to find someone had covered her with a blanket, and the cat was now curled up on her stomach.

Coffee. That was the scent that had awakened her. Freshly brewed coffee.

She propped herself up on her elbows and peeked over the back of the couch. Reece was pouring himself a mug from the pot, but his attention was focused on a notebook laid out on the counter, and every once in a while he'd mutter to himself and scribble something down. He was shirtless, in pajama pants and his glasses, and his hair stuck up from multiple passes of his hands. Definitely had a little bit of a mad scientist look going for him right now.

He walked away with his notebook in hand, completely forgetting his coffee on the counter.

Smiling, she picked up the cat, set him aside, and went into the kitchen to fix herself a coffee because it smelled too damn good to ignore. She gathered Reece's mug and followed him to his office. "You forgot something."

He glanced up, wide-eyed. "Shit. Did I wake you? I was trying to be quiet."

"No, I don't think it was you. Just a general sense I wasn't alone anymore. And the smell of coffee." She set his mug on his desk before taking a sip from her own. "It's my catnip."

He nodded and went back to whatever it was he was doing on the computer. "I hope you don't mind I put Poe back in his cage. I was a little worried Sam might wake up feeling peckish."

"Actually, they seem to be getting along. Or at least they're tolerating each other. Did you find Greer?"

He looked up again, startled. "How'd you know we're looking for him?"

"I had lunch with Libby. She mentioned it."

"He'll turn up. He always does." Reece's mouth kicked up in the corner. "I noticed we have some new paintings. Take it you also went shopping with Libby?"

She shrugged. "This place needs some color. Hence the pillows. And now the paintings. I just have to figure out where to hang them."

Another quick flash of a smile. "I'd like one in here if you don't mind."

Pleasure bloomed in her chest. "Really?"

"Yes, really. I agree this place needs some color." He pushed out a sigh, shook his head. "I didn't even realize I was living in a high-end institution instead of a home until you bought those crazy pillows."

"Wow. I feel like I just won some kind of war. What's all this?" She eased a hip down on the edge of his desk and studied his spread of notebooks. She picked one up. "Hey, wait. Aren't these the notebooks you took from your parents' house?"

Reece felt like a kid caught with his hand in the candy jar. "It's nothing." He started to close his laptop, but stopped short when she flipped through the notebook she was holding.

"Reece! These drawings are awesome. Did you do these?"

Heat crawled across the back of his neck. "Just sketches."

"They're damn good for sketches." She sent him a sideways glance. "What exactly are you working on so late? I have a sneaky suspicion it's not anything for DMW or Wilde Security."

"It's…nothing." He didn't know why he was so embarrassed to have been caught, but there it was. He snatched the notebook from her. "A hobby."

"You actually have *time* for a hobby?"

"Not as much as I'd like."

She craned her neck to better see the screen of the half closed laptop. "What is it? C'mon, we're full of secrets already. What's one more?"

He sighed. If anyone deserved a peek into this part of his life, it was her. After all, she was the reason he'd started pursuing this particular "hobby" again. Being with her, he realized he'd let go of too much of himself in the past few years, and he wanted to get back to a version of the person he used to be. These notebooks, retrieving them from his old bedroom, had been his first step in that journey.

Sucking in a breath, he pushed the computer open and waited for her laughter, her derisive comments.

Instead, she let out an ear-piercing squeal of delight. "It's a video game! You're designing a video game? Cool." She plopped down beside him and used the wireless mouse to click through the mock-up graphics he'd been fiddling with. "This is…really good. I mean it. I've played many a video game in my time, and these graphics are amazing. What's it about?"

A little thrill sung through his chest. Was that…excitement? It had been a long time since anything got him excited—well, beyond his recent sexcapades with Shelby. They were damn exciting and, admittedly, the only time he'd felt alive since his parents died.

But right now, his inner computer geek was thrilled at her compliments and chomping at the bit to show off. He took control of the mouse and clicked through some of the landscapes he'd mapped out. "It's a first-person shooter and starts as a war game. Gamers play as a group of soldiers tasked with a covert operation in a war-torn country, but as they move through the levels, it becomes more and more a survival horror story."

She gazed up from the screen and into his eyes. "So basically like real war."

He lifted a shoulder in a shrug. "But with monsters and zombies. The amount of horror the players face depends entirely on their choices throughout the game and, if they aren't careful, they eventually become the monsters themselves."

"I've never seen you this…animated. You love this stuff."

She poked a finger at his shoulder and grinned. "Don't lie. I can see through you, Hershey, and right now your nerd is showing. It's hot."

He huffed out a laugh. "I wasn't going to lie. This…" He waved a hand at the screen. "In high school, *this* is what I thought I'd be doing by now. Designing video games for a living. It's challenging and, hell, it's fun. But in college I realized video games were not going to provide financial stability for my brothers, so I tweaked the war game I was developing, and it became a simulation. When I finished school and entered the intelligence branch of the army, one of my superiors caught wind of my simulation program and it took off from there."

"And you created DMW Systems and got that financial stability."

"For nearly four years. But my government contracts aren't being renewed because of budget cuts and I need this contract with Irving James…" He closed his eyes and—shit, he was going to tell her, wasn't he? The secret he'd been holding deep inside, the one eating its way through his gut. "I hate it, Shelby." He opened his eyes, met hers. Expected to see surprise, but all he got was sympathetic understanding, and that spurred him on. "I hate DMW. I'm ashamed I ever associated my parents' initials with it."

"Oh," she whispered and touched the back of his hand. "David and Meredith Wilde. DMW. I just got that. But why are you ashamed of it?"

"It's falling apart around me, and I can't even figure out why."

She opened her mouth as if to say something, but closed it again after a moment and squeezed his hand. "You're thinking the blackmail is about more than money, like someone is sabotaging you. Lena, maybe?"

"It's not Lena. She's not smart enough." But the thought of sabotage had occurred to him before now. More than once, in fact. Except he didn't have any enemies that he knew of, so who hated him enough to want his company to fail? That was the part he couldn't wrap his mind around. He shook his head, defeat weighing down his shoulders. "It doesn't matter. Like I said last night, I'm fucked. I can't keep paying the blackmailer or I'll go bankrupt, but as soon as I stop, Irving James will find out all about you…and it'll be over. Might as well pack up my office and start handing out pink slips now."

She winced. "I'm so sorry. I thought marrying you would help solve the problem, not make it worse. I hate that my past is coming back to bite you."

He looked at her, saw a glimmer of tears in her eyes. Aw, fuck. He was wallowing, and he hated wallowers. Worse, he was being insensitive. He turned in his seat to fully face her and cupped his hand around the back of her neck, drawing her in closer. "Your past should have no bearing on this situation. Jesus, I'm scrambling for a contract from a man I don't like, a man whose politics and world views I don't even agree with. I've spent too much time trying to please him, forcing *you* to do the same, and it's starting to piss me off. If anyone should be apologizing here, it's me."

Her lips curved upward into a tempting bow, and he had to kiss her. He meant it to be quick, but the moment he tasted her, he was lost. How did she do this to him? Every time they touched, his higher thought shut down, and he became nothing but a bundle of raw need and desperate want. And right now, more than anything, he needed to feel her bare skin under his hand. He pushed up her nightshirt and curved his fingers around her hips, pulling her off the desk and settling her between his legs. Shelby breathed out a soft sigh and tangled her hands into his hair as he broke their kiss and dragged his lips down the slender column of her neck.

He nipped at her collarbone through her shirt, and she laughed. "Oh, please tell me you have a condom handy."

"Why?" He scraped his teeth over her peaked nipple. "You think you're getting lucky tonight, Mrs. Wilde?"

"No, Mr. Wilde." She walked her fingers down his chest until she found his cock peeking out from the top of his pajama pants. She caught a bead of moisture on her thumb and rubbed it in circles over his tip. "I *know* I am."

Every muscle in his body tightened in response. Thank Christ he'd picked up more condoms at the store on his way home, and there they were, still sitting in the grocery bag, right on his desk. He'd intended to put them away in his bedroom, but got wrapped up in his computer game and forgot. He dove his hand into the bag, pulled open the box, and yanked out a line of foil packets. One after another, they kept spilling from the shopping box like a clown's endless handkerchief.

Shelby grinned and ripped the last condom from the line. "Now you're talking, Hershey. But first, I think you should know a secret about me." She leaned in and traced the shell of his ear with her tongue. "Before I can really enjoy my candy, I need to lick it. All. Over."

He shuddered and freed his cock, squeezing it in one hand as her hot little mouth left trails of fire down his bare chest. He growled something that might have been her name. Or at least that's what he'd intended it to be, but it came out unintelligible.

"Hmm?" She paused and drew a circle around his navel with her tongue before smiling up with lust-brightened eyes. "I wonder…" She gripped him at his base, slid her hand up his shaft and back down. "How many licks does it take…?"

She sucked him all the way into the back of her throat, released him slowly, and then did it again, all the while doing wicked things with her tongue. His stomach muscles clenched with each lift of his hips to meet her mouth, and his every sense zeroed in on the woman doing her damnedest to suck the skin off his cock. He wound his fingers into her hair and tugged, probably harder than he should have, but she gave an approving hum that shot lightning up his shaft and nailed him in the balls. His body short-circuited. He groaned, trembled as his orgasm exploded from him, and she drank down every drop before releasing her mouth's hold.

She laughed softly and dragged her nails down his still trembling abs. "I love watching you come. All of your muscles tighten up, and it's gorgeous. My own personal eye candy." She gave the tip of his cock a little nibble, just a light scrape of her teeth that had him instantly going hard again. She stood, smiling like the cat that ate the canary.

"We're not done yet." He grabbed her hips and dragged her forward until she straddled his legs, then plucked the condom from her hand. "It's my turn to watch you."

He ripped open the wrapper and rolled the condom on, then found her with his fingers. And, yeah, she was soaking wet, so turned on and ready for him. But that wasn't enough. She was going to tremble and beg first. He slid two fingers into her slit, enjoyed the view as she bowed backward and worked her hips.

"There you go. Ride my fingers and I'll get you off." He pressed his thumb to her clit, drew circles around it until her rhythm grew choppy, her body shuddering each time she came down. And when she lifted herself again, he removed his fingers, stood up his cock and thrust his hips upward.

She screamed, climaxing as he filled her.

He loved watching her come, too, loved the way her body squeezed his as each wave of pleasure thundered over her.

Widening his legs to give himself more leverage, he pumped into her, again and again, deeper and deeper, until the spasms of her second orgasm finally milked another release from him. He came in hard, hot jets that left him dizzy.

Still shuddering, Shelby collapsed forward and rested her forehead against his. "Oomph."

Reece snorted a laugh—he was too exhausted to restrain it—and tugged on her hair. "Oomph? That's not exactly glowing praise."

"If you want praise, I'll write you a ballad as soon as I can feel my limbs again. My God, that first orgasm…" She lifted her head and imitated an explosion with her hands. "Wow. I mean. Wow."

Buried to the balls inside her, he felt the delicate shivers still racing through her body. He smiled and pushed her damp hair back from her face. "For me too."

"Yeah?" Color spiraled across her cheeks and she ducked her head. "We, uh, are good together. I-I mean, with sex. We're good together in bed."

Was that…a hint of shyness? From Shelby? No way.

Reece caught her chin between his fingers and lifted it until her gaze met his. "We're good together in a lot of ways,

Shelby. Come to bed with me."

The uncertainty in her eyes shifted to sheer panic. He saw it happen and tried to catch her, but she moved too fast, leaping away from him. He missed the intimate connection immediately and pushed out of the chair, taking a second to dispose of the condom in the trash bin under his desk and tuck himself back into his pants. This wasn't a conversation he wanted to have with his well-sated cock flapping in the wind.

Shelby smoothed a hand down the front of her nightshirt and backed several steps toward the door. "I should probably go. We have that opera thing tomorrow and—I need to go to bed. Alone."

A muscle ticked in his cheek just below his eye and he realized he'd clenched his teeth hard enough that his molars hurt. He did his best to unlock his jaw. "Shel—"

"No." She held up a finger, cutting him off. More than panic now, she radiated regret and her voice shook. "Tonight changes nothing."

The hell it didn't, but he let her go and didn't chase her. Hands on his hips, he stared at the empty doorway.

What the fuck was that all about?

Chapter Twenty-One

Reece left another note by the still-warm coffee. He'd gone to DMW's office, would be back in time to get ready for the gala.

Shelby crumpled the note. It had been sweet of him to leave it, but it wasn't enough. She'd wanted to talk to him, but she should have figured he'd sneak off to work first thing this morning. Retreating into work was what he did when things got too heavy. Just like her modus operandi was to run away.

She'd hurt him last night. The look on his face when she ran away from his suggestion of sharing a bed…yeah, she felt kind of like she'd kicked a puppy. She needed to apologize, try to explain things to him.

Except how could she do that without explaining everything? She'd need to tell him she never owed The Headhunters money and had used it as an excuse to get him to marry her. The marriage hadn't been her original plan, but when she found out about the blackmail, she really thought she was helping him out while still furthering her own goals.

Dammit.

Maybe it was time to lay it all out, Jason and his warnings be damned. She'd risk prison time if it meant she never had to see that hurt look on Reece's face again. But there lay the catch-22, because telling him the truth would most definitely hurt him.

She couldn't see a pain-free way out of this situation.

Shelby wasn't usually one to brood, but she couldn't seem to shake the horrible mood as she puttered about the apartment. She tried calling Libby, but she and Jude already had plans. And Shelby couldn't bring herself to talk to Eva yet, so she was left to her own devices for the day.

When the doorbell rang in the late afternoon, she jumped. She hadn't even known the apartment had a doorbell, and now someone was ringing it? She padded over to the front door in her socks, careful not to make any noise in case she wanted to pretend she wasn't here, and used the peep hole.

Oh, shit. Her stomach flipped. No way this was good.

She unlocked and opened the door, but only a few inches. "Mom. What are you doing here? Better question, how did you know where I was?"

Katrina Bremer wrung her hands. "I-I wanted to see you. Eva told me you moved here."

Yeah, fat chance. Eva wouldn't tell her the sky was blue if she asked.

Shelby studied her mother and a fist squeezed hard around her heart. Katrina was still going with the schoolmarm look, but underneath the prim and proper church-going facade was a thick layer of desperation. She was all pale and gaunt, and heavy bags under her bloodshot blue eyes spoke of many sleepless nights.

Katrina was back on the drugs.

Shelby didn't know why the realization hurt so much. After all these years, why did she always believe Katrina would stay clean? "Mom, you need to go."

Katrina's lower lip trembled. "I have nowhere to go. Eva won't take me in—"

"What about your new man?"

More with the lower lip. "He said he didn't need me anymore and left me."

Of course he did. Men always left Katrina. It was in her DNA, which made Shelby wonder if it was a genetic predisposition she shared with her mother. Reece was going to leave, and then she'd be in the same boat as her mother. No job, no home.

Shit. She wished she was more like Eva, but she just couldn't do it. She couldn't turn her mother away. Maybe because she saw too much of herself in Katrina.

She backed up a step. "You can stay here until Reece gets home in a few hours. Then…we'll see. I can't guarantee he'll let you stay longer."

Katrina launched through the door and threw her skinny arms around Shelby in a fierce hug. "I'm so proud of you."

Oh God. How many times growing up had she wanted to hear those words from her mother? Or from anyone? Shelby closed her eyes and savored the moment until Katrina tacked on, "Bagging a rich man like you have? You've done your mama proud."

Disgust rolled through Shelby and she pulled out of her mother's arms. "He's not a trophy."

"Of course he is. I was never able to find a sugar daddy, and Eva sure as hell didn't, marrying a cop. Ugh, I swear, I don't know what's wrong with that girl. But I should have known you'd wrangle one. You have my looks and your daddy's smarts."

Right. Her father was so smart, he landed himself in prison for twenty-five to life.

Katrina bumped her hip into Shelby's. "Now you just have to hang on to him. Oh!" Distracted, she wandered into the living room and did a little spin. "This place. My little princess found her palace!"

This was such a bad idea.

Shelby hugged herself to keep from shattering into a thousand heartbroken pieces. "Since when have I been your princess?"

"Since always."

"You attacked me three months ago. Gave me a concussion and a black eye."

Katrina put on her puppy dog eyes, blinking back tears she could turn on and off at a whim, and piled her hands over her heart. "Oh, Shel-bear, I wasn't well then, and you know it. You're my baby. My last baby. Of course you've always been my favorite."

Shelby rolled her lips together and drew in a deep breath through her nose. It was all she could do to keep from screaming, "Real mothers don't have favorites!" It would be a waste of breath anyway, because Katrina had a remarkable ability to ignore facts she didn't want to hear. "You need to go."

"Oh, honey. What's wrong?" She walked forward, arms outstretched, but Shelby ducked out of her reach.

"Don't." Her voice broke, and she hated herself for not being stronger when it came to this woman. "I'm sorry. You need to leave."

"What?"

"I made a mistake. You can't stay."

"You're kicking me out onto the street?" Outrage flushed her cheeks with much-needed color. "I am your mother!"

"I know. I know. And I'll give you money for a hotel, enough for a few nights, but you… you just can't stay here."

"Oh. I see. You married money, so suddenly you're too good for me now?"

Shelby flinched. "That's not it. I—"

"Fine." Katrina crossed her arms over her chest. "I see how it is. Get me my money and I'll leave you alone."

And there it was. Katrina's real motive. Her sudden appearance here had nothing to do with wanting to see her daughter and everything to do with money. She'd found out Shelby had married a well-off man and decided she deserved a piece of the pie by virtue of a shared biology.

Really, it had only been a matter of time until this happened.

Shelby held up her hands. "Don't move. Don't touch anything. I'll be right back." Afraid to leave her mother alone for too long, she ran into her bedroom for her purse. She had a couple hundred dollars in her wallet and it was pretty much all she had to her name at this point, but whatever. If it kept Katrina away, she'd pay it. She threw her wallet on her bed and started to turn, cash in hand—and broke into a run when she heard a thunk from the room next door.

Reece's office.

Katrina was rifling through Reece's desk like her life

depended on it.

"What are you doing?" Shelby lurched forward, but stopped short when Katrina pulled a gun and pointed it at her. "Mom!"

"You are not leaving me out on the streets to rot, you ungrateful little bitch," Katrina said through her teeth, spittle flying. She stuffed a box of blank checks in her purse, along with Reece's laptop and a bunch of notebooks, then motioned to the right with her gun. "Move outta my way."

Hands held up, Shelby did as she was told, stepping back into the hallway. "Mom, please don't do this."

Her pleas fell on deaf ears. But then, she'd known they would. Still, she had to try.

Katrina kept the gun raised as she edged out of the room. On the way, she snatched the few hundred dollars still clutched in Shelby's hand. "Give me your ring too."

Dropping her hands, she protectively cradled her wedding ring. "It's not worth anything."

"You're lying!" The gun bobbled dangerously, and her finger was on the trigger. It could go off at any second.

Shelby swallowed to ease the ache in her throat and took off the ring, shoved it into her mother's hand. "Okay, okay. Take it. Just, please, leave those notebooks here." The loss of them so close on the heels of the loss of his parents' house would break Reece's heart. "They're not worth anything."

"If that's true, you wouldn't want them so much."

"Just sentimental value. I swear, that's all."

"Lying again. Why are you girls always lying to me?" Katrina demanded, drug-fueled anger twisting her dainty features into something ugly and feral. She waved the gun again, and Shelby flinched expecting it to discharge.

"Mom." Her voice came out as little more than a squeak. "Put the gun down. You have everything you want. Just put the gun down and leave."

"Oh, I have everything I want? How about daughters who love me and take care of me like real daughters should? I don't have that. Instead, all my good babies got taken away from me, and I got left with two ungrateful little bitches who'd rather have their mom live on the streets. I brought you into this world! You owe me this! You. Owe. Me. Everything." She backed down the hallway until she reached the living room, then spun on her heel and ran.

Shelby didn't dare move. Katrina had been known to fly into irrational rages while on cocaine, and she was sure that was the drug pumping through her mother's veins right now. Katrina liked it all, dabbled in everything, but mostly flipped between coke and heroin depending on her mood. The former made her manic, paranoid, delusional. The latter put her to sleep, which had always been the more preferable of the two. The last time she was hyped up on coke, she'd hit Shelby hard enough to give her a concussion. This time…Shelby truly feared her mother might shoot her if she tried to intervene. So she waited, flinching at each crash from the living room, until finally she heard nothing but a resounding silence.

Oh. God.

She exhaled the breath she'd been holding and bent double, hugging herself, trying to breath and keep it together. A molten weight settled in her stomach, and her eyes burned, but she was too damned exhausted by it all to cry.

How many times had Eva warned her their mother would never change? And instead of accepting it as a fact, she kept letting Katrina back in to destroy her heart, over and over. Every time was like slicing open old wounds and pouring salt into them. Must be she secretly enjoyed the pain, was as addicted to it as Katrina was to drugs. Why else would any sane human being continually put themselves through this?

Gathering her strength, she straightened and trudged out to the living room. The short walk felt like a trip to the hangman's noose. Sam the Cat had backed himself into the corner of the room behind the entertainment stand and peeked out at her with wide, alarmed eyes. The coffee table was overturned, the couch knocked askew, and the cushions strewn across the floor. A lamp was shattered, drawers pulled open, and the paintings she'd yet to hang were gone.

Damn. That almost hurt more than having her mother pull a gun on her. Those paintings were virtually worthless, would get Katrina all of fifty bucks when she tried to pawn them, but they'd already had sentimental value. Reece had liked them, had enjoyed her efforts to make this place more colorful. For that reason alone, those paintings had been worth their weight in gold to her.

Oh, and the notebooks. Why had Katrina taken Reece's notebooks, of all things? And his laptop. His checks…

She needed to call him before Katrina emptied his bank account.

Numb, she retrieved her cell phone from her bedroom. Only when she tried to punch in the numbers did she realize she was shaking. She could barely keep hold of the phone, not to mention see to dial with the sudden wash of tears filling her vision. She dropped the phone, curled into herself, and finally, she sobbed.

Chapter Twenty-Two

The door was open.

Reece froze in the process of digging for his apartment key and stared. It was only about two inches ajar, but still. It was *open*, and it shouldn't be. With all of his recent problems, that was enough of a red flag to have a chill scraping across the back of his neck. He reached out, pushed on the door. The living room looked as if a tornado had hit it.

"Shelby!" His heart lodged in his throat, and he was moving through the apartment in floor-eating strides before his brain protested that the intruder could still be inside. His heart told his brain to fuck off, because he could handle anything an intruder dished out, and he had to find Shelby. Had to make sure she was safe. Had to—

A muffled sound from her room caught his attention, and he made a beeline for it. And there she was, curled up in a tiny ball on her bed, sobbing. Sam the Cat sat by her head as if protecting her, his tail swishing in aggravation. In the cage across the room, Poe squawked and waddled restlessly from one side of his perch to the other, obviously aware of Shelby's distress.

But she didn't look injured, and the knot in Reece's belly loosened. He sat down beside her, placed a soothing hand on her back. "Shelby. Sweetheart, what happened?"

She peeked up at him, her eyes red and puffy from crying. "Reece?" she breathed.

"Yes, I'm here now."

Without another word, she crawled into his lap and curled up again as if wanting to withdraw from the world.

She's…fragile. So much more than she lets people know…

Cam's words haunted him as he wrapped his arms around her and hugged her close. "It's okay, sweetheart. I'm here."

"She took your notebooks."

Her voice was so muffled against his chest, he wasn't sure he heard her right. "My notebooks?"

"For your video game." She sniffled. "And your computer. The book of blank checks in your desk. My ring…" She held out a shaking hand to show her empty finger. "Why'd she take my ring? It wasn't worth anything to her."

"Who?" Reece asked, although the sickening feeling in his gut told him he already knew the answer.

"Mom," she whispered and broke down in big, shuddering sobs again. "S-she said I owed her. She p-pulled a gun on me."

"I'm so sorry, sweetheart." He closed his eyes against the explosion of pure rage in his chest and held her tighter. What else could he do? Besides sic the cops on Katrina Bremer, which he fully intended to do.

Shelby wiped away her tears with the backs of her hands. "This is my fault. I shouldn't have let her in."

"This is *not* your fault."

"You need to call your bank and—and make sure she doesn't take all of your money. That's all she wanted. She found out we're married and wanted your money."

"It's insured. Whatever she gets, the money's insured."

She drew away enough to meet his gaze. "No. Call them right now. Freeze the account or whatever. I don't want her to get a dime. This is my home. However temporary this situation is, right now it is my home, and I'm not letting her get away with coming here and scaring the hell out of me. She took my ring and your notebooks and the paintings I bought yesterday just because she knew it'd hurt me. She didn't get her way, so she wanted me to hurt."

"There you go." He pushed her mussed hair back from her face and kissed her forehead. "Get mad."

"I *am* mad. She had no right to terrorize me in my home. I don't owe her shit." Sitting up, she pushed her shoulders back and inhaled through her nose. She blew out the breath slowly, then wiped her eyes and, when she looked at him again, she was calm, grimly focused. "Call the police," she said. "Call the bank. And then we will push her out of our thoughts and go to the gala and charm the pants off Irving James."

Jesus, she was amazing.

He cupped her cheek, dragged his thumb over lips that still trembled slightly. "Are you sure?"

"Yes." She lifted her chin, strength in every angle of her face. "I don't want to waste a second more of my time on that woman."

With the fire of determination in her eyes and the stubborn set to her jaw, she'd never looked more beautiful to him. He had to kiss her and leaned down, brushing his lips across her eyes, nose, taking his time with each light brush of his lips. Finally he moved his mouth over hers, drinking her in, wanting a taste of the flame that made up the core of her being, the wild heat that had first drawn him to her.

Shelby broke the kiss first and pressed a hand into his chest. "Go call the police. I need to shower or we'll be late for the gala." She squeezed his hand, then stood and disappeared into her bathroom.

Reece didn't move for several minutes. Should he call off this whole gala thing and join her in the shower? She obviously needed comfort, even if it was just someone to hold her. Because even as determined as she was to keep it together, he saw the cracks in her bravado. She was hurting. And he wanted to make it better.

The water came on and he finally stood. He couldn't be angry at her for shutting him out right now. She was using the gala as a distraction—he understood that—but later, he was going to hold her. If she needed to break down, she could do so without worry, because he'd be right there to help her glue the pieces back in place when it was over. They were stronger together than alone, and he planned to prove it to her.

He walked out to the living room, and the sight of it pissed him off. He wanted to start cleaning, but knew better and instead called the cops. They said they'd send a unit right over. Next, he called Cam. It took a couple tries before his brother finally answered.

"What?" Cam answered breathlessly.

Reece winced. He did not want to know what Cam was up to right now. "Bad timing?"

"Fuck you. I'm working out and—oomph!" His voice

faded away from the phone. "Eva, that didn't count. I called a time out." Then back into the phone, grumbling, "You're making me lose. What do you want?"

"Actually, I'm glad you're both right there. You might want to put me on speaker for this."

There was some shuffling, a muffled conversation, then Cam said, "Go ahead."

"What's up?" Eva asked.

This was not going to be a fun exchange. Reece exhaled hard to release the tension balled in his gut and launched into an explanation of the day's events. He ended with, "I wanted to warn you so you didn't hear it from the police scanner."

Eva's voice sounded small, miles away. "I keep telling her Mom won't change."

"I know. I know you do." Cam cursed. "Hey, baby, it's okay. He said Shelby is unharmed."

"She's shaken up," Reece said, "but also mad. Katrina took some paintings she'd bought for the apartment and her wedding ring."

"What?" Now Eva sounded more like herself. "Oh, fuck her. Just…fuck her! I'm going to kill her. I'm—"

"Don't say that," Cam soothed. "I know you're angry, but—"

"I'm pissed! That bitch deliberately took the things she knew would hurt Shelby the most. Reece, you better press charges, because Shelby won't. She never does."

"I wouldn't be so sure about it this time. As I said, she's as angry as you are. But," he added when she made a sound of protest, "if she won't do it, I will."

A knock drew his attention to the still partly open door, and he spotted two uniformed officers. "I have to go. The cops are here."

He spent the next half hour answering the police's questions as best he could, and then it was Shelby's turn. He was half afraid she'd lost her nerve, but she was steadfast in that she wanted to press charges. The cops left with a list of the items taken and a picture of Katrina Bremer.

Shelby stood in the middle of the living room after they left, staring at the mess. "I wish we had time to clean this up, but we have to finish getting ready. We're already going to be late."

With that, she retreated back to her bedroom.

Reece watched her go and considered following, but shook his head to dislodge the idea. She wasn't going to let him blow off the gala, even as much as he now wanted to. Stubborn woman.

He made sure the door was locked, then went to his own bathroom. It didn't take him long to shower and change into his tux, though he left the bowtie undone around his neck. As he strode down the hall toward the living room, Shelby called out to him. He backtracked, peeked in her room. She wasn't there, but the bathroom door was open so he walked over—and stopped dead in his tracks in the doorway. Her gown was black with a back that dipped almost indecently low, held together by dainty chains. And for a heartbeat he was struck dumb. She looked amazing. Sleek and sexy without being over the top.

Before he realized he was moving, he stepped forward and trailed a knuckle down her spine. "Shelby…"

The note of heat in his voice made her legs go to gelatin, and she suppressed a shiver of pure desire.

Get a grip, girl.

She needed to focus. So many of his recent problems were her fault—the blackmail, the fire at his parents' house, and now she'd allowed her mother to rob him—but she was going to make up for it by going to the gala and playing the part of a perfect wife tonight. And she refused to put Wilde Security in further jeopardy all because the sound of his voice sent her hormones into hyper drive.

Forcing a smile she didn't feel, she held out her tube of makeup. "Can you help me cover up the tattoos on my back? This dress dips too low, and I can't reach to do it."

He didn't move. "We should cancel tonight."

She lifted her gaze, met his in the mirror over the sink. "You know that's not a good idea, especially since we slipped away from dinner early the other night."

He hesitated, then took the tube from her like it would blow up in his hand. She laughed softly and handed him the application sponge. "All you have to do is squeeze some on the sponge, then rub it on. Just make sure it's an even layer so it covers everything."

Scooping up her hair, she turned her back to him and waited. But he still didn't move, just stood there frowning, the makeup in one hand and the sponge in the other.

She let her hair drop again and faced him. "What's wrong?"

"What if you don't cover them?"

She pressed a hand to his forehead. "Are you running a fever?"

"What?" Scowling, he waved her hand away. "No, of course not."

"Are you sure? Because you're obviously delirious. I can't show up to an opera fundraiser covered in ink." When his scowl only deepened, she sighed and clasped his cheeks in her hands. "Hey, we've come this far, right? Might as well see it through to the end."

"What if I don't want it to end?"

Her heart bungeed all the way down to her toes and back up into her throat. She dropped her hands and tried to back up a step, but the sink was blocking her escape. "Don't be silly. Of course it has to end. East and west, remember?"

"You're forgetting the rest of the poem," Reece said softly and set aside the makeup. His hands wrapped around her shoulders and pulled her closer. "*Oh, East is East, and West is West, and never the twain shall meet, till Earth and Sky stand presently at God's great Judgment Seat; But there is neither East nor West, Border, nor Breed, nor Birth, when two strong men stand face to face, tho' they come from the ends of the earth.*"

She couldn't look at him, not when he stared at her like that, with such earnest intensity. "I'm not a man."

"But you're strong. One of the strongest people I've ever met. We're opposites, there's no denying it. East and west, night and day. But we're also equals, and I'm starting to think we might be two different halves of the same whole." He caught her chin, lifted it until she could no longer avoid his gaze. He stared into her eyes like he was trying to see into her soul. "I don't want this to end."

Oh, God. He was serious.

She shrugged away from him and turned back toward the mirror. "We need to hurry or we're going to be late."

Chapter Twenty-Three

The ballroom was huge, sparkling with chandeliers, expensive gowns, and more jewelry than Shelby had ever seen in one place. It kind of blew her mind that they were mingling with celebrities like Tucker Quentin, a former child star turned businessman, who was one of the richest men in the country. *And* he seemed to know Reece as more than a casual acquaintance.

"Those brothers of yours still up to no good?" Tuc asked, flashing his camera-ready smile as he extended his hand.

"Always," Reece said and accepted the shake. Then he nudged her forward with a possessive hand that practically left scorch marks on the small of her back. "Tuc, this is my wife, Shelby."

"Wait, what?" Tuc did a double take. "You're married to this beautiful woman? Whoa. When did that happen and why wasn't I invited? I thought we were friends, man."

Reece winced. "It was...last minute."

"Uh-huh." Tuc turned that devastating smile on her. "Swept him off his feet, did you?"

She actually felt her cheeks heat with a blush, and she so wasn't the blushing type. But, holy crap, she'd had a poster of this guy on her bedroom wall growing up. And now here he was, in the flesh. Talking to her. She opened her mouth and hoped for something cool and sophisticated, but all that came out was a fangirl-y, "Mr. Quentin, I loved your movies."

He snorted a laugh. "Well, that makes a grand total of two people who actually saw them. You and my housekeeper. There's a reason I'm not in the movie business anymore — the least of which is that I'm a shitty actor. But thank you. And please, call me Tuc."

"Okay," she squeaked. Later she'd be embarrassed by the sound, but it was all she could manage. "Tuc."

Reece shook his head at her, his mouth turned up at the corners in amusement. "I've never heard her so quiet. I think she's starstruck." He kissed her temple before returning his attention to Tuc and switching right back into business mode. "If you have a minute tonight, I'd like to speak to you about a new idea in A.I. technology."

"Hmm. A.I. huh? That's not your usual wheelhouse, Wilde."

"No, it's something new we've been tinkering with at DMW."

"Okay, I'm intrigued," Tuc said and dipped a hand into his jacket pocket at the sound of a discreet chime. He took out his phone, read the text, and his smile faded. "Shit."

"Everything okay?"

"Nope. The HORNET boys are in trouble — again. Looks like I'm flying to Europe tonight." He pocketed his phone, but he didn't seem all that heartbroken about having to leave. He held out his hand to Shelby. "You keep this guy from working too hard. It was nice meeting you." Then he clapped Reece on the shoulder. "Call my office, and let's set something up for later this week. I should be back in town by then."

As he strode away, Shelby squealed. "Reece! You didn't tell me you know Tucker Quentin!"

Poor guy looked genuinely baffled. "Was...I supposed to?"

"Yes! He was only, like, every teenage girl's fantasy guy when I was in high school. I had a poster of him hanging over my bed. I always imagined him riding in on a limo like Richard Gere at the end of *Pretty Woman* and taking me away from my life. I blew that poster a kiss every night before I went to sleep."

His puzzlement faded into a scowl. "You better not still have it."

"No, of course not. I was a teenager."

"Good. I'm the only guy you should be kissing before bed." He snaked an arm around her waist, pulled her in to his side, and planted a possessive kiss on her lips.

It should have been an act. Days ago, it would have been. But something had changed tonight and the kiss...it tugged all the way to the bottom of her heart. It was *real*, and it scared the ever-loving hell out of her.

He drew away slightly, resting his forehead against hers, and gazed down into her eyes. "How are you doing? You okay?"

"Yes." And it was the truth. The events from the afternoon still played in the back of her mind like a broken record, but she wasn't as heartsick over it now. She was actually glad for this gala. It provided exactly the distraction she'd needed.

She poked him in the ribs. "Just don't spring any more former teen heartthrobs on me tonight. I don't know if my fangirl can take it. Oh my God, did you hear me? I squeaked like a freaking mouse!"

He laughed. "No more teen heartthrobs. It's a deal," he said and sealed it with another quick peck on the lips.

Over his shoulder, she spotted Irving James headed in their direction and winced. "Oh boy. Looks like it's show time."

Reece followed her gaze. Swore softly. "Yeah, looks like."

"Reece," James said, all fake smiles. "Sheila. It's good to see you both."

"Her name is Shelby," Reece corrected.

"Right, right. Of course." James waved a hand. "Was that Tucker Quentin I just saw you talking to? I'd love an introduction."

"He was called away," Reece said, and the note of dismissive coolness in his voice made Shelby glance over at him in question. He'd been so relaxed talking to Tuc, but now his shoulders were tense, his smile tight and no longer easy. What was he doing? He was going to ruin his chances to secure the deal with James if he kept this up. Was it because he was still feeling uber-protective of her? James was an ass toward women, so maybe Reece was bracing for an off-color comment. If that was the case, she should excuse herself.

Across the room, she noticed Charlotte James speaking to several other women, including Alicia Porter. She gave

Reece's arm a little squeeze to get his attention, then excused herself with a polite smile for James.

On her way toward the women, she snagged a glass of champagne from a passing waiter. She was going to need it.

"Shelby!" Charlotte said and leaned in for a hug and an air kiss. "I was just saying I hoped you'd make it tonight. We're so looking forward to the show, aren't you?"

Show? Reece hadn't mentioned she'd have to sit through a show tonight. "Yes, I'm excited." *For a nap,* she tacked on silently. Because that's what she'd end up doing if she was forced to sit through an opera.

The women spent several minutes chatting about the show, the singers, and spreading around some juicy bits of gossip about people Shelby didn't know. She nodded and smiled and made all of the appropriate noises until Alicia leaned in.

"I noticed you're not wearing your wedding ring," she said in a hushed tone. But not hushed enough because the other women stopped talking and focused in on their conversation. "Is everything okay between you and Reece?"

"Oh." She gazed down at her empty hand.

I don't want this to end.

Nerves fluttered in her chest at the memory of Reece's words, and she curled her fingers around the stem of her glass. Amazing how after such a short time as Mrs. Wilde, she'd gotten so used to wearing her ring that she now felt naked without it.

"Shelby?" Alicia's expression filled with alarm. "Is everything okay?"

"Yes, everything's fine. But we, uh..." She floundered for a moment, grasping for an excuse, then decided the truth was the best course of action. Since there was a police report, the robbery would probably be posted in the newspaper tomorrow. "Well, honestly, we were robbed earlier this evening."

The women all gasped.

"Then why on earth are you here tonight?" Alicia asked, eyes wide.

Shelby sipped her champagne to wet her suddenly parched throat. "Reece wanted to cancel, but I told him no. This is exactly what we need to take our minds off the robbery."

"Oh my goodness." Charlotte James pressed a hand over her diamond necklace as if protecting it. "Nothing too valuable was taken, I hope."

What a materialistic bitch.

Shelby winced at the venom in her thoughts. Maybe Reece was right and they should have cancelled, because she was finding it so much harder than usual to play her part for these women. She was exhausted, physically and emotionally, and all she really wanted to do was go home with Reece, curl up on the couch, and watch a Japanese monster movie together.

"No," she managed, beating down her annoyance. "Just my ring, a few paintings, and Reece's laptop. Not the business one," she added. She didn't want Charlotte saying something to her husband about DMW having shoddy security. "The business files are all perfectly safe."

Charlotte fanned herself with one dainty hand. "Oh, you poor thing. I don't know how you're so calm about it all. I'd be an absolute wreck!"

"I'll tell you how she's so calm." Lena Schilling, who had been lurking like a vulture on the outskirts of their little circle, pushed her way forward. "Shelby's used to dealing with scum. Isn't that right?"

Unable to keep a straight face, Shelby scowled at the woman. "I don't know what you're talking about."

"Sure you do." She leaned in close and her breath reeked of vodka. "I know all about you, Shelby Wilde. Or should I call you Shelby Bremer? Though you're certainly not from the California Bremers like we thought."

Oh, no. No, no, no. A cold sweat broke out at her temples, and she resisted the urge to swipe at it. "You're drunk, Lena. *You* don't know what you're talking about."

"Yes, as a matter of fact, I do. Shelby Bremer, *not* of the California Bremers, daughter of Katrina, a drug addict and occasional prostitute. And from the looks of things, the apple doesn't fall far from the tree." She pulled a handful of photographs from her jewel-studded purse and flung them. They scattered across the floor.

The blackmailer's photos. All of them. Stills from the video of her and Reece together at The Bean Gallery. The Vegas hotel photos. The not-so-flattering pictures of her before she decided she needed to straighten up her life…

All of it, laid out right there on the floor for everyone to see.

Charlotte scooped up several of the photos, her face white. "What is all this?"

"Blackmail," Shelby whispered and her stomach twisted. "It was you."

Lena scoffed. "I'm merely exposing a fake." Puffed up with righteous indignation, she faced Charlotte. "She doesn't belong in high society. She doesn't even belong in the middle class. She's nothing but white trash, and Reece only married her because he got caught slumming and was afraid of losing your husband's approval."

"Oh," Charlotte breathed, and her cheeks flushed bright red as she flipped through the photos. "This is…disgusting." She spared Shelby a contemptuous glance before scurrying away, pictures in hand. No doubt she was going to find her husband.

It was over. Just like she'd told Reece it would be. Only she hadn't expected the end to come so soon. Or so publicly.

Shelby whirled around, needing to get away, to go some-where else. Anywhere else. She felt as if every eye in the room was staring at her, judging her. Imagined the scornful whispers, the derisive jokes they'd all say about her.

She spotted a doorway not blocked by people and lurched toward it, but Alicia grabbed her arm.

"Shelby, wait—"

"No. I…can't stay here. I can't—" Voice cracking, she shook off Alicia's grip and raced from the ballroom.

White trash.

God. How foolish of her to think a dye job and a bit of makeup would be enough to hide what she was.

The more Reece listened to Irving James talk, the more he was sure he didn't want to tie his company to the man in any way, shape, or form. For so long, he'd thought it was wrong to let his personal feeling of distaste get in the way of business, but fuck that. It was his business and, from here on out, he was only making deals that felt good. No more of this acid-like feeling in his gut or worrying whether he'd do or say the wrong thing and offend the wrong person. He'd figure out another way to keep Wilde Security afloat that wasn't akin to selling his soul to this devil. In fact, he was ninety percent certain he'd already found another way thanks to the genius of Cliff McWilliam. He'd been so zeroed in on the deal with James that he hadn't noticed the way out of Wilde Security's financial crisis was sitting right under his feet in the basement of DMW.

He'd been so stupid. Stupid and tunnel-visioned. And if it wasn't for Shelby opening his eyes to all kinds of possibilities he'd never considered, he may very well still be that short-sighted man.

All right. Enough was enough.

Reece opened his mouth to tell Irving James the deal was off, but he never got the chance. Charlotte bustled over and shoved something into her husband's hand. Crossing her arms, she glared at Reece like he was a cockroach.

And he knew. Even before James's eyes bugged and his face flushed red, he knew the jig was up.

"W-Wilde," James sputtered and held up the photos. "Explain this!"

He should probably be panicking right now, but all he felt was a giddy rush of relief. He laughed. "I don't owe you a damn thing." He turned to go find Shelby and get the hell out of here, but stopped short. "Wait. Yes, I do have something to say. I've been so busy trying to kiss your ass I was ruining the best thing I've ever had, forcing her to change herself to suit your antiquated view of how a woman should act and what a marriage should be. Yeah, well, fuck you. DMW is pulling out of this deal." He grabbed the photos from James's hand. "Have a nice night."

There was a distinct bounce in his step as he left the ballroom. He'd just committed social suicide, and he felt like dancing. Hell, maybe he would take Shelby dancing.

Except then he saw her standing on the front steps of the building, shivering, tears freezing on her cheeks, and his good mood died a slow, painful death. He took off his coat and wrapped it around her.

"Shelby, baby. What are you doing out here without your coat?"

"Y-you have the valet ticket. And the car keys. I couldn't leave, but I couldn't stay in there. The pictures are out. It was Lena. Your blackmailer."

She was like an ice cube, and he pulled her into him, rubbed her back to generate some warmth. "It's okay."

"I'm sorry."

"Don't be. It doesn't matter anymore."

"How can you say that?" Yanking free of his arms, she plopped down on the steps and hid her face behind her hands. "I've ruined everything for you. I always ruin everything."

"You didn't ruin anything. I promise you didn't." He wanted to tell her that he'd spent the entire day at DMW, discussing Cliff's A.I. side project and that he saw so much potential there, he didn't think they needed Irving James after all. They only had to shift DMW's direction a bit—but it all hinged on selling the idea to Tucker Quentin, and he didn't dare say anything out loud for fear of jinxing it.

So, instead, he pulled her hands away from her face and crouched to put himself in her line of sight. "What can I do to make tonight better?"

"Nothing."

"Of course there's something. What do you like to do to

blow off steam?"

She hesitated.

"Shelby?"

She exhaled hard. "Usually I'd go to a club, lose myself in the music and the crowd, but—"

"All right. Where to?"

"You want to take me to a club? Dressed like this?"

"I want to do something that makes you happy for once. If that means going to a club in black-tie attire, let's do it."

She eyed him like he'd lost his mind. "Who *are* you? You're not the Reece Wilde I know."

He wasn't entirely sure, but he liked this new version of himself. He felt lighter than he had in years. Chains he hadn't even known he'd been wearing were breaking, falling off, and he suspected she played a major role in his new-found freedom.

"Well, someone once said I wouldn't know spontaneity if it slapped me upside the head." He grinned and stood. Held out a hand. "Help me prove that person wrong."

Chapter Twenty-Four

There was a line around the block waiting to get into the club. Reece eyed the throng of people as he climbed out of the Escalade. "Why is everyone dressed in white?"

Shelby showed the first hint of a smile since leaving the gala. "You'll see. C'mon." She grasped his hand and pulled him to a side entrance. "We don't have to wait in line. I know the bouncers."

The big tattooed man guarding the side door grinned toothily when he saw her coming. "Hey, baby doll. Look at you, all dressed up. What you been up to?"

"Oh, you know, Eddy. Same old, same old. Getting in trouble. Getting married." She held up their interlaced hands. "Think you can let a couple of newlyweds sneak in?"

Eddy's wide face lit up. "You got yourself married, baby doll? Well, didn't see *that* coming." He stepped aside, waved them in, and handed Shelby a card. "Go on. And give Meg at the bar this, tell her I says your drinks are on the house tonight. Wedding present."

"Thank you, Eddy. You're the best." She stood on her toes to kiss his cheek, then pulled Reece into the crush of light and sound and people. It was blinding, disorienting, but Shelby seemed to know how to navigate it, so he followed her lead to the bar. She had to lean over the polished metal surface and shout to be heard, but Meg the bartender seemed to understand what she was saying just fine. Meg took the card and disappeared, returning a moment later with two tall glasses of neon-blue liquid.

Reece choked out a laugh when Shelby handed it to him. "What the fuck is this?"

"I don't know. I told her to make us something yummy and strong. To spontaneity." She clinked her glass to his. "Cheers."

He had to admit, the concoction was "yummy," as Shelby had called it. Fruity, but with a kick to it. Before he knew it, his glass was gone and there was a pleasant buzz inside his head. He was enjoying himself and liked watching Shelby relax into her own skin. She had a smile for everyone she ran in to, even if she didn't know them.

A fast, infectious beat started and Shelby grabbed his hand, dragging him out onto the dance floor, which was packed with people. She melted into the beat, eyes closed, hips swinging, hands in the air, and the sight of her throwing herself so completely into the music reminded him of when he was young and his parents used to dance together across the kitchen. They'd been so in tune with the music, with each other, and even as a child, he'd known he was witnessing something beautiful.

He was witnessing something beautiful now, too.

Shelby laughed and grabbed hold of his shoulders, wiggling them. "Loosen up, Reece! Dance!"

He hadn't danced since his parents died. And, dammit, they had both loved to dance. Together, apart. It hadn't mattered. If there was music playing, David and Meredith Wilde had been dancing.

What a way to not honor their memory.

Reece swayed a bit on his feet, but he felt awkward and foolish. No way was he getting his hips or arms involved in this disaster. He'd end up looking like one of those inflatable arm-flailing tube men and scare Shelby right into an annulment.

She moved in close and tugged on his bowtie until it fell loose. Having her so close, moving like she was, sparked a blaze inside him. He needed to touch her, skin to skin, and circled his hands around her hips, found himself moving with her. His heart kept time with the beat and he lowered his head, intending to kiss her—

The music screeched to a halt, and the room plunged into darkness, only to be relit by the eerie purple glow of black lights.

Shelby smiled up at him. "Here it comes."

"What?"

Something like a cannon fired, and the music exploded back to life as neon glow-in-the-dark paint rained down over the thrilled crowd.

Shelby laughed and tilted her head back, letting the paint splash across her face and chest. She should have looked out of place in her gown, with her hair piled on top of her head in an elegant twist, as paint rained down on her—but she didn't. She looked more like Shelby now, covered in streaks of neon green and pink and purple, than she had since they left Vegas. And that, more than anything else, made him feel like a complete ass for asking her to change. All of the color and brightness that made up the core of her being *belonged* on her clothes, in her hair, and written on her skin in ink.

Reece snaked a hand around the back of her neck, crushed her to him, and captured her mouth. She yielded to the domination of his lips and together they moved to the beat of the music. He didn't hear cannons spew more paint or the shouts of joy as it rained down. He didn't worry about looking stupid or about the bridges he'd burned tonight. Everything else faded away as his world narrowed to her.

And they danced.

It was late by the time they returned home, laughing and covered in dried paint. Shelby started stripping as soon as she set foot in the apartment, suggestively sliding one strap of her dress off her shoulder, then the other...

Dumbstruck and a little drunk, Reece watched her striptease, the way the sleek fabric caressed her body as she let it slide down to pool around her waist.

She turned to him, crooked a finger. "I think we need a shower, don't you?"

Oh, yeah. They definitely, absolutely, without a doubt needed a shower.

He made sure the door was locked and reached to pull off his bowtie, only to discover he'd lost it somewhere during the night. Fine by him. One less article of clothing between him and the woman he wanted more than he wanted his next breath. He wasn't careful with his vest or shirt, popping buttons as he fumbled to get them off. Shelby laughed and whirled around like she intended to race him, but only made it a few steps before skidding to a halt in the still torn-apart living room.

She crumpled to the floor as if the weight of the night had finally gotten too heavy to hold on her shoulders. Three long strides had him by her side and scooping her into his arms.

She curled into him. "I almost forgot."

"We are forgetting it, okay? Just until tomorrow. Tonight was too good to end it on a sad note." He carried her into the master bathroom and started the shower, setting her down under the warm spray. Fuck. He was still in his pants. He left the shower again long enough to strip and grab a washcloth from the linen closet. When he returned, she still hadn't moved.

This wasn't what he'd wanted. The whole point of taking her to a club had been to forget about the rest of the night. Stupid man that he was, he hadn't even considered how she'd feel to return home to the mess her mother had made. Should have called one of his brothers to come over and straighten things while they were gone.

With his heart breaking for her, he soaped up the washcloth and ran it down her arm. Layers of paint and the makeup obscuring her tattoos washed away, and he reveled in each new inch of ink he uncovered. He smoothed his lips in the wake of the cloth, over the flowers and dragon crawling up her arm. He kissed each of the colorful birds taking flight on her collarbones. They were perfect representations of Shelby—bright, unrestrained, and full of vitality.

He straightened and stared down into her eyes, combing her wet hair back with his fingers. "I don't ever want you to cover these up again."

Tears brimmed in her eyes and spilled over to mingle with the shower water already sprinkling her face. "Are you sure? I don't want to ruin you—"

"You can't." He cradled her face in his hands. "Listen, Shelby, you *can't* ruin me. How could you? I'm a better person with you."

Her breath hitched. "But all of your friends—"

"Fuck them. They're not my friends. They're all uptight, snobby assholes, and I want nothing more to do with them. *You* are more important to me than maintaining whatever unattainable status quo they've set. I'm in love with you."

"Oh no." Sobbing openly now, she broke away from him and covered her face with both hands. "Oh, Reece, you can't be. You *can't* be. You have no idea what I've done…"

"I don't care."

"You have to care."

"Sweetheart…" How to make her understand? He was under no illusions—he knew her past wasn't pretty. But tonight, as he'd watched her crumple under the scrutiny of his contemporaries, then rebuild herself while dancing covered in splatter paint, he'd realized her past didn't matter. It didn't matter because the future was what mattered, and they could build an amazing one together. More than that, he *wanted* a future with her. He loved the color and unpredictability she brought into his life.

But he saw that he wasn't going to convince her of it right now. No matter what he said, she wasn't going to believe him.

He pulled her into his arms again, smoothing a hand over her hair and back. The water had run cool and goose bumps roughened her skin, tremors racing just underneath. "Let's go to bed."

She sucked in a sharp breath. "You mean the same bed?"

"Yeah. The same bed." He wasn't about to give her a chance to protest and scooped her into his arms again. But she didn't seem to be in a protesting mood, which was troubling. Shelby always had a comeback ready. Her sharp tongue was one of the things he loved about her.

He deposited her on the counter by the sink and opened the linen closet for a towel to warm her up. She'd gone pale, and he didn't like the glassy, shell-shocked look in her eyes, but who could blame her? Although it had ended on a high note, the rest of the day had been one devastating blow after another. She had the right to a bit of distress. He wrapped her in the biggest towel he owned and briskly rubbed her arms until some color returned to her cheeks.

She finally stirred, pushing him away. "I can do it myself."

"Okay." Reece went back for a second towel, silently cursing as he dried himself with a lot less care. He'd bungled the whole I-love-you thing. He knew it, didn't know how to fix it, and that bugged the hell out of him. He was good at fixing things, but this was completely uncharted territory for him.

Reece discarded his towel in the laundry basket and turned to see Shelby had hopped down from the counter. The towel now wrapped around her was as big as a dress, swallowing her up in folds of terry cloth. She always seemed bigger than life to him, and he often forgot how petite she truly was until a moment like this came along and smacked him with the realization.

Someone could so easily hurt her.

Someone had already tried to. Multiple times.

He swallowed the growing lump of dread in his throat. No matter how things shook out between them, tomorrow he was going to put an end to her problems. He wanted her safe and, if The Headhunters wanted money, he'd pay them every dollar in his bank account to keep her that way.

She stared across the bathroom at him as if she wasn't sure what to say. She even opened her mouth, but no sound emerged.

He wished he knew how to reach her, but the gap opening between them was more than the few feet of physical space separating them. She was on guard now, closing down, shutting him out.

"Shelby," he began and stalled. Last thing he wanted was to spook her more than she already was. "Don't feel pressured. If you're not comfortable sharing my bed, I won't make you."

She pressed her lips together in a thin line and hugged the towel tighter around her. "Why?" she blurted after another long silence.

"Because I'm not a complete asshole. Despite recent evidence to the contrary."

She rolled her eyes, a hint of that old Shelby spark. "No. Why do you think you love me?"

"Why do you think I don't?"

Uncertain again, she picked at a loose thread on the towel. "Nobody's ever said those words to me before. I didn't think anyone could."

His heart cracked. "Jesus. You think you're unlovable."

She breathed out in a soft, tear-choked laugh. "I think you'd have to be crazy to love me, and you're not crazy, Reece Wilde. Not even a little bit."

Fuck this awkwardness. He strode forward and wrapped her in his arms, hugging her tight. "You've been hurt. I believe in ways I don't—can't—understand because before my parents—" He stopped, had to clear away the sudden roughness in this throat. "I came from a good, strong family with a solid foundation. I know what love looks like, feels like, and I know it's what I feel for you. I also know it scares you because it's not something you've had a lot of experience with."

Her breath shuddered out, hot against his bare chest. "Can we talk about this tomorrow? I-I need to sleep."

"Okay." He schooled his features to keep his disappointment from showing and dropped his arms to his sides. "Okay. I'll see you in the morning then."

"Wait." She captured his hand before he turned away. "Your bed. Please. I'd like to stay in your bed with you."

Chapter Twenty-Five

A phone's buzzing woke Reece from a dreamless sleep. Text message. Had to be because the vibration stopped a half second later. Shelby was still in bed with him, wrapped around him with her head resting on his chest. Surprising. He'd half expected her to slink back to her room after he fell asleep.

He liked waking up like this, with her hair tickling his neck and his arm numb from cradling her all night long. All mornings should start like this.

He craned his neck to see her face. She was still sound asleep, completely relaxed. She looked fragile and, although he knew she was anything but, a fierce protectiveness heated his blood.

He'd keep her safe.

Which meant he had to see who that text was from. Hopefully Greer finally coming back from wherever he'd ghosted off to.

Reece stretched for the phone on the nightstand, doing his best not to disturb Shelby, and rubbed his eyes with one hand before pulling the phone close to his nose. Damn, even though he'd worn glasses since he was five, he still hated not being able to see like a normal person. Maybe Vaughn had a point about getting laser surgery to fix his eyesight.

He rubbed his eyes again and squinted. Yeah, not Greer. Cam.

Have news about fires. Get to WS office asap.

And time to go back to work. For once, he'd rather not. His bed was warm and comfortable, especially with his woman curled up beside him. He lingered a few minutes longer, playing with a strand of her hair as he convinced himself he had to get up, then finally kissed her forehead and slid out of bed.

She stirred and lifted her head, blinking up at him with sleepy eyes. He loved seeing her like this, all soft and sexy, cozy in his bed.

"Are you leaving?" she asked, her voice throaty with sleep.

"Just for a bit." He leaned over and kissed her again. "Go back to sleep."

She reached for his hand and pulled him to a stop. "Reece…"

The note of vulnerability in her voice cut through him, and he sat down on the edge of the mattress, stroked his thumb lightly across the back of her hand. "Everything will be fine, okay? Don't worry about my companies. I can fix this."

"It's not that. I…" Hugging the pillow to her chest, she sat up. "You're right. We're good together and I'm not ready for it to end either."

He couldn't have stopped his grin even if he wanted to. "Are you saying you want to make a go of it?"

"I love—" She stopped. Drew a breath. "I love being here with you."

Not exactly what he wanted to hear, but it was a start. He pushed her hair back from her face, kissed her forehead. "I love having you here."

"You might not after I tell you—God, I don't even know where to start, but we need to talk."

His phone buzzed again with an incoming text, and he lifted her hand to his lips before he stood. "How about over dinner?"

She hesitated. Nodded. "Promise you won't hate me."

"Shelby." Ignoring his phone, he leaned over again, placing his hands on the mattress on either side of her body. He met her gaze, held it. "*Nothing* could make me hate you. I love you, and I don't say those words lightly. Whatever it is that has you so anxious, we'll figure it out. We'll make it work. We'll make *us* work."

The worry in her eyes softened as she reached up to touch his cheek. He leaned into the caress and sincerely thought about climbing back into bed with her. But his phone sounded again, and she yawned.

He gave her another quick kiss and straightened. "I can tell you're still exhausted. Go back to sleep. I should be home for dinner, but I'll call if I'm going to be late. I love you."

"Okay." She rolled over onto her belly and hugged his pillow to her head. Within moments, her breathing evened out, and she was asleep again, a small smile tugging at her lips. Sam the Cat, sensing an opportunity, jumped up into his vacated spot, kneaded the bedspread, and curled up next to Shelby, purring like a motor.

"Paws off. She's mine." But he rubbed the cat's head anyway, because he was actually going to miss the furry beast when Jude and Libby's lease was up this summer and Sam returned to them. "Keep an eye on her for me."

Sam blinked as if he understood and scooted his body closer to her side.

Reece made sure she was covered and strode to his closet. Started to pick out his usual—dress shirt, suit, tie—but stopped short. Jesus, he was an uptight bastard. He didn't need a tie to go meet his brother. Instead, he grabbed a dark gray sweater. He didn't even own a pair of jeans, and how ridiculous was that? The closest his closet came to the casual staple of men's clothing was a pair of chinos.

He really needed to fix that. Among so many other things.

Reece pulled into Wilde Security's parking lot, saw all of his brothers' vehicles—minus Greer's—in front of the office, and his gut clenched. What were they all doing here? This was supposed to have been a private matter between him and Cam. There was absolutely no need to get Jude and Vaughn involved. And, shit, was that Eva's car?

There went his good mood. He had a few things to say to Eva, and it wasn't going to be pretty.

He stalked to the door, unsurprised to find them all waiting right on the other side with Cam at the center of their semicircle. All of them were grim-faced, even Jude.

All right, then. If this was some kind of gauntlet he had to run before he got the information he needed, so be it.

"Care to tell me what this is about?" he asked the group as casually as he could manage.

Cam was the first to speak. "This is an intervention. We're worried about you."

Disbelief roared through him, and he stared at each of his brothers in turn. The disturbing hollowness in Vaughn's eyes since Lark disappeared was even more pronounced. Cam looked exhausted and frazzled, probably stressed out from a mix of worrying about his twin's increasing emotional distance and his wife's emotional health. Even Jude was a bit haggard. Apparently baby-making was exhausting work.

Reece shook his head. "An intervention for *me*? Have you all looked at yourselves lately? I'm not the one who needs it here."

Cam stepped forward and slapped a tablet against his chest. "You're the only one here who's lost his fucking mind."

He caught it before it fell and looked at the picture on the screen of him and Shelby at the club last night, covered with paint. There were several other photos on the popular tabloid website, including one of him kissing her.

And he didn't care. He. Didn't. Care.

Holy hell, that was freeing.

He shrugged. "So what?"

Vaughn's brows slammed together. "That isn't you."

"Uh, yeah, it is."

"He means," Cam said in exasperation, "that's not like you."

"How would you know?" He didn't raise his voice, but

the room went pin-drop silent. He set the tablet aside on Jude's desk. "Really, how would any of you know? None of you know me. To you, I'm the workaholic, the uptight asshole who strangles himself with a tie every day because he feels powerless without one, and he's so fucking afraid to fail. But I don't want to be that guy anymore. At heart, I don't know that I was ever him, and Shelby's the only one who saw it."

"Shelby's a liar," Eva said, a catch of emotion in her voice. "I'm sorry, Reece. I love my sister, but—"

"No. If you truly loved her, she wouldn't think of herself as unlovable."

Eva flinched and shut her eyes, sucked in a breath through her nose. "She makes it very, very hard sometimes." When she opened her dark eyes again, they were glossy with tears. "Reece, I know she told you she owes The Headhunters money, but she doesn't. They'd never come after her because her father is Alec Hudson. Their leader." She nodded toward Cam, who held out a folder.

He didn't want to take it, didn't want to see what was inside, which was exactly the reason he snatched it from his brother's hand and flipped it open. On top of the pile of papers was Shelby's birth certificate, listing none other than the notorious Alec Hudson as her father. Her birth name had even been Shelby Hudson, and there were a few old photos from the 80s attached to the documents. A very young girl in pigtails—obviously Shelby—on Hudson's shoulders or sitting in front of him on his motorcycle while he sported The Headhunters' patch on the back of his jacket. There were other papers, including documentation of her name change from Hudson to Bremer, her mother's maiden name, after her father was sentenced to life in prison for murder, drug charges, and a handful of violent racketeering-related offenses.

Reece suddenly couldn't breathe. Needed some space from his brothers and Eva before he did something stupid like pass out from lack of oxygen intake.

Smacking the folder closed, he slapped it down on the nearest desk and walked to the back of the room, toward his tiny office. But he didn't go in. Just stood there in front of the door, eyes closed against the riptide of betrayal threatening to suck him under. "Why would she lie?"

Eva pushed out a breath. "I don't know. She's been lying to me for years. It's just…what she does, part of who she is."

"No." He couldn't accept that Shelby was simply a pathological liar. Wouldn't accept it. He'd seen her at her most vulnerable, had seen her beaten down and broken by her mother's constant lies. "She has to have a reason."

"C'mon, man," Vaughn said on a groan. "She made up this sob story about owing bad guys money so you'd marry her. Look at the evidence in front of you."

"You're one to talk," Reece snapped. "Chasing after a woman who doesn't want to be found."

"Yeah, well. You're smarter than I am. Always have been."

No. He shook his head, pushed past his brothers and out into the cold bite of January. He wasn't deluding himself here. He *knew* Shelby. She didn't want his money, hadn't even taken the credit card he'd offered when she went shopping with Libby.

No, there was another reason for her lie, and he'd damn sure find out what it was.

Chapter Twenty-Six

The apartment was empty when Shelby finally dragged herself out of an exhausted sleep. She wasn't surprised to find Reece still gone and smiled, spotting the note he'd propped up on the nightstand.

Don't worry about the living room. I called my cleaning service, and they'll be by this afternoon to take care of it. Love, Hershey.

Her heart did a funny little dance behind her ribs. She picked up the note, reread it, and had to blink back a fresh rush of tears. Not only had he used the L word again, but he'd signed it with her favorite nickname for him.

Oh, she was in so much trouble. Because, damn it all, she loved him too. It meant she had to come clean about everything—and that wouldn't be a pretty conversation—but maybe things didn't have to end between them.

There was just one thing she had to do first. Well, two

things. She wasn't about to let him pay a cleaning service when she was responsible for the mess.

She threw back the blankets and ran into her room for some clothes. While there, she took the time to feed Poe and opened his cage to let him stretch his wings. Then she went to the kitchen to feed Sam and, sure enough, Reece had left the coffee on warm for her.

Yep. She loved that man.

As she fixed herself a mug, she called Jason and told him she needed him to stop by. He was reluctant to be seen anywhere near the apartment until she mentioned that Reece wasn't home, and she had important new information for him. Which was true. She did have new information—it just wasn't going to be the kind of information he wanted to hear.

She. Was. Done.

The doorbell sounded forty minutes later just as she finished straightening up the living room. She checked the peep and, yes, it was Jason. For once, he was dressed in a suit and tie. Must be he was done with his latest undercover operation.

She opened the door for him…

And her heart dropped like a stone as, down the hall, Reece stepped off the elevator.

A bald man Reece recognized stood in front of his door. Dressed in a suit and tie now, but there was no doubt in his mind this was same man who had chased him and Shelby with a gun in Vegas.

And Shelby was inviting him inside. At least, she'd been about to until she spotted Reece. Now she stood frozen, every drop of color fleeing her complexion. She sucked in a sharp breath. "Reece, it's not what—"

"Not what I think?"

"Yes. I mean, no, it's not."

"Then what the hell is it? Because from where I'm standing, this doesn't look good. This guy was chasing us with a fucking gun in Vegas, and now you're inviting him into our home?"

The bald man stared at Shelby for a long moment, contempt in his eyes. Then he turned and held out a hand. "Maybe I can explain. My name is Jason Mallory. I'm an agent with the ATF, and I'm Shelby's handler."

"Handler?" He looked from Mallory to her, but she was bent double, hugging her middle, her hair obscuring her face. She wouldn't meet his gaze.

Mallory nodded and motioned toward the apartment. "Come inside and we'll talk."

The guy had some balls, inviting him into his own fucking home. For that alone, he wanted to remain in the hallway, but he had a feeling this was going to be a long story, one that could potentially rip his heart out of his chest. More so even than Eva's bombshell had. And if that was the case, he needed to be seated when it happened. He walked past the two of them and found the living room had been straightened. Shelby cleaned it despite his note telling her not to worry about it.

He sat down in a chair and waved his hand in a get-on-with-it gesture.

Shelby sank to the couch, still refusing to look at him.

Mallory chose the spot next to her. "Six years ago, I busted Shelby for possession of around a quarter million dollars' worth of cocaine."

"It wasn't mine," she said softly. Almost too softly to hear.

"No, none of it was actually hers. Upon investigating, we discovered she was holding the merchandise for her father, Alec Hudson, the leader of The Headhunters motorcycle gang. My superiors and I realized we had a golden opportunity to get eyes and ears inside the club, so we made a deal to keep her out of prison. Nobody would suspect *her*. And it worked like a charm. She gave us enough evidence to put dear old dad away for life."

From behind her curtain of red hair, she made a faint sound, something like a whimper.

Reece couldn't look at her without his blood boiling, so he focused all of his attention on Mallory. "I assume you have a point for telling me all of this. Get to it."

Mallory nodded. "We've been working our way up The Headhunters' chain of command to find their supplier. They have weapons they shouldn't, military-grade stuff they couldn't possibly have access to without the help of someone who has high level security clearances. At first, we suspected you were that someone. Shelby was told to get close to you and find out what she could."

This time he did look at Shelby, and the hot edge of betrayal flayed open his chest. "When did it start?"

She finally drew in a breath and sat up straight, pushing her hair back. "I told them you weren't involved from the very beginning. You have to believe me, I never doubted you, but—"

"But the trail ends with DMW Systems," Mallory

finished. "Someone with a measure of power and military connections is working with The Headhunters. You have both, and we were able to trace the money to your doorstep through an anonymous tip. Not to mention, you have access to all kinds of weapons through your brother—"

"Which brother?" He finally turned away from Shelby and saw Mallory's brows lift in surprise.

"Greer."

"How would Greer give me access to military-grade weaponry? He's been out of that world for a long time now."

Mallory was silent for a beat, then shook his head. "Ah, that's something you'll have to ask him. Suffice it to say, you had the means and opportunity. Shelby was supposed to discover whether you had a motive as well."

"And did you find one?" he asked Shelby directly.

"No," Mallory said before she could speak. "But we think you do have employees involved in this. Like I said, the money trail stops with your company. We'll need access to investigate further."

"You should have saved yourself a lot of trouble and come to me first." Reece stood. "I'll talk to my lawyers, and we'll cooperate with your investigation in every way we can." After he did some digging of his own. If someone he'd hired—someone he put his trust in—had been using his company as a front, he was damn well going to find out about it. "But for now, you need to leave."

The agent stood. "I'll be in touch, Mr. Wilde."

Yeah, he had no doubt.

"You did good, Shelby," Mallory added, squeezing her shoulder.

"Don't," she whispered. "Just…go."

Mallory's features tightened as his eyes tracked back and forth between the two of them. He opened his mouth as if he were going to say something more, but then must have thought better of it because he closed it again without making a sound and left.

For a long moment after the door closed, neither of them spoke. Reece didn't think he could with the hard lump lodged in his throat.

"I'm sorry," Shelby finally whispered.

"Yeah, that's not going to cut it."

"I didn't want any of this. They've had me under their thumb since I was twenty-three years old and—I just wanted out. Buying The Bean Gallery was an attempt to escape that world, but then it burned down and—and I realized I'd never escape. Not really. Not until ATF lets me go. Jason promised this was the last thing I had to do for them, then they'd erase all of my records, and that would be it. I'd be free."

"And you believed him?"

She swallowed. "I wanted to. I don't want that life anymore. All I want is to make my sister proud of me. And to make you happy. I love seeing you happy and the sex is amazing and I love living with you and having you write me a note every day and…" She paused to take a breath and stayed silent for so long he turned to face her again. Tears poured down her cheeks.

His throat was tight and he could barely squeeze any words out. "And what?"

When she said nothing more, he asked, "How long have you been spying on me? Since we first met?"

"No!"

"That night at The Bean Gallery?"

She shook her head. "It was that night, but Jason approached me after you left."

"He was there?"

"I had no idea. I swear. They already had surveillance on you, and when they saw us together..." She trailed off. "I thought they were done with me until then because I'd cut ties with The Headhunters after my father went to prison. But Jason just keeps finding ways to drag me back."

He grunted. "So everything in Vegas was staged?"

"Not everything. I just...wasn't ever in any danger."

Rage boiled in the center of his chest. He honestly couldn't remember a time he was this pissed off. "You're an excellent actress, I'll give you that much."

Her gaze dropped to her hands knotted in her lap. "I've had to be to survive."

He pressed his lips together to keep from saying something he'd regret. He wished he had Vaughn's ability to freeze out all emotion, because he didn't want to feel for her, couldn't let himself feel for her anymore. She'd brought this on herself, just as Eva had warned him she would. Should have listened, should have used the head on his shoulders rather than the one between his legs.

He stalked toward the door. "I'm staying with Dylan tonight." He couldn't face his brothers yet. "Tomorrow, I have to leave town for a few days, but first thing Monday morning, I will be at the courthouse applying to have this marriage annulled."

That lit a fire under her ass and she sprang to her feet, capturing his arm before he reached the door. "You said you wanted to see if we can make it work."

"That was before I knew you were lying about

everything."

"Not everything! I love you, Reece."

"You don't know the first thing about love." He expected her to flinch, had calculated the barb to sting. And by the way she momentarily squeezed her eyes shut, he guessed he'd hit his mark. But there was no satisfaction in it. Only more hurt, for both of them.

Shelby didn't stay hurt, though. Color infused her pale cheeks and she let go of his arm, shoved him. "And you know all about love, is that right? You don't even know who you are! You can't love somebody until you love yourself."

"Then it's a good thing I was wrong about loving you."

She sucked in a sharp breath and backed up a step. If he had gutted her, he thought he'd see less pain in her expression than he saw now and, despite his anger, part of him wanted to go to her, soothe away the hurt he'd just caused. Because of that, he continued to the door.

"That's not true. I know that's not true," she said behind him. "You've spent your entire adult life pretending to be this unfeeling, uptight asshole, and you're not. You're not that guy. Why can't you let the real Reece out? Why not do something wild and crazy and illogical for once and take a chance?"

He glanced back over his shoulder. "On you?"

"Yes! On us."

"Because that's worked out so well for your sister all these years. Every time she's taken a chance on you, it's blown up in her face."

She flinched. "It's not the same."

"Yeah. It is." Rubbing at the ache blooming right where his heart should be, he opened the door. "When I come home Saturday, I want you gone."

"Reece." Her voice broke. "Please don't do this to us."

"I'm not the one doing it," he said and closed the door behind him, blocking out her sobs.

Chapter Twenty-Seven

Although returning to her sister's house with Poe's cage in hand and tears splotching her face felt a little — okay, a lot — like defeat, Shelby had no place else to go. So here she was, standing on the front stoop, praying she wouldn't be turned away.

Eva opened the door and just stood there, unmoving, staring through the screen, disappointment in her eyes. How many times had this scene played out over the years? Dozens. She was the yo-yo sister, always bouncing back after a bad breakup or quitting yet another job.

God, she sucked at life.

Finally, Eva heaved out a sigh and stepped back. "I haven't touched your room."

"I'm sorry," she whispered and shut the door behind her. She set Poe's cage in its usual spot on a table near the door. "It will only be for a few days this time. I'll find my own place."

"Ugh, that's not the point, Shelby." Exasperation in her every move, Eva scrubbed her face with both hands, dragged her fingers through her dark hair, and tugged on the strands. "You shouldn't have lied to Reece. Shouldn't have married him, knowing you were lying. Shouldn't have made me make the choice between keeping your father's identity a secret or telling my husband. You know how much that sucked?"

"I know. I'm so sorry. I hope you and Cam didn't fight about it."

"We did." She dropped her hands to her sides and her shoulders slumped. "I just…I really wish you'd tell me the whole truth. It's always lies and half-truths and it's like walking through a minefield, waiting for one to blow up on me. I'm exhausted by it, Shelby. I don't know how you aren't."

Shelby swallowed, trying to ease the tension in her throat. "I am. I've wanted to tell you everything so many times, but I couldn't. Didn't have a choice."

"There's always a choice."

"Not really." Sucking in a fortifying breath, she met her sister's gaze. "For the past six years, I've been a snitch for the ATF. It was my information that put my father in jail."

Eva blinked once. Again. She opened her mouth, but no sound emerged for a good thirty seconds. "Excuse me?"

"That's why I had to lie to you. If anyone ever found out I was the one who snitched, I'd be dead."

"Oh…Jesus Christ." Eva paced away, hands carving into her hair again. She held it back from her face for a long moment, then let it drop and whirled around. "I'm not *anyone*, Shel. I'm your sister! You should have—"

The doorbell rang and they both froze.

"Are you expecting company?" Shelby whispered.

"No." Eva slid over to where her coat was draped across the back of the couch, found her holster, and unhooked her gun. Then she moved soundlessly to the window and peeked out. Her spine straightened. "It's that guy Mom had with her in Vegas."

Shelby went to the window on the other side of the door. It was the same man, but now he was dressed in business casual—trousers, shirt, blazer, no tie—under a long trench coat. A scarf hung loosely around his neck, the ends flapping in the January wind. At his feet was a large cardboard box. He must have noticed her moving behind the curtain because he picked up the box and turned toward the window, tilting it to show her what was inside.

She gasped. "He has Reece's laptop."

Eva didn't put away her gun, didn't even bother hiding it as she opened the door. "Can I help you?"

He nodded once, a quick up-down jerk of the chin. "My name is Miles Weiss. We met briefly at your wedding."

"I remember. Why are you here?"

He looked past Eva at Shelby. "I'm returning some things that belong to you."

"How did you get them?" Eva demanded before Shelby had a chance to open her mouth.

Weiss push out a long breath. "It's a complicated story."

"We have time."

He set the box down, nudged it forward with his foot. Eva didn't so much as glance at it and crossed her arms over her chest.

Shelby bent down and did a quick inventory, her heart jumping into her throat when she opened a small padded envelope and found her ring. "Everything's here."

"Well?" Eva said.

Weiss smoothed a hand over his silver hair. "Listen, I was just doing my job. Your husbands are private investigators too. They know how it is."

"You're a PI?"

"Yeah, and I was hired to dig up dirt on her husband." He motioned to Shelby with his chin. "First time I saw them together the night that coffee shop burned down—and after I watched the surveillance video before giving it to my client—I figured she was the best way to get close to him."

"And you thought what better way to get close to her than through her mother," Eva finished, her lip curling.

"Only I didn't know how fucking insane Katrina is," Weiss said. "When I realized it, I broke it off. That afternoon, she shows up at my door with all this stuff, begging me to take her back, saying she can help me. Didn't take long to figure out the laptop was hot, or who it belonged to." He shook his head. "Batshit crazy woman."

Shelby stood, and her stomach rolled over in disgust. For such a handsome man, he was an ugly, ugly person. "And it took you this long to return everything?"

He held up his hands in defense. "Hey, I had to track you down."

"Right," Eva muttered. "You're an unethical jackass, and I should report you, have your license stripped."

He dropped his hands. "I don't want any trouble now. I was just doing the job I was hired for."

He turned away but Shelby wasn't about to let him leave without more answers. She shouldered past her sister. "Who hired you? Lena?"

He snorted out a disbelieving laugh. "I don't know

anyone named Lena, but if I did, I wouldn't tell you. Client privilege."

Wait. It *wasn't* Lena?

She grabbed his arm hard enough to spin him around on the icy steps. "If you don't want my sister riding your ass—and believe me, you don't—then you *will* fucking tell me."

Chapter Twenty-Eight

"I was an idiot," Reece muttered and knocked back the two fingers of Maker's Mark Dylan had poured him. They sat in the living room of Dylan and Alicia's townhouse, surrounded by the antiques passed down through Dylan's wealthy family and the expensive artwork that Alicia collected. It was a home, a place where two people had melded their personal styles into something welcoming and cozy. He'd been on his way to that with Shelby and her crazy pillows and paintings and...

Fuck.

"You look like hell," Dylan said and leaned forward in his seat to grab the bottle of whiskey. He held it out in offering, and Reece shook his head. His stomach was too sour, and the alcohol wasn't settling well.

"I feel like hell."

Dylan nodded and refilled his own glass. "You can stay here as long as you need, buddy."

"Just for tonight," Reece said. "I have a couple home security installations in Virginia Beach. I'm leaving tomorrow."

"Maybe you should reschedule."

"No." Now more than ever, he needed to work.

Dylan gave a half laugh. "That's what I figured you'd say—hell, it's what I'd say in your shoes—but as your friend, I was obligated to pitch the idea."

"Dammit!" Alicia's voice floated out from the kitchen, and she appeared a second later, hands on her hips. "Hon, where are the tomatoes I asked for?"

"I got spaghetti sauce."

She pushed out an exasperated sigh. "I am *not* making your mother's lasagna recipe with canned sauce. If she found out, I'd never hear the end of it." She pointed to the door. "Grocery store. Now."

Dylan groaned, set aside his glass, and stood. "Look on the bright side, buddy. An annulment means no wifezilla ordering you around."

Alicia swatted him as he passed her on his way to the door. "I wouldn't have to order you around if you did things right the first time. I swear," she said to Reece. "I gave him a list. How do you screw up a list?" Then, noticing the bottle of Maker's Mark on the coffee table, she clucked her tongue and scooped it up. "Drowning yourself in alcohol will not solve anything. You should go talk things out with Shelby."

"We're past the point of talking things out."

"Men." Alicia shook her head and turned to go back into the kitchen. "If you want something to drink, I'll make you coffee."

Reece winced. Coffee didn't sound any more appealing than the alcohol had, but he didn't want to be an ungracious guest. It was bad enough he was being a mopey guest. "Thank you. I'd love some."

Once he was alone, he sat back in his seat and scrubbed his hands over his face. Coming here had been a mistake, but going to Cam and Eva's house was out of the question and his other brothers…yeah, he didn't want to talk to them, either. What he really wanted was to be alone so he could stew in his anger without interruption.

He should get a hotel for the night.

Actually, the more he thought about it, the better he liked the idea of anonymous, impersonal solitude.

Yeah, as soon as Dylan came back, he'd make his excuses and take off.

Alicia returned from the kitchen with a mug and pushed it into his hand. "Drink. Coffee always makes everything better."

He obligingly took a sip, and she smiled, but there was a slight strain to it, a tightness that wasn't normally there.

She touched his shoulder. "I'm sorry."

He mustered up a hint of a smile in return and covered her hand with his. "I'll be okay."

She turned away fast and hurried toward the kitchen. "I need to finish a few things in here, then I'll come sit with you."

Before he could protest, she was gone. He heard dishes clinking, water running, and the sounds were soothing. Normal. He nearly fell asleep sitting there, listening to her fix dinner.

He yawned. Hadn't realized how exhausted he was until he had a few minutes alone. Drifting, he didn't know how much time had passed before she came back with her own mug of coffee and curled up in the seat her husband had vacated.

"Okay, Reece," she said. "Talk to me."

He shook himself awake and took another gulp of his cooling coffee. Although he'd known Alicia since college, they'd never before had this kind of personal conversation, and the thought of doing so now had him shifting uncomfortably in his seat. "Uh, you don't have to—"

"I have nothing to do until Dylan brings me my tomatoes, and I know you guys don't talk, not really. It's all"—she deepened her voice and did a fair intimation of her husband—"'Hey, man, relationship problems suck. Let's drink and pretend nothing's happening. Maybe bump shoulders in a manly show of support before the big game starts.'"

Reece laughed and it was genuine, if not a little weak. "What big game? And since when have either of us cared about sports?"

"Yes, you're right. With you two, you're more likely to bury yourselves in work." She sighed, sipped her own coffee. Which reminded him he was still holding his mug, and he drank, too.

"Not that I'm any better," she added, setting her coffee aside. She sat forward in her chair and scanned his face. "Which is exactly why I'm going to ask about the deal with Irving James. I received a request from his accountant for our books."

His temples started pounding in tune with his heart. He took another fortifying gulp of coffee. "I'm sorry, Alicia. Work is the absolute last thing I want to talk about right now."

She said nothing for a moment, then stood. "It's a bad

idea."

"What is?"

"The deal with James. I've told you that from day one."

He opened his mouth to tell her there was no longer a deal, but his tongue felt too big for his mouth. The room started to tilt-a-whirl around him and he tried to get up, but couldn't find his feet.

Alicia stepped around the coffee table and took the mug from his numb fingers. "I really didn't want it to come to this. The blackmail should have been enough."

"W-Wha...?" Even to his own ears, he sounded unintelligible.

"C'mon. Let's get you into the bathroom before Dylan gets home." She slid an arm around his waist, wedged a shoulder under his armpit, and lifted him. He tried to push her away, fight her, but none of his limbs were responding to his commands. He had two fucking black belts and he could do nothing but stumble along beside her and try to keep his head upright.

In the bathroom, she none too gently dropped him on the floor. The tile was cool against his cheek. His skin felt on fire. "Wha...didya...give me?"

"Xanax. And I didn't give it to you. You were so distraught over your fight with your wife, you came in here, found my prescription, and took too many." Alicia pulled a pill bottle out of her pocket, opened it, and put it in his hand. His fingers wouldn't close around it, and the pills scattered across the floor. She stepped back. "Unfortunately for you, I won't realize it until Dylan gets home. By then, it'll be too late."

He pushed himself up to his hands and knees, wobbled,

and crashed back to the floor. Pain thundered through his head as it bounced off the tile, and the room wavered. He flopped to his back, stared up at the wife of his best friend, a woman he'd known for close to fifteen years. And all he could think was...

"Why?"

She crossed her arms over her chest. "I can't let anyone see our books or they'll know I've been laundering money through the company. Dylan—" She paused, seemed to gather herself. "He has a gambling problem. You didn't know that, did you? I've done my best to keep it quiet, but he was in trouble. A lot of trouble with the wrong people. So I made a deal to keep him safe, but then you started this whole thing with Irving James... I knew I was about to be exposed. I thought blackmail would stop you, but that didn't work. Then I gave the pictures to Lena, knowing she'd try to ruin you with them, but that doesn't seem to have worked either. So now, you have to commit suicide because if you're dead, Dylan will have control of the company and there will be no deal."

"Already no deal," he tried to say but it came out garbled. He tried again, enunciating, "No. Deal."

"What?" Alicia knelt down, turned her ear close to his mouth. "What did you say?"

He fleetingly thought about biting her, chomping down on her earlobe, but that wasn't going to help him get away from the crazy bitch when he couldn't move. "There's. No. Deal. I... ended it. Last...night."

"Oh God." She reeled backward, tripping over her own feet and slamming into the wall. "Oh God."

"I'sokay. Call amble—ambulance. We'll forget this."

"I can't. They'll arrest me. I'll lose Dylan. He—he doesn't know about any of this. He'll hate me." She shook her head hard, strands of dark hair escaping her ponytail. "No, I'm sorry, I can't. I can't lose him."

Alicia fumbled for the door. Just before it shut, she looked at him again, and he thought he saw real regret in her eyes. Or maybe that was only the Xanax blurring his vision.

"I'm sorry," she whispered. "I was only trying to protect Dylan."

And the door shut.

Reece drifted somewhere between wakefulness and un-consciousness. His thoughts scattered and blurred, but every once in a while, one would pop back into sharp focus.

Shelby.

If he died here, he'd never see her again and, Jesus, he wanted to. If he died here, he'd never be able to apologize.

He made another attempt at pushing to his hands and knees. Got up and wobbled there, but didn't go down.

Progress.

Now he had to get some of the drug out of his system before he passed out or he was toast.

The toilet was about a foot in front of him and he dragged himself over, pulled himself up. Leaning over the bowl, he jammed a finger down his throat. His gag reflex kicked in, his stomach emptied. He gagged until there was nothing left, until his throat was raw and his stomach spasmed with cramps.

Body heavy, he slid to the floor again, the tile a wonderful relief to the internal combustion going on inside him. Fire blazed just under his skin even as shivers wracked his body. There was a sudden burst of noise, but he couldn't pinpoint where it was. What it was.

Didn't matter.

He had to focus, stay awake.

Shelby.

Yes. Had to focus on her. She was his wings. She helped him fly when he hadn't even known he could.

And he loved her. No matter what she'd done, he would always love her.

Light pooled around him, and there she was, hovering over him, her face streaked with tears, her hands cool on his cheeks.

He must be hallucinating. Dying. Still, he reached up for her, and her hand closed around his. She felt so real. She had to be real.

Her lips were moving, but her voice sounded far away. "Reece. Reece, can you hear me?" When she blinked, he felt the saltwater of her tears splash against his face.

Wait.

She *was* real.

"Shelby?"

"Yes, I'm here. We're here, and the paramedics are on their way. So hang on, Hershey."

His head lolled, heavy on his neck. There was something he needed to say to her. He mustered every drop of energy he had and wrangled his tongue into submission. This had to come out clearly. She had to know…

"I love you," he managed. "Stay with me. Please."

And then he drifted away.

Chapter Twenty-Nine

"He's going to be okay."

Shelby gazed up at her sister standing in the door of Reece's hospital room. In her leather jacket, jeans, and boots, she looked every inch the kick-ass cop that she was.

"Docs say he'll be out of here in a few days," Eva added, rocking a little on her feet, hands stuffed in her pockets.

"I know." She returned her gaze to the bed, where he'd been drifting in and out of consciousness since the doctors treated him for the Xanax overdose. "But he asked me to stay with him, and I just can't bring myself to leave until he comes around."

Eva nodded and stepped into the room. "Shelby, I'm sorry. I was pissed when I found out about you and Reece, I'll admit it. Reacted..." She winced. "Badly."

"To say the least. You punched him, Evie."

"I was afraid for you. I thought, how can this possibly

work?" She looked at the bed, heaved out a breath. "But, you know, I was wrong. It does work. For the two of you, it does. Cam said he's never seen his brother so...at ease. Even with the shitstorm flying around him this past week, Reece has been happier. You do that for him."

"Not after yesterday."

Eva came the rest of the way into the room and sat down in the chair next to Shelby's. "Yeah, well, he had a right to be pissed off. You fucked up, Shel. Why didn't you ever tell me about this Jason Mallory character?"

"I didn't want you to be ashamed of me. *More* ashamed of me," Shelby blurted, unable to keep the truth from slipping out when all of her emotions were so close to the surface. She stared into her sister's eyes, saw tears there, and her own vision blurred. "I see how you are with Mom, and I've always been afraid I'll just keep doing the wrong thing and someday, I'll reach for you and you'll turn your back on me like you have her. I'm terrified of that."

"Oh," Eva breathed and closed her eyes as if in pain. She leaned over and wrapped Shelby in a hug. "That's not going to happen. I will *always* be there when you reach out, no matter what. And I might get mad and I might say things I shouldn't, but that doesn't mean I'll stop loving you. Ever. Until Cam, you were all I ever had. Nothing can break that bond, okay? So tell me when you get in trouble from now on."

Sniffling, Shelby drew away. "I don't plan on getting in any more trouble."

"That'll be a nice change of pace." Eva straightened her shoulders, whisked away tears with impatient wipes of her hands. "Okay, enough waterworks." She stood. "I'm gonna go, but when that man wakes up"—she indicated Reece with a jerk of her thumb—"you make sure he knows how you feel about him. Life's too fucking short to miss out on spending it with the man you love."

Shelby gazed over at Reece. He was pale, so still under the bleached white blankets of the bed. Her heart clenched. Life was short—and his had almost ended far too soon.

"Oh, and one more thing," Eva said from the doorway and tossed a small padded envelope to Shelby. "Thought you might want that back."

Heart thudding, she waited until her sister was gone before opening the metal prongs that held the envelope closed. She dumped the contents into her palm...

And wasn't sure whether to laugh or cry.

Her wedding ring.

She slid it onto her finger and immediately felt whole again. A sob caught in her throat. Okay, the tears were going to win out, as they had so many times in the last few days. She loved this ring, loved what it symbolized.

And it killed her that it wouldn't mean anything after the annulment.

Sobbing openly now, she slid the ring off her finger and returned it to the envelope.

It was two days before Reece was able to stay awake for more than a few minutes at a time and although he still felt fuzzyheaded and nauseous, he was happy to at least be upright again.

He knew Shelby had been with him for the last forty-eight hours, because he remembered seeing her at his side the few times he'd resurfaced. She'd appeared hazy, apparition-like as if he were dreaming her, but he was positive he hadn't been and waited restlessly for her to walk through his door. Except she didn't. The day wore into afternoon, then into evening, and she didn't.

But Dylan did. He tapped on the frame and hesitated. "Can I come in?"

Reece's immediate gut reaction was a massive hell-to-the-fucking-no he couldn't come in. But he couldn't be held accountable for his wife's sins, and their friendship ran too deep, went back too far, to dismiss him outright.

Reece nodded and sat up straighter in the bed. "All right."

Dylan shuffled inside, and the guy looked like he'd been dragged through the innermost ring of hell. He was wearing the same clothes he'd been in the last time Reece saw him, all wrinkled and sweat-stained. His eyes were bloodshot, his hair a mess. Several days' worth of growth darkened his jaw. He scrubbed at that stubble with one hand and wouldn't quite meet Reece's eyes. "I'm, uh, sorry."

"Yeah, I know, buddy."

"No, you don't." He finally lifted his gaze. "Reece, I suspected—no. Fuck. I *knew* what she was doing. I knew she was laundering money through the company to cover my debts. I—" He stopped, drew a sharp breath. "I'm the one who anonymously tipped off ATF. I knew James would ask for our books, and I knew she'd be caught when he did. I had hoped by tipping them off, they'd focus on you long enough for me to get Alicia out of the country."

"Oh Jesus." If Dylan had hauled off and punched him,

it would have hurt less. "Why didn't you come to me? Why didn't you both just come to me? I'd have helped you, found you a good treatment center. I'd have even footed the bill if you needed me to. All you had to do was ask."

Dylan shook his head. "I didn't want to admit I had a problem. And Alicia...she was just protecting me."

"And you were protecting her. I get it. I do," Reece said softly. "And I forgive you for it, but don't ask me to forgive her. She tried to kill me."

Dylan said nothing for a long time as emotions battled over his features. "I stand by her. For better or worse."

"I respect that, but you can't be a part of DMW anymore. You're fired, Dylan."

"I figured as much." He nodded once and went to the door but glanced back. "I am sorry for all of this and I hope someday—someday you can forgive her."

It'll be a cold day in hell, buddy, Reece thought and sank back against his pillows as Dylan walked away. He rubbed at his chest because, fuck, that conversation had hurt. It was like losing a brother.

Or, no, he decided when another knock drew his attention and his brothers—minus Greer—filed into the room. Not like losing a brother, because his brothers would never stand by a woman who tried to kill him.

Jude's hands were full of smiley face plastic bags from their favorite Chinese restaurant and Reece smiled, some of the ache easing out of his chest. General Tso's in hospital rooms was starting to become a Wilde family tradition.

"Dudes," Jude said as he passed out the white cartons. "This hospital thing is getting old fast. Knock it off."

Vaughn scowled and popped open his carton, grabbed

his ever-present bottle of Tabasco sauce out of his pocket, and liberally doused his shrimp chow mein with the stuff. "You can't blame me for nearly getting blown up."

"Or me for being poisoned," Reece added.

"I can, too." Jude pointed his chopsticks at Vaughn. "You set yourself up as bait. And you?" He jabbed them toward Reece. "You should know better than to take coffee from strangers."

"She wasn't a stranger."

"Still," Jude muttered and stabbed a piece of chicken. "You're supposed to be the smart one."

Reece smiled slightly. His little brother usually had the best disposition out of all of them, was a silver-linings kind of guy, and only got crabby like this when he was scared. "I'm okay, Jude."

"Yeah, well. You better be."

After that, nobody said anything for a while. Just the sound of the TV and the occasional call for a doctor over the hospital's PA system. After a nurse came in to check his blood pressure—apparently low blood pressure was a concern after a Xanax overdose—Reece finally broke the silence to ask the question that had been nagging at him since he regained consciousness. He shut off the TV with the remote by his bed and waited until his brothers all turned to face him.

"How did you guys know Alicia was behind everything?" He knew now that it hadn't just been Shelby there that day, but also his brothers, Eva, and the cops.

His brothers all shared a look, each passing the conversational ball. Cam, being Cam, was the one to finally take it and run with it. "Shelby and Eva were confronted by the

PI Alicia hired to dig up dirt on you—the guy their mother brought to our wedding. Apparently, he was using Katrina to get closer to Shelby, and therefore, to you, but it blew up in his face when he decided it wasn't working and dumped her. She went off the deep end, dove right back into the drugs, and robbed you thinking she'd win her lover's affection by bringing him information—your laptop."

"Which is encrypted," Reece said.

"Yeah, and maybe that's part of the reason the guy decided to cut his losses. He couldn't get any info off it, and things were spinning out of his control, so he took everything back to Shelby and bailed."

"Assholes like that give PIs a bad name," Vaughn muttered.

"No doubt," Cam agreed and several beats of silence passed.

"What about Katrina?" Reece asked.

"She was picked up yesterday for buying drugs from an undercover cop." Cam rubbed the center of his forehead, eyes closed. Then he shrugged. "Maybe this time, she'll get the help she needs."

Vaughn grunted. "Doubtful. The system sucks."

"You know," Jude said, "I suddenly feel the need to call my mother-in-law and tell her how awesome she is."

Reece could only work up the energy to glare, but Cam summed up his thoughts with a succinct, "Jude, you're an ass."

"What?" He held up his hands. "All I'm saying is I didn't realize how good I got it with Mrs. Pruitt. Could be a lot worse than the occasional meddling and the when-are-you-going-to-give-me-grandbabies talk. Next to you two, I won the mother-in-law lottery."

"An ass," Cam repeated.

"Yeah, I got one. It's a fine one, too. Ask my wife."

At the resounding groan from everyone in the room, Jude grinned and pushed himself out of his seat. "And speaking of my beautiful wife, I'm going home to her now."

The twins stayed for a few more minutes, but eventually they left Reece alone with his thoughts. He didn't like it. Too much nasty going on inside his head right now, too many conflicting emotions, and the longer he stared at the TV, the more depressed he got.

Why hadn't Shelby come to the hospital today? Did he want her to? What would he even say if she showed up right now? He didn't know. He wanted to forgive her, but a small sliver of him was still pissed off at all her lies. And if he did forgive her, pretend like none of this happened, would that sliver fester into something more than anger? Would he eventually grow to hate her?

Jesus.

Restless, he muted the TV again and grabbed his cell phone from the over-bed table. On a whim, he tried Greer's number for the simple reason he missed hearing his older brother's voice. Didn't really expect an answer—

And sat up in shock when Greer's deep voice came on the line. "What's wrong?"

He exhaled the tension he hadn't known he'd been carrying since Greer disappeared. "What isn't wrong? Where the fuck are you?"

Greer said nothing for several seconds. "There was something I needed to take care of."

"And you're not going to tell me what it is?"

"No. But I might not be around for a while, so you'll have to watch over our brothers for me. Especially Vaughn. I'm afraid he's driving himself straight off a cliff."

Reece snorted. "I feel like I'm right there with him, riding shotgun."

Static silence dragged out over the line.

"Reece," Greer said eventually. "I don't know what all's going on there, but you *can* handle it. Dad always knew you'd make something of yourself. Something big, something more than any of the rest of us. He'd be proud of you."

A hard lump took up residence in Reece's throat. "I miss him. Every day."

"We all do." Greer's voice was rough, and he cleared his throat. "But Mom? She'd kick your ass for pushing Shelby away."

Reece groaned. Greer wasn't even here and hadn't been for days. How could he possibly know this was about Shelby?

"Because I'm not an idiot," Greer said and shit, did the guy have mind-reading abilities or what?

"This call has nothing to do with Shelby."

"If not, it should." Greer pushed out a sigh. "Listen, I was wrong to tell you to end things with her. We were all wrong, and Mom would smack the rest of us for sticking our noses in your personal life."

"No, you weren't wrong. Shelby's been lying to me from the start."

"Yeah," Greer said softly. "I know."

Figured. Reece leaned back in bed and shut his eyes, too tired to care that Shelby wasn't the only one he loved who had been keeping secrets. "I'm not even going to ask how."

"Good. Don't. And what you do now about Shelby is

your choice, but we *were* wrong to interfere. Thing is, all of us, we've always felt like we've had to protect you because you're…"

"A computer nerd?" Reece suggested dryly.

Greer snorted out a gruff laugh. "Well, yeah. You're not like the rest of us. You don't have the same…brutality in you. I don't know if it's because you never saw combat or if you were just born without the gene that makes the rest of us—"

"Aggressive? Belligerent? Combative? Thick-skulled?"

"Yeah, yeah. I get it. We're knuckle-dragging mouth breathers."

Reece rubbed his eyes under his glasses. "I'm not like you guys, but that doesn't make me weak."

"I know. In some ways, it makes you the strongest of us all." There was a short pause, then Greer said, "I have to go, but first lemme say I think you should forgive Shelby. She hasn't had a lot of good in her life until you came along. But that's your decision, not mine. However it shakes out…just do what makes you happy."

"I could say the same to you," Reece murmured, but the line had already gone dead. He pulled the phone away from his ear and stared at it for a long time.

Do what makes you happy.

Well, he sure as fuck wasn't happy sitting here in this hospital. In fact, he hadn't been happy since he walked away from Shelby. Sure, he had every right to his anger, but was he angry enough to completely give up on her?

She hasn't had a lot of good in her life…

No. He wasn't that angry. Despite it all, he still loved her. It hadn't been the Xanax or fear talking when he reached that conclusion on the bathroom floor. And if he'd learned anything from his parents—and from his brothers—it was that love wasn't easy, wasn't neat and tidy, and sometimes wasn't even fun. But it was worth the trouble.

And he didn't want to lose it, wasn't ready to give up on her.

Reece shoved up off the bed and shuffled over to the closet for his bag of personal belongings. Fuck this. If his wife wasn't going to come to him here, he'd just have to drag his sorry ass home to her.

Chapter Thirty

"What the fuck are you doing here?" Jude said when he opened his door the following morning to see Reece standing there. "You should still be in the hospital."

"I checked myself out last night."

Jude shook his head and stepped back, opening the door wider. "You're supposed to be the smart one, remember?"

He stepped inside. "Yeah, but I'm also a Wilde."

"And there's no hope for us as a species. C'mon, sit down before you fall down." Jude motioned to the living room in a sweeping gesture with his coffee mug. "Libby's in the kitchen making breakfast. I'd offer you coffee, but that didn't go so well for you last time."

"Oh, man." He groaned as he lowered himself to the couch. "I'm never going to live that down."

"Eh, eventually." Jude sat in a recliner and leaned forward, elbows on his knees, hands linked in front of him. "Okay. Why are you here?"

"I went home last night. Shelby wasn't there."

"Well, what did you expect? You told her to leave, didn't you?"

"Yeah. I did. I'm good at opening my trap and saying things I don't mean." He lifted his gaze and felt like a heel all over again for some of the things he'd said to Jude in the past. If anyone understood what he was getting at here, it'd be his youngest brother. "I see you when I look at her."

Obviously uncomfortable, Jude glanced away and sat back in his chair. "Dude. I love you, but that's just nasty."

"Not like that. Jesus, you can be such a douchebag sometimes."

"Takes one to know one."

"A douchebag with a five-year-old's comebacks."

Back on familiar ground, Jude grinned, all smug and un-apologetic. He picked up his coffee mug again, lifted it to his lips. Drank. Waited in silence for Reece to continue, which said something about the level of his smugness, because the youngest Wilde brother was not known for his patience.

Reece heaved out a breath in frustration. "What I mean is everyone has always kept her down, talked down to her. Like we did to—no, like *I* did to you. Nobody has ever giv-en her a chance to be something more. Including me." His throat tightened. "I want to be the one to finally give her that chance."

Jude's smile faded into a rare serious expression. "Bro, I'm going to ask you something, and I don't want you to think about it. Just answer from your gut. Do you love Shelby?"

He hedged. "She's my exact opposite…"

"Answer from your gut." Jude patted his abs. "Stop thinking about it. Does the idea of not seeing her every day make your chest tighten up like you can't breathe?"

"Yeah."

"You love her?"

"I love her." He tried out the words, and the world didn't burst into flames around him. He couldn't even remember why he thought it would, because the words felt satisfying as hell, like the last puzzle piece snapping into place and showing him the image of the rest of his life.

With Shelby.

If he could make it up to her.

He slumped back on the couch. "Oh shit. I fucked up. She'll never forgive me."

Jude lifted his mug in a toast. "You'll be amazed at what your woman is willing to forgive."

Surprisingly, that bit of sage advice gave him a sliver of hope. After all, Libby had forgiven Jude his stupidity. Of course, it was after eight years, and the wounds between them had time to heal. Would he have to wait that long too? He didn't want to, but if that's what it took, he would. He'd do anything to win her forgiveness for being such a jackass.

Even if that meant he had to beg his annoying younger brother for help. "What do I need to do?"

Jude gave his best Dr. Evil laugh and rubbed his hands together. "Oh, am I going to enjoy this."

"I swear," Reece said through his teeth, "I will slug you."

"Nah. You adore me."

"Won't stop me."

Jude waggled his brows, then got serious again. "Tell me how you fucked up with her."

Resigned, Reece explained the whole situation. The drugs Shelby was caught with, the undercover work she'd done, and even the marriage manipulation to get closer to him and his company. Before he finished, he paused and grabbed Jude's coffee because his throat felt too tight, and he was afraid his voice would crack. "So that's it. I didn't react well. Basically told her to fuck off."

Jude sat up straighter in his chair. "Wait. Shelby's been working for this ATF agent for how long?"

"Six years."

Jude scowled and sat back in his seat again. After a moment of thought, he called out, "Hey, Libs. Can you come in here for a sec?"

Libby appeared in the doorway drying her hands on a paper towel, and glanced between the two of them. "Something wrong?"

"Nah, just need your lawyer-y opinion." He tilted his head back and tapped his lips with one finger. Smiling, she bent to give him a kiss.

Reece turned away from the couple as a hollow ache opened up in his chest where his heart used to be. He'd had that same playful, easy intimacy with Shelby until recently.

Jesus, he really had fucked up. Big time. But he'd make it better. Somehow.

"So," Libby said, straightening away from her husband. She planted a hand on her hip and looked at Reece. "Don't tell me you're in legal trouble, Mr. Responsible."

"No, not me."

Her smile dissolved into a grimace. "It's Shelby, isn't it? I should've known. Sorry."

"It's not what you think, babe," Jude said. "Can you answer me something hypothetically? And don't jump to conclusions."

She perched on the arm of Jude's chair. "All right. Ask away."

"How long is the statute of limitations for drug possession?"

She didn't even have to think about it. "Five years."

Reece came half out of his chair in surprise. "You're sure?"

"Well, unless there are other mitigating factors…"

"For example?"

"Uh, if the hypothetical person we're talking about has been in possession of the drugs for that entire length of time. The statute of limitations only kicks in once a crime ends, so if Shel—I mean, this hypothetical person were to still be in possession of the drugs, they could still be charged."

"She's not."

"Then if no charges were ever brought against her in the first five years, she's free and clear." Libby raised a brow. "Can we stop being hypothetical now? What's going on?"

As concisely as he could, Reece explained everything. When he was done, Libby shook her head. "No. That's all wrong. This Agent Mallory is holding an empty threat over her head."

Or at least he was until the firebomb at The Bean Gallery. Then he offered her protection as long as she continued to do his dirty work. That motherfucker.

"I need to look into this Agent Mallory."

"If you want, I can help," Libby offered.

Reece nodded. "I'd appreciate it."

Jude grinned and pulled Libby down onto his lap, kissing her soundly. "Isn't my wife brilliant?"

"Yeah, she is. Still don't know what she sees in a knucklehead like you."

"I ask myself that every day," Jude murmured and gave his wife another quick kiss before setting her on her feet. He also stood. "And while Libby's checking into your shifty ATF agent, we need to get moving. We have a lot of work to do if you want to win Shelby back."

Wincing, Reece followed his brother. "I'm going to hate this, aren't I?"

"Yup. And I'm gonna take lots of pictures." Jude grabbed his coat from the nearby rack and held open the front door, motioning him to go first. "The Wall of Shame at the office will no longer belong only to me. It's gonna be awesome."

Chapter Thirty-One

The drive to the courthouse Monday morning was the longest of Shelby's life. She'd stayed away from the hospital after Reece came back to consciousness, but had received updates on his condition by Cam and Eva, learning he had checked himself out several nights ago, and he'd been asking about her. Still, she'd kept her distance and ignored his calls. Partly because she was afraid of what he'd say now that he was lucid again. Partly because she was afraid she'd throw her pride to the wind and beg him for a second chance. She didn't know if she could take getting shot down again, so she played the coward and avoided him, putting off the inevitable for as long as possible.

But today, the inevitable had arrived. He was going to file for the annulment, and she couldn't stay away. Sometime over the weekend, her fear had mutated into anger. He couldn't throw them away like this. Yes, she'd fucked up—big time—but what they had together was the kind of thing people spent their entire lives looking for. And call her self-ish, but she wasn't willing to let that go. She'd beg and plead and straight up sacrifice her pride in front of everyone at the courthouse if she had to. Whatever she needed to do to prove her love to him.

She was so wrapped up in her thoughts, she didn't see the man with the shock of blue hair in front of her until it was too late. She walked straight into him, and stumbled.

"Whoa." He held out his hands to steady her, then did a double take. "Shelby?"

She was pretty sure her jaw hit the ground. "Reece?"

Then, at the same time, they both asked, "What are you wearing?"

For the first time since she'd known him, he was dressed down in jeans and sneakers. Under his jacket, he wore a graphic T-shirt of Pac Man eating a Hershey bar. He hadn't shaved in a few days and a sexy scruff darkened his jaw. Oddly, he looked a lot like Jude, except for his glasses. And the blue he'd dyed into his hair.

"Oh." Tears filled her eyes and she reached up to push a lock away from his forehead. "What did you do to your hair?"

"What happened to *yours*?" he countered, winding a strand around his finger.

She self-consciously ran a hand over her new color—a honey blond, as close to her natural color as she'd been in years. "I thought…maybe if I toned it down, you'd find me more…I don't know. Acceptable, I guess."

"Oh, Shelby." His features softened in a way she'd never seen before and he held out his arms. "Come here."

She hesitated, still playing with the ends of her new dye

job. She couldn't look at him, didn't want him to see how vulnerable the admission had made her. Especially when the terror of rejection had her cold from the inside out.

"Shelby." He hooked a finger under her chin and lifted her gaze to his. She saw tenderness there and the ever-present fire of desire, but there was also a bit of shame and some worry lurking in the depths of his eyes. "I have never found you unacceptable." He tugged at a strand of her hair. "I find this unacceptable. A normal hair color? A business suit? For fuck's sake, you're even wearing pearls."

She swallowed hard. "I thought you'd like it."

He clasped her shoulders, rubbed. "This isn't you, Shelby."

"I thought— I don't know. I guess I thought if I looked more the part of your wife, then maybe we could stay married."

"I don't want a Stepford Wife."

Even dressed like this, he still didn't want her. God, that hurt. So much that she suddenly couldn't breathe because of the pain in the center of her chest. She nodded and tried to turn away before the tears blurring her vision spilled down her cheeks.

Reece pulled her into his arms. "Don't cry."

"I'm sorry. I was—" Her breath shuddered out on a sob and fat tears spilled from her eyes, screwing her carefully applied makeup all to hell. "I was hoping this would change things between us."

"I don't want things to change."

"I understand."

"Hey." That was all he said, then he waited in silence until she reined in the sobs and gazed up at him again. He cupped her cheeks in his palms, swiping away her tears with his thumbs. "Why are you crying?"

She sniffled. "I don't want an annulment. I love you."

The dimple in his left cheek flashed and he pulled a stack of folded papers out of his jacket pocket. "I never filled out the paperwork."

"You…" She blinked at the empty pages. "Why not?"

"Shelby." Again he waited until she lifted her gaze to his. "I let Jude pick out my clothes and dye my hair blue. Do you honestly think I'd show up to court looking like this if I wanted to end our marriage? I love you, and I want you as my wife. But I want the real you, not this cookie-cutter person you're trying to turning yourself into. A person I foolishly tried to turn you into. I want—" He stopped short, closed his eyes and shook his head, then corrected himself, "No, I need the color you bring into my life. Before Vegas, I was not happy. I was existing, not living. I just didn't realize it until you showed me that happiness is coming home to find you doing yoga to reggae music. It's sneaking away from dinner parties for closet sex. It's crazy pillows and paintings, whipped cream fights and getting dragged to a club in my tux and ending up covered in glow-in-the-dark paint."

A fluttery feeling started in her belly and tingled through her body. "Really?"

"Yes, really." He smiled and swept her hair back from her face. "Happiness, for me, is the two of us, together. I want us to stay together, so I sold DMW to Quentin Enterprises, gave my brothers their shares of the profit, and have enough left over that we can run away, change our names, and disappear. Mallory will never be able to use you again."

"You'd do that for me?" she whispered. "Give up your life here, your brothers?"

He cupped her face in his palms and feathered kisses over her eyes, nose, and finally, her mouth. He took his time there, kissing her softly, thoroughly. When he finally broke the contact of their lips, he rested his forehead against hers. "I'll do anything to keep you safe. I love you."

"But I lied. About…so much." She bit her lower lip. "I never owed The Headhunters money. My dad set up a bank account for me when I was little. I never touched it, never planned to, until The Bean Gallery went up for sale. I just told you I owed them because I knew you wouldn't go for the marriage thing unless you thought you were protecting me."

He winced. "Yeah, you're right. I wouldn't have."

"But you need to know I could have gotten the information Jason wanted without marrying you. It just seemed like a good way to help you with the blackmail situation."

He quirked a brow. "Killing two birds with one marriage?"

"Oh God. That sounds so horrible when you put it like that, but yes. And…" She swallowed hard, determined to get everything out in the open this time. If they were starting fresh here, she didn't want any more secrets. "And, part of me, I wanted it. I think even then I was a little bit in love with you already. I just didn't know it or maybe didn't want to admit it to myself. As crazy as it sounds, I did truly want to marry you."

"Good. Because I truly want to stay married to you."

She laughed softly, wrapped her arms around his waist, and hugged him. "And we're not going anywhere. I did my part. Jason has to let me go now."

"I was hoping you'd say that."

"You were?"

"Well, I would have run away with you, but when I sold to Tuc Quentin, he may have offered me a position as lead developer of DMW's new video game arm."

He said it so offhandedly, it took her a few seconds to process it. "Reece! That's fantastic!"

He raised a shoulder in a shrug. "It suits me better than CEO and allows me time to still work at Wilde Security with my brothers. Dealing with Tuc on the sale of DMW gave me an idea about how I can get Wilde Security operating in the black. Personal security. My brothers have the marketable skills for it and, thanks to Tuc, we already have our first client."

She laughed. "Something tells me Tucker Quentin doesn't need help protecting himself."

"He doesn't, but if he hires us, it'll make us more appealing to other celebrities. We both know that world is all about appearances." He hugged her briefly then set her back and smiled down at her. "But that's not our world anymore. Which reminds me…" He laced their fingers together and tugged her toward the Escalade. "I have something to show you."

It was all such a whirlwind, she couldn't imagine what that something might be. She'd come here expecting to beg for his forgiveness, plead for another chance. Never in her wildest dreams did she think it would go this well.

It wasn't a long drive to their destination: the strip mall where Wilde Security was located, except he didn't pull into his usual parking place in front of the office. Instead, he parked in front of the next empty store in the line and climbed out of the car, scrambling around the hood to open her door before she could. As soon as her feet touched the ground, he clamped a hand over her eyes and cradled her elbow, guiding her forward.

"No peeking," he said.

"Kinda hard with your hand over my eyes."

A door opened and he ushered her inside, into a blast of warm air scented with sawdust. "Here we are."

"Where?"

He removed his hand, and Shelby took in the empty store. It had been stripped to the studs, the floor pulled up, the ceiling ripped out, but even so, she could tell it was a good space with lots of room. "What is this?"

"It's yours." Reece took her by the shoulders and spun her to face the back wall and the sign propped there.

The Bean Gallery.

Slightly singed, but still legible. Warmth radiated through her. Trembling, almost not daring to believe, she gazed over her shoulder at Reece. Had to blink to see him through the flood of tears. "Here? Next to Wilde Security?"

"If you want it."

"Yes!" She flung her arms around his neck and kissed him. "Oh God, yes. Of course I want it! I—" A loud thunk from the back of the building made her jump. Shouts and curses followed. Some kind of struggle? She looked toward the noise. "What's that?"

"Sounds like my brothers are taking care of a pest problem." He gave her a quick, reassuring squeeze, then walked to the door at the back of the space.

She chased after him. "You have pests here?"

"No, but you do," he said and unlocked the door, shoving it open.

Outside, the twins had a man flattened out on the icy

pavement, and Jude was scooping snow onto a blazing trashcan fire. Eva was there too, directing a pair of uniformed cops to the downed man. The arson investigators followed close behind.

Shelby stepped out into the cold, her gaze tracking over the scene, trying to make sense of it. "What…?"

The twins hauled the man upright. She sucked in a sharp breath, dragging the cold deep into her lungs where it seemed to sit like concrete and made drawing in more oxygen impossible.

Jason Mallory.

His face was scratched from the pavement, and his eyes spit fire at the brothers as he cursed and struggled. But fighting against them was as hopeless as a mouse trying to escape a pair of cats. The twins held him without even breaking a sweat. In fact, they seemed to enjoy it, wearing identical grins.

She gaped at the man, then at the blazing trashcan.

Jason was the arsonist?

"Shelby, you need me," he said through gritted teeth. "You need me. Without me, The Headhunters will find out you put your father in jail. I'll make sure of it, and they'll kill you."

Fury blasted through her and, before she knew she was moving, she crossed the short space between them, hauled back, and punched Jason hard enough to have pain singing up her arm. He stumbled sideways, and the twins let him fall.

She stood over him, staring down at the man who had terrorized her in more ways than she'd even known. "Go to hell. I don't need you." She reached back, found Reece's hand, warm and strong and comforting. "I have everything I need right here."

The arson investigators moved in, dragged Jason to his feet.

Jude grinned at her. "You knocked him flat! Remind me to never piss you off."

Behind her, Reece snorted. "You piss everyone off at one time or another."

"I'm not the only one in the family with a kickass right hook," Eva said and looped an arm around Shelby's shoulders, giving her a quick squeeze. "I'm proud of you."

Stunned and kind of numb, she watched the cops take Jason away. "All this time...it was him?"

Reece's hands settled on her shoulders, rubbed. The weight of them was comforting, and she leaned back into the warmth of his body.

"Libby figured it out," he said. "Mallory never actually charged you for drug possession, and the statute of limitations ran out last year, right around the time he demanded you break up with your ex-boyfriend. He had no legal control over you."

"So he used fear instead." Hands on her hips, Eva scowled, watching the officers stuff Jason into the back of a waiting patrol car. She sighed. "Shel, I'm so sorry you didn't feel confident enough in me to tell me about him. I could have helped a long time ago."

Shelby shook her head. "But why would he...?"

"You were too valuable for him to lose," Eva said. "Over the years, your information has helped him collar some huge names in the criminal world, made him a big deal in the ATF, and when you tried walking the straight and narrow by buying The Bean Gallery, he saw his career going out the door. Must have figured if he scared you enough, you'd go to him begging for protection." She smiled over at Reece. "He just didn't count on you going to Reece instead."

Shelby glanced at Reece, then at each of his brothers, then back at the building behind her as she mentally connected all the dots. Pain sliced through the center of her belly. "Steven, my ex-boyfriend. He wasn't the pyromaniac, was he?"

Eva rolled her lips together, shook her head. "He was innocent. Or at least as innocent as a guy with a rap sheet can get."

"He'd done bad things, but he wasn't a bad person." The pain grew teeth and Shelby shut her eyes. "And I killed him."

"No." Hands still on her shoulders, Reece spun her to face him. "Your father killed him, and Mallory set it up. He saw you slipping out of his control and decided Steven had to go."

She sniffled. "I cared about Steven."

"I know you did, and it's not your fault he died, okay?"

She wanted to believe him, but the guilt was too heavy. "Jason was going to burn your building down. Just like he did my neighbor's house, your parents' house."

"Nah," Cam said and slid an arm around Eva's waist. "We were ready for him. Made sure he saw us taking The Bean Gallery's sign down and moving it here. The last thing he wanted was for you to reopen, so we hoped he'd take the bait and resort to his usual tactics when Reece brought you here."

"Aaand," Jude said, finally smothering the last of the trashcan fire, "he did. Obviously."

Her heart sank. "So, the sign...it was only part of the

sting?"

"No." Hands still on her shoulders, Reece spun her to face him. "If you want to reopen The Bean Gallery, this space *is* yours."

So many things flung through her mind, a whirlwind of questions and thoughts and feelings, and she didn't know what to say. Reece had forgiven her. She was finally free from Jason. And now this?

"Please." Jude clasped his hands in a pleading gesture. "We *need* some good coffee around here."

She gazed around at all the hopeful faces. Even Vaughn's eyebrows were raised in question, which was about as hopeful as the big guy got.

So this was what family looked like, felt like. She could get used to this.

"Okay," she said and saw Jude punch a fist toward the sky in triumph out of the corner of her eye as she turned to Reece. Her heart swelled at his grin. "But right now, I really just want to go home with my husband."

They barely made it inside the door before they were on each other, hands roaming, mouths fused.

"God," Shelby said between kisses as she tugged at his shirt. "I thought I lost you. When I saw you lying on that bathroom floor…"

"Shh. You didn't lose me. You never will." He ducked to let her pull his shirt off over his head.

She laughed and ran her fingers through his hair. "I can't believe you dyed it blue."

The dimple in his left cheek flashed as he straightened. "Yeah, that's not all I did." He pointed to his side, and her gaze tracked down his lean body to the healing ink along his ribs.

"Oh my God. You got a tattoo!" She dragged her fingers over the design, and he squirmed as if it tickled. "It's beautiful, but why an anchor?"

A slight flush worked up his chest and neck. "It's a not-so-subtle reminder to myself that I have a tendency to drag you down—"

"Reece, no. You don't hold me down. You—"

He touched her lips to silence her. "Yes, I do. But it's not a bad thing. I keep your feet on the ground..." He unbuttoned her blouse, drew the two halves apart, and kissed one of the birds tattooed to her collarbone, then the other. "And you're the wings that keep my heart in the clouds. We balance each other. It works."

She swallowed to ease the tightness in her throat. "Yes, it does."

"So..." He dragged the word out and he reached into his pocket. "I have a question for you. One I never really got to ask."

Her heart fluttered as he dropped to one knee and held out her ring. "You were my first, and I want to be your last. Will you do me the honor of continuing to be Mrs. Wilde?"

"Yes," she whispered and accepted the ring, sliding it on her finger. Back where it belonged.

Epilogue

Reece paused on the sidewalk in front of what would become the new Bean Gallery and smiled as he watched his wife through the window. She was talking to someone he couldn't see, laughing while she stocked a glass-fronted refrigerator with soda. She'd jumped into the renovation with her usual gusto, full steam ahead, and had transformed the once empty space into something even better than the first Bean Gallery had been.

Her hair fell in a rainbow from her ponytail, bouncing as she hurried around with last-minute preparations for the grand opening tomorrow, and he wanted nothing more than to walk in there, wrap all that bright color around his hand, and draw her in for a kiss…

A car door slammed behind him, and he turned in time to see Vaughn stalk into Wilde Security next door.

Cam jumped out of his 4Runner and was right on his twin's heels. "Vaughn! We're not done. What the fuck is wrong with you?"

Reece sighed and glanced over at Shelby again. After a long day spent transitioning DMW over to Quentin Enterprises, the last thing he wanted was to deal with a fight between his brothers. All he wanted was some quality time with his wife, but he'd promised Greer he'd look after their younger brothers.

Greer, who still hadn't returned from wherever he'd gone.

And that was starting to worry him. He hadn't heard from Greer since the night he spent in the hospital over three weeks ago, but he could only deal with one problem at a time and the fact the twins were fighting was a major one. He could count the number of times they'd fought with each other on one hand.

Reece followed them into the office and nearly ran into Vaughn, who was shoving back through the door with the keys to his Hummer in hand.

"Get out of my way," Vaughn said through his teeth.

"No." He stood his ground, blocking the exit, and looked backed and forth between the two of them. "What's going on?"

"Ask him." Cam threw up his hands in complete frustration. "He's the one with the fucking death wish."

Oh, shit. This wasn't good. "Guys. What happened?"

"This asshole," Cam said and pointed at his twin, "talked me into a winter jump, then scared ten years off my life when he waited until the very last second to pull his damn chute."

Vaughn growled and swung around to face off with Cam again. "You know how many jumps I did in the navy? I can fall out of a plane in my sleep and still pull the cord with plenty of time to spare."

"Do you have any idea what it felt like to watch you go flying past me and not be able to do a damn thing but pray your backup opened? Jesus, Vaughn."

Reece dropped his head into his hands and massaged his temples with his fingers. "Enough. Both of you."

"Fuck this," Vaughn said and shouldered past him.

Reece let him go. There would be no reasoning with him while he was like this. So instead, he turned his attention to the more rational twin, who had sank into one of the office chairs and looked utterly defeated.

"He considered not pulling the cord," Cam said softly and then gave a humorless snort of laughter. "Did he really think I wouldn't realize it? We're identical. I know how he thinks, and he's spiraling. I just…" He looked down at his empty hands. "I don't know how to fix it."

And Cam, usually the family's peacemaker, the glue, hated not being able to fix things. Especially when it came to his twin, who had always been just a little bit broken.

Reece walked over and pulled himself up to sit on the desk beside his brother. "The only way to fix it is to find Lark Warren."

Cam shook his head. "I don't get it."

"Neither do I, but this all started when she disappeared. He's not going to stop until he settles whatever it was that happened between them."

Another shake of the head. "I can't do this now. Not tonight. Is Eva still next door?"

"I don't know. I didn't make it inside."

Cam pushed out of the chair, and they walked to the door together. "Shelby's done good work with the place. She has a talent for it."

Reece smiled to himself as he stopped to shut off the light and lock up. "I know." And he couldn't be prouder of everything she'd accomplished in only a few weeks. His woman had vision and a good head for business. He still felt like an ass for doubting her.

Next door, Shelby had turned up the music, and Taylor Swift was telling everyone to shake it off. She danced circles around her sister with a broom, trying her damnedest to convince Eva to join her.

Some of the tension eased out of Cam's shoulders as he crossed to his wife. "C'mon, Shelby. You know your sister doesn't dance. Stop torturing her with pop music."

"Fine." Shelby spun over to Reece, pecked him on the lips, then grabbed his hand. "I'll dance with my husband."

The music changed to something with a strong, fast beat and he fell into easy rhythm with her, hands on her hips.

Cam's jaw hit the floor. "Since when do you dance?"

He spun her. "You think I can be married to her and *not* dance?"

"Ah…" Cam held up a finger, but dropped it again after a second. "Good point. Look at you. You inherited Mom's rhythm."

He drew Shelby in close again and kissed the tip of her nose. She laughed, weaved her fingers into his hair—which was no longer blue, thank God—and drew him down for a real kiss, the kind of kiss he'd wanted but had held off on because of Cam and Eva.

"Ugh," Eva said. "Stop it, you two. I'm okay—mostly—with the whole marriage thing. Not so much with the public displays of affection."

Shelby broke the kiss, but only by inches. "Maybe you should leave then, because I want to do a whole lot more to him than just kiss." She grabbed his ass with both hands, and his body lit up like a flare.

Eva groaned. "Oh God. My eyes." She cupped one hand around her eyes like blinders and used the other to tug a laughing Cam toward the door. "We're leaving. Just…don't do anything more until we're gone."

Shelby snorted as she watched them go. "Eva can be such a prude sometimes."

"Aw, give her a break." He tugged on her ponytail. "You're her little sister. Honestly, I get it. The thought of my little brothers having sex weirds me out."

"Because you're a prude too."

He traced his fingers along the curve of her breast. "A prude wouldn't do the things we did last night. And he certainly wouldn't take you back to your office and tongue fuck you until you scream his name."

"Hmm, Mr. Wilde. You're getting an awful dirty mouth."

"Maybe you should punish me for it, Mrs. Wilde."

"I'm thinking I should." She smoothed her hands over his open collar. "You know, I kind of miss your ties."

Grinning, Reece reached into his jacket pocket and drew out a length of silk.

"Well, then." She dragged the tie from his fingers with a slow, sensual tug. "I believe we have unfinished business in my office. We were interrupted last time."

He watched her walk toward the back, swinging the tie and giving her hips a little extra sway with each step. He hardened, but didn't immediately follow and instead glanced around.

The Bean Gallery was all color and light, with deep-cushioned couches and chairs, a place where people would want to come to unwind, relax. It had Shelby written all over it, with little bits of him scattered throughout since he'd drawn and painted most of the tabletops for her.

"Hershey," she called from the back. "I'm starting without you, but I'd really like your mouth on me instead."

His throat went dry at the mental images her words conjured, and he strode over to lock the door. On his way back across the room, he stripped off his shirt, but then paused and glanced around again before shutting off the light. They were building something together here, something better than the high-society life he'd lived for the past five years, something he'd never thought he'd have. Yeah, some people might think he was crazy for giving up so much, but this coffee shop and the colorful woman who owned it were his heart.

And he abso-fucking-lutely belonged here with her.

About the Author

Tonya Burrows wrote her first romance in eighth grade and hasn't put down her pen since. Originally from a small town in Western New York, she's currently soaking up the sun as a Florida girl. She suffers from a bad case of wanderlust and usually ends up moving someplace new every few years. Luckily, her two dogs and ginormous cat are excellent travel buddies.

When she's not writing about hunky military heroes, Tonya can usually be found at a bookstore or the dog park. She also enjoys painting, watching movies, and her daily barre workouts. A geek at heart, she pledges her TV fandom to Supernatural and Dr. Who.

If you would like to know more about Tonya, visit her website at www.tonyaburrows.com. She's also on Twitter and Facebook.